I0662031

CRUEL PROMISES

CRUEL SECRETS BOOK 2

KHARDINE GRAY

FAITH SUMMERS

AUTHOR NOTE

Please note Faith Summers is the Dark romance pen name of USA Today Bestselling Author Khardine Gray

IMPORTANT NOTE

Dear Reader Friend,

Thank you so much for picking my book to read.

Please note this story is a dark new adult romance which is intended for mature audiences due to the graphic content of this novel.

Please also be aware there might be content some readers might be sensitive to or find triggering.

This book is part two in the Cruel Secrets Duet. This book is the second part of the duet.

For your enjoyment, please read this book first. If you don't, you won't be able to follow the storyline or know who the characters are.

I hope you will enjoy this book. It is the first in my Raventhorn world.

Happy reading.

Hugs and love,

Khardine (Faith)

USA TODAY BESTSELLING AUTHOR
KHARDINE GRAY
writing as

FAITH
SUMMERS

BLURB

Our vicious past dragged us into a whirlpool of dark secrets.

The villain isn't supposed to be the hero.

Willow was always mine.

So, I'll become whatever I need to be to save her.

Including breaking the oath I made when I became a Knight.

The oath is our life and our death.

But she is my path to redemption.

My obsession.

My love.

My wife.

I'll walk through the fires of hell to protect her.

And the sky will rain the blood of our enemies.

I won't stop until I get what I want.
Even if it kills me.

RAVENTHORN

COME BACK TO ME ...

PROLOGUE

11 years ago, Russia - Age 8

As the image of Willow's beautiful smile and vibrant red hair floats into my mind, I know I'm dreaming.

It's only in my dreams that I will see her now.

Since I got taken, I keep dreaming about the last time we played in the meadow near our home. That was only a few months ago, but it feels like forever.

I was chasing her through the cattail reeds. When she looked back and smiled at me, the twinkle in her eyes made me stop in my tracks as I noticed for the first time how pretty she was. I thought she was the most beautiful girl I'd ever seen.

I'd never thought that before.

"Caspian, you can't catch me." Her sweet little voice drifts into my mind, and I run toward her with the biggest smile on my face.

Just as I reach her, that bloodcurdling sound forces its way into my head and she disappears right before my eyes.

Clank. Thud. Clank. Thud. Clank. Thud.

The scenic view of the meadow fades, and terror snaps my eyes wide, ripping me out of the dream.

In an instant, I'm pulled back to reality, where I'm lying on the grimy, blood-soaked floor of the dimly lit cell those men put my family and me in. It's at the bottom of a well where rats and insects run free.

Both my legs are broken, so I can't run, hide, or protect myself.

Clank. Thud. Clank. Thud. Clank. Thud.

That sound—it's a combination of heavy boots clashing against the concrete floor and that terrifying metal bar clattering on the wall.

The men used that bar to beat Uncle Nicholai to death. It still has his blood on it.

They've been beating me with it daily.

They're coming for me again.

The turbulent pounding of my heart reverberates off the walls of my soul. I try to straighten against the cold cobbled wall, keeping my eyes away from the decaying remains of Uncle Nicholai, my cousin Anushka, and Aunt

Evangeline. When the men kill me, I will rot away just like them.

Will they kill me today?

I think they're going to. They've been torturing me for weeks, and I think they're getting bored.

Tears sting my eyes as the sound gets louder and closer. My body shakes, and I find myself looking at Anushka's rotting face. The dim cell light cast a glow on the metal nails hammered into her head, showcasing the gruesome sight of my once beautiful cousin.

Every time I look at her, I remember what those men did before they killed her. There was nothing I could do to help her.

They all raped her in front of me and Uncle Nicholai.

Rape...

I didn't even know what that word meant until they told me.

Just before Anushka died, I remember the terrified look in her eyes. The terror wasn't there because of what was happening to her.

It was for me.

It was because I wasn't supposed to be here.

Thorne was.

Thorne, her brother.

Thorne, my cousin, who is so much like a brother to me I switched places with him and allowed the demons to think they took him when they broke into the safe house to kill his family.

Nicholai and Anushka knew what I did, and although they gouged out Aunt Evangeline's eyes before she got the chance to see me, she knew I was here, too.

No one knew that I switched places with my cousin because of the blood oath we made when his family started getting death threats.

We promised to have each other's backs.

I never knew I'd be taken the following week when we came to Russia.

Uncle Nicholai told us to get to the basement as the men stormed the house.

But as they started shooting, we had to hide where we could. Thorne in the coat closet and me in the cleaning cupboard.

When I saw the men heading for Thorne's hiding place, I jumped out of mine.

That's how I ended up here.

Clank. Thud. Clank. Thud. Clank. Thud.

Shadows steal the light, then the devilish faces of the men appear with bright menacing smiles.

The leader unlocks the cell door. "Time to play, you little shit," he taunts, rushing toward me with the bar raised.

I piss myself. Tears stream down my cheeks, and I push back into the wall as if that can help me.

Growling like an animal, he strikes me right across my cheek, and I scream.

The agony which jolts through my head makes me vomit instantly, and I scream even more when the monster beats my legs. More bones crack under the weight of the bar as I'm struck repeatedly.

Unimaginable pain pounds into me as the man continues to beat me, and I feel like death has finally come for me.

This is it. They're going to kill me now.

It's happening.

Through the searing pain, I place the image of Willow in my head.

She'll cry when she finds out I died, and I won't be there to comfort her.

I'm about to embrace death when the familiar sounds of gunshots and men shouting fills my ears. I'm so disorientated, however, that I'm not sure what's happening.

The beating stops, and flashes of light bounce around the room along with the sound of battle.

It registers in my mind that there are other people around who shouldn't be here.

At that moment, I see a face I never thought I'd see again—my father.

At first, I think I'm imagining things, but when he lifts my broken body and stares down at me, I know it's him.

"I got you, son. I got you, my boy. No one will ever hurt you again, I promise you," he vows.

My lips part, but I can't speak. I'm in too much pain and my head is spinning.

"You're going home," he adds.

Home.

Home makes me think of Willow.

Beautiful Willow.

I'll get to see her again, but...when I do, everything will be different.

I will be different.

She'll still be the girl in the meadow, but I'll never again be the boy she knew.

The darkness and evil of what I saw have consumed my soul.

I don't think it's ever going to leave me.

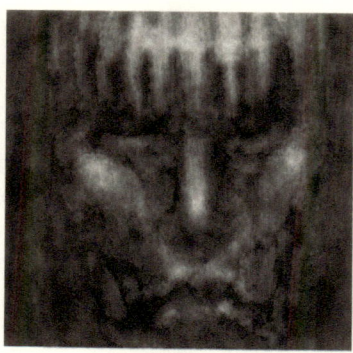

CHAPTER 1

CASPIAN

Present day, Boston, Age 19

I gaze up at Willow's apartment and toss my cigarette.

I know we're going to argue and it's going to be bad.

Willow will hate me even more than she already does, but I have to make her see I did what I had to do to save her.

She's right to be enraged; my father owns her now.

My motherfucking bastard of a father held on to Willow's rights because he wants the company.

Over the years, he obsessed over the loss of his previous partnership with Dynamic Corp nearly as much as he grieved for my mother.

The spell of shit with my implication in Dorian's

death just gave him an opening to seize back what was once taken from him.

I'll never forget the maddening smile that lit up his face as I told my tale and betrayed Willow with every word that left my mouth.

When I reach the side of her apartment, I glance up at the bridge. There I see the vague outline of two people. One is a tall, hooded figure with a build that looks like the guy I saw that night weeks ago. The other person is a woman.

I stop my stride to watch them for a few seconds, but when the woman goes limp in the guy's arms like a rag doll, instinct moves me.

The guy steps into the moonlight, and dark dread fills me as I catch a flash of red hair on the woman's head. Realization of who she is slams into me like a bolt of lightning, and I run.

Willow!

My God, it's Willow!

He has her.

I torpedo down the path, blood hammering through my veins as I run as fast as I can.

Everything inside me shatters, and what's left of my soul dies when the man releases Willow and throws her over the side of the bridge.

Then she's falling.

Falling into darkness.

The man steps away, blending into the shadows, but I can't think of him now. I have to get to Willow.

As the darkness swallows her whole, I push forward,

willing my body to move faster. Except, even as I do, I know I'm too fucking far away to get to her.

The terrifying thought suddenly takes me back to one of the earliest memories I have of her running through the meadow. She was seven and I was eight. That memory kept me alive when I was kidnapped in Russia.

Now it haunts me as I recall the words she said to me.

"*Caspian, you can't catch me.*" The ghost of her voice fills my head and pierces my heart as I realize I can't catch her.

No matter how tough I think I am or how ruthless, not even I can save her from falling off a bridge when she's already been thrown to her death.

Jesus Christ. No.

I mustn't think like that, and I can't let her die.

I can't allow death to steal another from me.

She's mine. Which means I can't fail.

I keep my eyes riveted on her until she plunges into the river, and I imagine her being pulled deeper underwater because of the height she fell from. That's a big enough fucking worry in itself. The other worry is that I don't know what that motherfucker did to her before he threw her over the bridge.

Roaring like a wild beast, I implore every muscle in my body to work harder and faster. My brain speeds, too, working overtime to conjure a plan.

I race to the emergency box attached to the wall, resisting the urge to jump into the river to find her. Precious seconds are ticking by, but if I jump in now, I won't be able to see her. The water is too dark, and it will only get darker when I'm beneath the surface.

I find the emergency floodlight, switch it on, and position the high beam shining at the area I saw Willow land in. Thankfully, there's still a ripple. I then throw a life light around my neck, which should light up the moment I'm immersed in the water.

With that done, I kick off my boots and strip down to my boxers then dive into the water, slicing through the current. Instantly, the life light turns on, guiding my way, so I head toward the ripple spiraling ahead.

I search the murky water for her but can't see her anywhere. Terror stabs at my heart as the seconds continue ticking by.

Time, my old enemy, is against me as I fight the clutches of helplessness to find the girl I love.

I swim further down, going deeper and deeper. When I'm near the riverbed, hope sparks my heart as a lock of bright red hair floats into the light ahead of me. Then I spot Willow floating amongst the reeds.

Fueled by adrenaline, I rush to her. When I secure my arm around her waist, I can already tell from how she feels that finding her doesn't mean I have hope, but I refuse to give up.

I swim with her to the surface and get her out of the water.

Since she's not breathing, I check for a pulse. When I don't feel one, my heart sinks deeper into hell. But again, I don't give up. I start CPR and give her the rescue breaths and compressions, checking after each round if she's come back to me, but all I see is her pale, lifeless body.

I keep going and going and going, but it's not working.

It's not fucking working.

"Willow, come back to me!" I shout. "Please. I'm sorry. I'm sorry for everything. Please come back to me. Please."

I stop talking and push harder on her chest, so hard I worry I might break her.

On the last hard pump, water spurts out of her mouth, and she gasps for air.

Relief stirs my soul to life, but I know she's not out of the woods yet.

She's barely breathing, and her eyes are still closed.

CHAPTER 2
CASPIAN

S*omeone tried to kill Willow.*

Someone actually tried to kill her right there on campus *in front of me* and in a sea of the most invincible people on the planet.

And I was right when I thought she wasn't out of the woods. She wasn't by a long shot because she was poisoned.

The doctors said she'd been injected with a lethal dose that shut her body down. Had I not gotten to her when I did, she'd be dead.

I've practically been at the hospital all night. I left at around two in the morning because Willow was taken away for various tests that would take several hours. I didn't want to leave, but the doctors insisted and advised I get some rest because I'd only be sitting where I am now in the hospital's private waiting room—*waiting*.

When I returned two hours ago, I got hit with more bad news.

Since Willow's body had gone into shock, the next twenty-four hours are crucial. Should she make it, they'll be keeping her in a sleep-induced coma for the next few days while they take care of her.

So, here I am, actually praying to whomever will listen, that she makes it.

Blowing out a ragged breath, I reach for the Styrofoam coffee cup on the little table before me and down what's left of the acrid liquid that tastes like shit.

This is my sixth cup, and it's barely eight in the morning.

Coffee and the two joints I smoked earlier are the only things keeping me sane right now. It's possibly also what's stopping me from unleashing my inner beast, who wants to rampage through the campus grounds and find the motherfucker who tried to kill Willow.

I'm waiting for the results of her last blood test and for my father to arrive.

He was among the many phone calls I made last night.

Adrian, Elaine, and Eilish were the only people allowed to see Willow for a brief visit after the doctors stabilized her.

I'm still trying to process what happened because it doesn't feel real to me.

None of this feels real, and I'm not sure what the hell any of it means or what I'm going to do.

There's no way this spell of shit is a coincidence. So many events occurring in one go can't be. My heart and my gut tell me everything is linked to the past.

Willow was nearly killed. Lucian was nearly killed.

Dorian *was* killed. He's in the fucking morgue beneath me.

Zak was murdered, and that same feeling in my gut tells me Lillian might have died for the same reasons, too. I think they both saw or heard things they shouldn't have.

But how do I prove it?

How?

Sheriff Tanner said something must have changed, but back then, all I was thinking of was the notes Willow was getting and the threat of death.

If I'm to go with my gut thought that everything is linked to the past, then the answer is still the same. Something changed that instigated all these events at *this* time.

Besides Willow starting at Raventhorn, the only other thing I can think of that's imminent is her receiving her inheritance. Which is happening on her birthday.

Factoring that in, however, makes everything else confusing because I previously thought anything to do with Zak's death was about stopping him from revealing information. I don't think I'm wrong about that or the connections.

So, maybe everything I've thought is correct, but there are other links I just can't see.

I feel like the walls are closing in on me with the pressure to solve the puzzle before I lose someone else.

I nearly lost Willow. The difference was mere seconds.

I don't know what I would have done if she'd died, and the fucked-up thing about this is when she wakes up, she'll hate me because I've pulled her back into a world where we must live under my father's thumb.

The door creaks open, and the devil himself walks in.

My father lifts his chin, keeping his gaze trained on me. He's wearing a light jacket and black slacks. Both look too casual on him even if they do make him look younger.

He strides over with that air of authority that commands attention, and I hate the way my body automatically gives it.

I already told him what happened to Willow, and he started investigating.

I hate to need his help, but the things happening have reached a stage where I'd be a fool to keep my silence. My father has the resources to dig deeper. I don't, so keeping certain things to myself at this point is only going to cause more harm than good.

I already broke Willow's trust when I told him she still believed her sister died at Bluff Island. I gave him the keys to open the door, take control of her guardianship, and own my girl. I don't want to make things worse.

Father pulls out the chair before me and sits.

"How is she?" he asks, and I wish he wouldn't bother because I know he doesn't care.

Only God must know what stopped him from

punishing Willow in front of the entire council when she told him to fuck off and called him a fucking asshole.

If I weren't already in the shit, I would have commended her, like I'm sure many others silently did because she showed more balls than all of us put together.

Not even I have spoken to him in such a way, and the last guy I know of who did is six feet under. Fuck knows where the others might be who displeased him.

"They're still running tests. The next twenty-four hours will determine what happens next." I sound a lot calmer than I feel.

"Sorry to hear that."

His insincere words grate on my nerves. He's not sorry in the least. If Willow doesn't pull through, the only thing he'd be sorry about is her death throwing off his plans to own Dynamic Corp.

"Did you find anything?" Better to cut to the chase.

"Nothing." When he tilts his head to the side, the bright sunlight picks up the gray in his hair, making it look silver. "We're still investigating. It doesn't help that they screwed with the cameras."

I grit my teeth. That isn't what I wanted to hear, but it's not surprising. The person we're dealing with is clever. They know how to outsmart us and stay off the grid. That just confirms this is above me. So, it's time to delve into deeper conversation, but at the same time, I have to remember to watch myself and be careful of what I say.

Despite everything, I still have a personal stake I

need to protect that I've managed to keep between myself and Thorne. And that's finding out who killed my brother.

Everything else started happening the moment Willow arrived at Raventhorn, but I've been preparing for the last twenty months to position myself to get answers for my brother's death. I've come too far to fuck that up.

Everything I do from now on needs to be well thought out and well played, like a poker player who might lose everything on his last hand.

I reach into my jacket pocket and pull out the note Willow gave me about Lillian. It's more than relevant now and what I'm hoping will sway my father into helping me.

I hand it to him, and when he reads it, a frown wrinkles his face.

The note says:

Lillian died for the sins of your father.
Stay at Raventhorn, and you'll end up just like her.

THAT FROWN IS ETCHED into his already hardened expression for two reasons. The first is the mention of Lillian. The next, the mention of her father.

Any subject at all regarding Timofey Raventhorn always gets my father worked up the way he is now.

"What is the meaning of this?" He balls a fist.

"That's the note Willow received a week ago. She's been getting notes like that since she started college. She was also nearly killed in town. And I'm sure I saw the same guy who attacked her on the bridge watching her apartment weeks ago. Someone wants her dead, Father, and I want to know why."

"That's why I'm investigating. Why didn't you report this to me?" He holds up the note.

"I was dealing with it myself, and I'm telling you now because it was one of the reasons I went to Bluff Island. I think it's connected."

He sighs with frustration and steeples his fingers. "Caspian, how is this connected?"

"It mentions Lillian. My gut tells me there's some connection between the past and the present that we should investigate. Lillian told Willow they were in danger. The note says she could end up like her sister, and she nearly did."

"We do not know if her sister died at Bluff Island. There's no evidence of that, but there's evidence she ran away."

"Father, for fuck's sake, you're seriously telling me you believe a fifteen-year-old girl can escape us—*the Knights*? Really?" I raise my brows and stare at him askance.

He bites down hard on his back teeth and narrows his stare. "If your little girlfriend hadn't told you her *story* about her sister, you wouldn't be thinking any of this. Lillian was in a position and a place where it was easy for her to escape."

"I agree. But don't you think we would have picked up something on her after all these years?"

"She was the Pakhan's daughter. Maybe she knew how to hide well. Her piece-of-shit father knew how to hide many things. Perhaps he taught her well. What I see here is love blinding you from reality. Love has turned you into a fool."

"It fucking hasn't." I straighten and glare at him. "You're so quick to cast off Willow's testimony, but you won't even consider the possibility that she's telling the truth."

"There's no evidence of her version of the truth. *None.* Only her word. I am the leader of the Knights and the Pakhan of the Komarovski. I can't be an idiot and fill in the blanks with something that has no fucking evidence to support it."

"The sheriff I talked to in Bluff Island believed her story. Why can't you?"

"Did he have evidence of Lillian's murder, Caspian?" Knowing the answer, he smirks at me.

"No, but that doesn't mean there's none. Maybe it's just well hidden."

"Or it didn't happen."

"What the hell is the matter with you? I find it hard to believe you can't see this is all suspicious as fuck. And, Jesus, I just handed you a note saying Lillian Raventhorn died. Don't you even want to check that out?"

I'm lashing out, but I know it's like talking to an iron wall. He's not going to want to contemplate the past because it will throw a wrench into what he plans for

Dynamic Corp. If everything Willow said is true, then he'll be forced to accept that there was nothing wrong with her sanity. It will be clear she never lacked mental capacity, meaning he won't get what he wants.

"I never said I wouldn't check it out." He sets his shoulders back. "What I'm doing is refuting your arguments that this note has anything to do with the past. To me, it looks more like someone is messing with Willow."

"I think it's more than that."

"Of course, you would," he mocks me with a sneer. "Caspian, listen to yourself. You are so desperate to find some link to the past when there is none. Besides, this note is a warning. Why warn her and kill her after?"

I clench my jaw. "I think there might be two people involved, and they both know Lillian died. I don't think the notes are coming from the same person who wants to kill Willow. But I think the two people know what really happened to Lillian, or why would the note make reference to ending up like her?"

He shakes his head at me. "Timofey Raventhorn committed many sins. So, this could be someone who most likely suffered because of one of them and knew what Willow believed about her sister's death."

"Hardly anybody is supposed to know what she believed," I counter. "She wouldn't have talked about that because it would have sent her back to St. Jude's." I don't even want to mention that hospital because I don't like the way my father's eyes light up when I do. Like he has more ideas up his sleeve to ruin Willow.

"St. Jude's is exactly where she belongs if she still believes Lillian died at Bluff Island."

I throw my fist down on the table. "No! She doesn't belong there."

"Yes, she does."

"You don't plan to give her back her freedom, do you?" I challenge, speaking my fears.

"She's sick, Caspian. Mentally sick."

I shake my head. "She's not." I don't care what anyone says. I believe Willow, and I know she's not *mentally sick.* "Don't think I don't know you're after the company, Father. You want Dynamic Corp more than anything."

If he can show Willow's unfitness to own the company, it will be his. That's what he's up to.

As if hearing my thoughts, he gives me a devilish smile and chuckles, flicking his palms over and raising his shoulders.

"Of course, I want Dynamic Corp. I taught you long ago that it matters not how something comes to you and who you have to hurt or kill to get it. What matters is that you have it. That is the way of the Knights, and if you don't have that mindset, then you have no business calling yourself one."

I bare my teeth. "I earned my Knighthood fair and square."

"Maybe so, but once again, you're allowing your heart to stand in your way. Your heart is what is making you believe *that girl.* She'd have you running off the edge of the planet if she could. I will not allow that shit to happen to my son."

"You talk like you love me." The words spew out of my mouth before I can think to hold my tongue. Maybe it's because, in the last forty-eight hours, my old man has done nothing but shock me when it came to saving me from death. It was clear he was desperate to find anything to keep me alive and even enticed me with the lure to marry Willow.

Fuck, I haven't even thought about that part properly. Marriage—me and her.

It's the least of my worries right now but a worry nonetheless that I need to factor in. Things are far from okay between Willow and me, and marriage is a fucking big step I never took seriously until my father offered her to me.

The devil mirrors my position, leaning forward so we're eye to eye. He gives me that probing look again that makes me want to shut down my thoughts, so he won't know my fears.

"I protect what's mine. Years ago, as I rescued you in Russia from the bottom of that well, I told you no one would ever hurt you again. That includes *her*. She will not destroy my legacy."

I don't think I'll ever forget that image of him finding me in my darkest hour.

It was redemption and safety for my soul that had been darkened by that hellish event. But what he's talking about is against me, and I will never be in agreement with him because I love Willow.

"My men are investigating this incident and that surrounding Dorian Belkov and Lucian Sokolov. You are not to interfere. That goes for both you and Thorne." He stands but continues glaring at me. "You are also not to pursue this crazy talk about Lillian Raventhorn. One word from Willow's lips about her sister, and I'll toss her insolent ass right back into St. Jude's. I will speak to that girl of yours when she wakes up and put her in line myself—"

"You will not go near her." I bolt up.

"Don't you fucking take that tone with me, boy. Remember, I own her, and you are to do as you are told. I don't think I have to remind you of the pact we signed in blood. Or the consequences of breaking it *and* the Knights' Oath."

The consequence is a fucking catch twenty-two. It's death, and the alternative is death, too. This way just made sure he doesn't marry Willow.

"You don't have to remind me." I bite down hard on my back teeth.

"Wonderful. Keep in mind I didn't have to give her to you and there are several ways of taking her away without breaking our pact."

The smile on his face sends a shudder through me, so I remain silent.

Being Willow's guardian means he owns her, but that pact we made means he owns me, too—more than before.

I promised him an alibi and my allegiance to him, and he promised me these three things: marriage to

Willow, his word that he wouldn't screw with my legacy and membership in the Knights, and he wouldn't interfere with my relationship or marriage to Willow.

I might have felt like I was his pet before; now, I am exactly that with the threat of Willow's life hanging over my head.

If I die, she dies; because he'll destroy her.

To top it off, my hands are tied behind my back until I can come up with some solution from the universe of fuck knows where to get that guardianship out of his hands.

"With the hope she pulls through, then all you need to worry about is your wedding. I'll allow her an extra week after she is released to recover. Hopefully by then we sort out these unfortunate incidents. Do you understand me?"

"*Yes.*"

"Yes, what?"

Fuck, he wants me to call him sir like I have to when I'm amongst the other Knights. He's insisting on it now to remind me I'm his subservient piece of shit.

"Yes, sir."

"Good boy. Do as you're told, and you'll be fine." He smiles and taps my shoulder. Then, without another word, he leaves.

I grit my teeth and stare at the door as it swings shut with a heavy thud.

Do as I'm told?

Yeah, I should. I'm playing with fire, and I'm at square zero with nothing but air to work with and all these loose ends. But I can't let that stop me or take the back seat like a little bitch and expect my father to find out who hurt Willow.

I don't trust him enough to do that, nor to not find some way to still hurt her to get the company.

I didn't tell Father about Zak either, and I'm not going to. He doesn't know I was at Dorian's apartment because of my suspicions about Zak's murder, and he doesn't know why I enlisted Lucian's help.

There's no point taking the risk and telling him any of that until I know more, especially since Dorian is dead.

Timofey Raventhorn committed many sins indeed, and it looks like I'm going to have to find out what they are to get what I want and protect Willow.

Even though I'm the last person she'll want help from, I'm her best bad choice.

If she hopes to survive, she has to marry me and be my wife.

She has to be mine, whether she wants to be or not.

CHAPTER 3
WILLOW

"Willow, we're in danger! We need to get out of here!" Lillian cries, but her face is blurry. As if she's not really there.

Not real.

This is another dream, and I'll be stuck inside my head until my mind is done playing out my most haunting memory.

I stare back at my sister and note how young she looks. She's younger than I am now.

My heart hurts deeply at the thought that she died just before her sixteenth birthday.

How can that be?

I lost my parents, but to also lose my sister at such a young age was too much.

Just like always, the images in my mind scramble together, and like I'm having an out-of-body experience, I see Lillian holding my hand as we run through the woods. Behind us are those two men chasing us like a pair of hound dogs out for blood.

Who were they?

Who the hell were they?

Lillian and I fall into the ditch, and she sprains her ankle. When I help her get up, we continue our escape.

Then, suddenly, we're on the cliff and she's holding me, looking at me like I'm the most important thing in the world to her.

"I love you, Willow," she tells me, but her voice comes out like a whisper. Like she's already a ghost.

The moonlight shines down on her face and her necklace. That look in her eyes freezes in my mind as if someone took a picture of the image and cemented it there.

This is the part where I'm supposed to fall, but I don't. The two of us are frozen until Lillian changes into the man with the hood and we're on the bridge by my apartment.

He's going to kill me. I know he is.

"No...o," I mumble, but my lips feel like lead.

He stabs something into my neck, and I fall.

I land in the water, except this time, I die.

My eyes snap open as I'm ripped from the nightmare.

Panting like I've just ran a marathon, I look around and take in the beeping sounds of machines attached to my arm. Within two seconds, I realize with panic that I'm in the hospital.

In the hospital again.

Which one, though?

Am I at St. Jude's?

Please, God, don't let me be back there. Please no.

Caspian's handsome face enters my view, and my heart leaps with joy. He comes closer, and I notice the usual spark of life in his pale green eyes is swallowed up by worry—worry over me. I can tell.

Caspian is the last person I'd describe as an open book, but I just know certain things.

Another quick glance around the area at least confirms I'm not in one of the barren-looking, window-less rooms at St. Jude's but in a regular hospital. I'm so disorientated, though, I can't remember when I last saw him or what happened to put me here.

What the hell happened to me?

I try to think of the last thing I remember; what comes to my mind is us walking through the meadow. That was such a good day, but I don't think that was the last thing to happen to us.

"Willow," he says, resting his hand on mine.

I open my mouth to talk, but my voice comes out croaky, like I haven't spoken in days. On hearing that, he moves to the tray with the jug of water and pours me a small cup.

When he returns, he lifts my head and places the cup to my lips so I can drink. The cold water soothes my dry throat, so I drink it all, feeling better almost instantly.

"Thank you," I mutter. My voice is still husky, but at least it's there.

Feeling awkward lying down, I try to sit up, taking

note of the mass of tubes with fluid and wires connected to a monitor attached to my left wrist.

Something terrible must have happened to me. I've never been attached to so many tubes before.

"How are you feeling?" he asks, setting the cup back down.

"Confused and weak."

"You've been through a lot. You need to take it easy."

"What have I been through?" I draw in a deep breath, hating that my memory is so fuzzy. My mind literally feels like someone covered it with fluff. "Why am I here?"

His brows pinch, and his worry deepens. "What's the last thing you remember?"

"You taking me to the meadow."

He groans and bites the inside of his lip, a definite sign there's a lot more I need to remember.

"Nothing else?" He searches my eyes.

I think hard, pushing past the fog in my mind, and remember the dream. I don't want to talk about Lillian, so I decide to tell him about the other parts.

"I dreamt there was a man on the bridge near my apartment. It was a guy with a hooded sweatshirt, like the one you told me about. In my dream, he tried to kill me. I guess my mind is conjuring all kinds of things because of the notes. What's going on, Caspian? Why am I in the hospital?"

He presses his lips together in a thin line of displeasure then gives my hand a gentle squeeze. In response, I hold on to his fingers.

"That wasn't a dream, Printsessa," he replies, and a

cold weight drops into the pit of my stomach. "That ... really happened."

Shock jolts my brain, and my mouth falls open. In the same moment, the image of the hooded man pushes to the forefront of my mind and I remember what happened to me.

My God ... I remember the man on the bridge, but he wasn't alone. There was another man in my apartment.

"Oh, God ...I ... I remember." I shudder, reaching for him with the hand attached to the wires. As my pulse skitters, the monitors beep louder.

"Easy, there, Willow."

"Caspian, there were two of them," I say quickly, stopping his next words.

His nostrils flare. "Two men?"

"Yes. There was a masked man in my apartment when I got back. I ran away from him. He chased me onto the bridge. That's when I crashed into the other guy. He stabbed me in my neck with something."

"Did you see his face?"

I shake my head, and it hurts. "He was masked, too. Whatever he gave me knocked me out straightaway, so I don't know what happened after. I don't think he just knocked me out, though. What did he do to me? I feel like hell."

I feel wrong. My body feels weird, like I've borrowed it and don't quite fit this version of myself. Caspian also looks like he's withholding information.

"It's not a good idea to get worked up when you need to stay calm and rest." He nods.

"How can you say that to me? I need to know what happened. My body feels like it died."

He looks at me for a long contemplative moment and sighs.

"Tell me, please. I need to know," I add.

"The man... threw you over the bridge, and you drowned," he answers in a low voice.

Terror twists my insides into tight knots. "I drow ... ned?" I stutter. No wonder I dreamt that I died. I nearly did.

"Yes. And you feel the way you do because he poisoned you. You've been in here for the last two days, and when you're released, you're going to need at least a week of downtime, if not more."

"Jesus ... How am I still alive?"

"I got to you before it was too late."

My heart surges with gratitude. "You did?"

"Yes, but it was close, Willow."

"Oh, Caspian." Emotion swells within me, making my eyes well with tears.

Staring back at him, I feel a safety I only remember experiencing when I was younger. That was with him, too, before the pain of my secret severed our friendship. I would be dead now if not for him.

"Thank you," I mutter, holding back tears.

"You don't have to thank me for that."

"Of course, I do. Thank you for saving me."

I expect him to move closer and hold me, but he doesn't. His expression is reserved, and that confuses me even more. I feel like I'm waiting for the other shoe to drop and there's more I should remember, except my mind is still fuzzy.

"I'm just glad I found you," he says, and that does it.

Those words rip away the rest of the fog in my mind like a wild dog tearing the flesh off a carcass. A hard tremor rushes through me next. One that sparks the memory of him saying he would always find me.

That was a threatening vow that told me there was nowhere on this planet I could run to escape him.

I remember us arguing at Raventhorn Hall. Him in his Knight's tunic looking like he'd just stepped out of a dark medieval fantasy, and me in those awful robes.

I remember fighting against his hold when I tried to run away.

When I said I didn't want to be with him, that's when he told me he would always find me.

As that memory processes, everything else returns, flowing into my mind like a raging river in a storm.

I feel like such a fool for my temporary amnesia. I remember it all now, including what happened to Lucian.

Lucian is in a coma, and Dorian is dead. I found them at Lucian's apartment.

That was mere days before my fate was decided. At the same time, all plans to find out what happened to Lillian went to hell.

That stern look on Caspian's face is there because we are enemies again, but I knew we would be when we next saw each other.

I knew we would be after what he did.

He told the worst person on this earth my biggest secret—the only thing that could destroy me.

Now, his father owns me, and I'm getting married to Caspian.

That makes me a prisoner to them both.

When I drop his hand like a deadweight, realization dawns on the beautiful devil's face. He chases my hand and secures a tighter grip as I try to pull away.

"Willow—"

"I remember everything," I cut him off. "I remember your father owns my rights." An uncontrollable tear slides down my cheek.

He squeezes my hand even harder, to the point it's almost painful. "Then you should remember I did what I had to do."

Yes. I remember that part, too, and I feel just as torn as I did when he first explained his nightmarish reasons.

He told his father he went to Bluff Island because the evidence from his visit eradicated him as a suspect in Dorian's murder.

If Caspian had been found guilty, he would have suffered the death penalty under the law of the Knights. His father would have also married me.

I can assure anybody who thinks I look ungrateful that it's not that at all.

I'd be a fool if I didn't feel gratitude in abundance that none of those things happened.

What I can't get my head around is the fact that exposing my secret means my life will be little more than living in a cage.

The cherry on top of the shit is the threat of being sent back to St. Jude's if I don't follow every order issued to me.

"Listen to me, Willow. I did what I had to do. I told my father about Lillian to save you. That is the only fucking reason I broke your trust. You have to understand that."

"I understand, but, God, Caspian, you *must* know your father is never going to let me have my freedom."

That man has always wanted my family business, so I don't need to be told it will be of great financial benefit if I don't get my freedom back.

When I first thought things were bad, all I had to contend with was Dorian having possession of my legal guardianship for a year. Now, the possession of my rights is indefinite, and I belong to the leader of the Knights.

The defeated look on Caspian's face tells me I'm right. He knows I am, and there's not a goddamn thing he can do to change the situation.

And that's just the beginning of my worries. Caspian is a Knight, so he has to follow orders anyway, but there's a side of him that will do anything to please his father.

He'll defy him within a certain limit, but when his father pushes back, he'll crumble because above all else, he seeks his father's approval.

Although I don't know this for sure, my guess is it's become worse since Zak's death. It was always clear his father favored his brother.

"You know I'm right," I break the silence, almost afraid to talk. "You know your father will still find a way to ruin me. I guarded that secret for so long, and it kept me safe. I kept *myself* safe."

He releases my hand and straightens. "Clearly, you weren't safe by yourself."

"I'm not safe with you either," I snap back. "You'll do whatever he tells you to do. How safe can I be if that's the case?"

The vicious look in his eyes mirrors the viper tattooed on his neck. He leans closer, and a shiver runs through me. "You are safe with me because I say so. You are promised to me now, so stop fucking around and do what I tell you to do."

There. That's the Caspian I know—*the monster.*

He sounds more like himself now, not like the guy I gave myself to.

Seeing the monster again infuriates me because I was truly foolish to drop my guard and trust him.

"What are you going to order me to do now?" My voice drips with sarcasm.

Pushing his shoulders back, he squares off with me, and his face hardens. "You will do whatever I tell you to do. Right now, that's to rest and get better."

"How am I supposed to rest? Someone tried to kill me."

"That is being taken care of. We're investigating."

That means I'm still in danger, and I've only just told him about the second guy.

The last note warned Lillian died for the sins of my father and if I stayed at Raventhorn, I'd end up just like her. This is to do with the past. It has to be, and the same people who killed Lillian have come to kill me now.

Two men in the woods, two men at my apartment.

Was it the same two?

Were they who Lillian thought we were in danger of?

If this is about the past, then the answers must lie with what happened to her and why.

"What about Lillian?" I choke out.

His lips thin again, which tells me all I need to know. "We're not to do anything more about Lillian. There is nothing more anyone can do. I didn't get any information from Sheriff Tanner that we didn't already know, so we need to leave the past alone."

My already dry throat seizes, and I have to swallow hard to make way for my words. "Leave the past alone? Do you seriously expect me to just forget someone killed my sister?"

"I'm not saying that."

"Do you no longer believe me?" I utter in a hushed undertone.

"Willow, you can't talk about Lillian anymore," he replies, and the knife in my heart twists a little more.

He's not confirming or denying his belief. That can only mean one thing. "These are your father's orders."

"Yes. We can't look into something when we don't have anything to work with."

"What about the notes? I fail to see how those mean nothing. That last note was pretty damn clear. If your father saw that—"

"I showed it to him," he cuts in, holding my gaze.

36

"And what?"

"He thinks someone is screwing with you."

Jesus, what am I supposed to do now? "Not many people know the truth about Bluff Island."

"He doesn't think the notes are enough to connect this to the past. The note isn't specific about when Lillian died."

"So, that's it? I'm seriously to do nothing?" I can barely get the words out.

"Willow, it's out of our control, so I need you to listen to me and leave the past alone."

God...he's not going to help me. I'm alone and lost again. Telling him my secret was all for nothing because now I can't do anything. I should have kept my mouth shut.

"My father has given us an extra week after you're released so you can recover for the wedding," he states, releasing a heavy sigh as he changes the subject. "The wedding date has been set for the last Saturday in October. When you get out of here, the wedding is what we'll focus on."

Wedding?

Rage roils within me. Normal people wouldn't even be talking about something as trivial as a wedding when my life hung in the balance mere days ago. It's all going ahead, though, because my inheritance comes through in a matter of weeks. I'm sure his father—*our fucking Highness*—wants to make sure everything is in order to seize my family's legacy.

"Did you hear me?" Caspian prods.

"I heard you." I know he wants me to comment on the wedding, but I'm not going to. That's going to piss him off, but I don't care.

I don't want to talk about any damn wedding. The fact that I'm being forced to marry him makes it so much worse because it's *him*.

I hate that my heart feels anything for him. My own body has betrayed me and continues to do so when it comes to him.

I've never met anyone who could make me feel everything amazing in one breath then shatter me into a million pieces in the next.

Right now, I can barely look at him, and it's probably best I hold my tongue.

There is one more question I need to ask, though. One that's definitely going to piss him off, but it's more important than me. So, I force the angst writhing through my mind away and meet those eyes of his with a boldness I don't feel.

"How is Lucian?"

As predicted, Caspian's face contorts into a frown. "He's the same."

My heart shrinks. "Did you actually see him?"

"Yes."

I don't believe him. "Can I see him?"

His gaze hardens once more. "You need to rest, Malyshka."

Calling me Malyshka is another mark of ownership. I hate hearing the endearment now more than ever.

"After I've rested, can I see him then?" I throw back.

"We will talk about that when I'm *convinced* you've rested."

Asshole. God knows just how much I'm going to hate this. "When can I go home?"

"You aren't. You're going to live with me—"

"No." I shake my head.

"We're not arguing about this. You can't go back to your apartment, and there's little point if we're getting married in a few weeks."

"Then I want to stay with Adrian and Elaine while I'm recovering." I hold his gaze. "I need to be with people who can take care of me."

"I will take care of you. You are mine."

"What do you think I am, Caspian? I'm a fucking person." I'm so sick of him treating me like a thing. "You can't just tell me I belong to you."

"But you do, Malyshka. And the sooner you start realizing that the better it will be for you."

"I need my godparents," I insist, hating the weak edge in my voice. I need Adrian and Elaine, and I need to be away from him for a while so I can process what's happening and what's not. "Someone tried to kill me. How the hell do you think I feel? Adrian and Elaine are my family. No one can take care of me like they can. I need them."

Although his expression is still hard, something softens in his eyes. I hope he agrees because I'm too weak to fight any more.

"Three days." He gives me a curt nod. "I'll give you three days with them. After that, you'll live with me, and we'll focus on planning our wedding. Understood?"

"Yes... understood."

I understand perfectly, much more than what we're acknowledging.

I'm in this mess because we weren't supposed to be together. I followed whatever I felt for him knowing I was going to get burned one day. Well, here I am in the fire, burning up.

As I stare at my very own monster, I look past the dark obsession and find the hatred that still lurks in his eyes.

The hatred for the secret I kept that took his mother away is the thing he shares with his father and a warning the beast I feared in Dorian is nothing compared to the devil I know.

That prevalent hatred tells me in the end, it won't matter how close we got because Caspian won't choose me. He will always choose to please his father.

Which means there's nothing to stop him from allowing his father to use and punish me, no matter how evil he is.

Why would he when they both want revenge for what I did?

CHAPTER 4

CASPIAN

My blood is still boiling like a volcano nigh on eruption when I march into my apartment. I've come home because it's the only place I can go to unleash.

I knew when Willow woke we were going to have a difficult conversation. I just never realized talking to her was going to enrage me.

It's been forty minutes, and my blood vessels still feel like they're gonna pop.

I'm fuming because I can't do more than what I'm doing and because she's right to not want me.

That is the essence of what's happening.

After everything I've gone through, Willow doesn't want to be with me.

I broke my vows and even defied my father to be with her, but this mess is what I got. Like an idiot, I landed in this shitty situation headfirst with my ass in the air.

The girl I love to hate and hate to love wants nothing

to do with me. Not even my forgiveness for the secret she kept in the past.

I noticed the moment she shut down.

When she woke up, I had her back for a few minutes. Then it was like someone had walked into her head and raised the walls of Fort Knox to keep me out. It didn't even matter I saved her life.

I then made everything worse by telling her we couldn't talk about Lillian anymore. That was when I lost her for good.

I had to be the asshole because I don't want her snooping around and my father catching her. He's serious about taking her away from me.

He'll do it, and I'm pissed he has so much power over me.

And yes, I'm fucking pissed at the way she asked after *Lucian* when I was talking about the wedding.

I loathe the way her fucking beautiful face lights up when she talks to him or about him.

She doesn't look at me like that. She's *never* looked at me like that.

And she never will.

Fuck. How did I get myself into this mess? I was supposed to stay away from her. Except I didn't.

Jesus Christ, I'm gonna flip the fuck out.

I head to the living room like I'm ready for war and reach for the first thing I can get my hands on. Unfortunately it's the paperweight Thorne gave me for Christmas years ago.

I launch it into the wall. When it smashes, shards of

glass blast everywhere, but I don't feel the relief I hoped. I doubt I would if I smashed the whole fucking place.

"Maybe I should come back another time." Thorne's voice stops me from reaching for the vase on the bookshelf.

I whirl around to face my cousin, meeting his worried gaze. I haven't seen him since the other night when I briefed him in full on everything. I even told him the things I'd previously held back about Lillian.

"No." I sigh with frustration. "Stay."

"I take it the princess is awake."

"Good guess. I'm sure my craziness gave me away."

"What happened?"

"Everything went to hell, Thorne." I move to the sofa and sit. "Everything is a mess."

He walks over and plants himself opposite me. "Anything I can do to help?"

"No."

He takes a quick breath. "Unfortunately, I have some more bad news."

"Christ, what now?"

I hold my breath, hoping he hasn't done something and fucked up. I already told him my father doesn't want either of us involved in the investigation, but Thorne is as bad as me.

"Someone wiped Timofey's files."

My jaw slackens. "Wiped?"

"They're all gone."

"Fuck."

We suspected Dorian must have been at Lucian's

apartment because he was checking to see if Lucian found something in Timofey's files. The fact that the files have been wiped confirms there was definitely something in them that posed a threat, and Lucian could have seen it.

Those files were my only genuine lead. Prior to finding out Zak was looking through them, all we had was the call log that listed Dorian's number as the last call Zak took before he died. Now Dorian is dead, and the files are gone, too.

Great.

"I was worried something like this would happen," Thorne adds. "I did my best to go through them as quickly as possible, but there were a lot. Lucian must have used some kind of cloaking device because I can't tell what he was looking at."

"This just keeps getting worse."

"Sorry, man." Thorne sighs. "I don't know what to do now."

Neither do I. What I know is someone is watching us, which means I need to watch my back and those helping me—a.k.a Thorne.

"You have to stop." The words fall from my lips, laced with the regret I feel coursing through my mind.

"Stop what, cousin?" He glares back at me.

"You have to stop helping me with everything."

His brows snap together. "Are you fucking kidding me?"

"I can't get you in trouble. I won't stop looking for justice for my brother, and now I have to protect my girl.

Everything I do from now on to pursue either of those could mean death, or at the very least getting kicked out of the Knights." *Which is the same thing as death.*

Cynical laughter falls from his lips. "You don't realize what you're saying."

"Like fuck. Of course, I do."

He inches forward and stares me down. "You can't do this by yourself, Caspian. That's not me taking a dig. It's the truth."

"You do know my father is watching us, right?"

"Of course, I know that. But you must know he's not the only one watching us." He quirks a hard brow.

"I know. If we weren't being watched, Timofey's files would still be there."

"Precisely. Lucian wouldn't be in the hospital either."

As guilt waters the jealousy and rage I previously felt, I stare at him for a few labored beats and nod, trying to ignore the lump forming in my throat.

"I went to see Lucian straight after I saw Dorian." That was the one and only time I questioned Dorian about Zak. I threatened to kill him and everyone he knew if I ever found out he had anything to do with Zak's death. "Then Lucian came here to Erebus."

"Clearly, they kept tabs on him after. Dorian's death is a wild card I never saw coming but being found in Lucian's apartment makes me suspect him even more regarding Zak's death. However, since Dorian is dead, and they didn't find any guns at the scene, we know we're dealing with someone else. Someone who wanted them both dead."

45

I hang my head in dismay and stare at the patterns on the stone floor. There's too much going on, and I don't know how to begin making the connections.

"I'm going to help you regardless of what you say. You're only going to get burned in the worst way possible if you keep going as you are."

Since I already feel like I've been through the infernal fires of hell, I can't exactly refute his prediction.

With reluctance, I nod, accepting his help. "We have to lie low, Thorne."

He smirks. "Yeah, genius, I know."

"All right... Well, the first thing you should know is, I don't have a plan."

"We'll come up with something. For now, I suppose the wedding needs to be priority to get your father off your back."

"Yeah." That's going to make my problems with Willow worse, but I can't worry about that now. "What can we do now that the files have been wiped?"

"I'll keep checking the Knights' database. I also factored in that if we were being watched, maybe our conversations were being listened to as well."

I straighten. "Damn it."

"Don't worry. I sorted something out to screw with any listening devices. We're good here and at the club." He looks at me tentatively. "Is there anything else we can look into right now?"

"Willow told me it was two men who attacked her."

His brows disappear into his hairline. "Two?"

"Yes, two masked men. One guy inside her apartment who chased her onto the bridge, where she ran into the other guy. The girls at the house were all questioned, and no one saw anything."

"Did you tell your father about the second guy?"

"I did, but you know he doesn't care, right?" I messaged my father when I left the hospital. He simply replied that he would add the information to the notes. "Willow is more valuable to him alive, but *alive* could mean anything to him. And when she turns nineteen, he'll care even less because he will have gotten everything he wants by then."

Thorne bites the inside of his lip because he knows I'm right.

"What happened to Willow appears to be a separate matter from everything else, but I don't think it is." I drag in a breath.

"I don't think so either," he agrees. "Finding out Zak was looking through her father's files days before he died makes me think it's all the same problem."

"Yes, so what if she was the main attraction and everything else was just loose ends that needed to be tied up?"

Thorne studies me with a contemplative expression. "You said she got that first note on her first day on campus."

"She did, so whatever is happening was already under way. It was probably put in motion when Lillian died. But now they want Willow dead."

"But, why?"

"The only thing that comes to mind is her inheritance, and if I am right, then there's no reason to want Willow Raventhorn dead, unless you're a judge."

His eyes widen. "You seriously think so?"

"I can't think of anything else."

"But there are at least three judges on the council who care deeply for her."

"And there are others who don't care. My father is top of that list but is the only person we can rule out since he already has a way to *all* her wealth if she lives. Add my marriage to her, and we have control of the bank. He'd have everything."

"He would."

"Now, if she dies before her nineteenth birthday, her inheritance gets divided amongst the eight judges. That's the law of the Knights."

"But that's always been the law. They could have killed her before now. Why didn't they?"

Once again, I think of Sheriff Tanner's words. "Maybe something else changed. Something that's relevant now that put her in more danger."

"What the fuck could that be?"

"I have no idea."

"Okay, let's start with what we know." He runs a hand over his beard. "We know Zak went looking in Timofey's files, but something must have happened to make him do that. Perhaps if we figure out what that *something* could be, it could give us a good baseline."

I take a moment to think, allowing my weary mind to mull over the clues. As I do, I recall something Willow said about Lillian. "Willow told me Lillian went to the library when they were at Bluff Island. I doubt she went to the library to borrow a book. What if she went there to use the computer to check something out? The same *something* Zak could have been checking?"

"You remember Lillian, right?" Thorne raises his brows. "Nice girl, but she was on drugs. A lot. You seriously think she had the type of skills to get into her father's files?"

"No." Not even we have those skills. That's why we involved Lucian. Lillian had no interest in computers, but she was a clever girl. "I don't think she could hack a system, but what if she had her father's password?"

Realization dawns on his face. "Jesus. That's… entirely possible."

"It is, and if so, something outside of computers would have made her want to check her father's files. Or someone." I knit my fingers together, knowing I'm making a lot of assumptions.

"What if it was Peter?" he suggests. "He was close to their family, and he's close to ours. We initially thought a judge could be responsible for Zak's death. Peter is a judge. What if Dorian was working for his father? This is all looking like Lillian and Zak saw something that got them killed. What if it was to do with Peter?"

The phone Dorian used to call Zak before he died previously belonged to

Peter. Right now, it's the only connection to suspect him, along with the fact that whoever killed my brother had enough help to keep their involvement hidden. Peter would have the means to do that.

"I think we should definitely consider that and keep looking into him."

"Sure thing. However, he's gonna be a little harder to check out. I can't just hack his systems; he'll know." He bites the inside of his lip. "I'll have to be extremely careful. That man has skills beyond my years."

He's right. Peter is the computer infrastructure architect at Ivanov Tech. He also takes care of the computer systems at Dynamic Corp, and the bank, too. He's one of the few people who work across all the companies because of his skills.

Those skills also make him the perfect candidate to wipe the files, and the perfect villain to be wary of with his leadership roles as judge number two in the Knights and the Sovientrik in the Komarovski.

To say we're going to have to be careful when we investigate him is an understatement. Add the fact that he just lost his son to the mix, and it's going to be near impossible to get close to him.

"Check out what you can, and we'll do the rest the old-fashioned way and hunt," I reply.

I'm going to have to do the same thing to find out who tried to kill Willow.

"What about Dorian and Lucian? Who the hell tried to kill them, Caspian? The person who screwed with the cameras would have needed serious computer skills, too, but I don't think Peter killed his son. Killing Dorian would also eradicate the wealth he would have stood to gain from the marriage to Willow."

"The only person who can give us answers to what

happened that night and maybe why it happened is Lucian Sokolov."

I won't lie to myself. I'm jealous of whatever Lucian has with Willow, no matter what it is—friendship or otherwise. However, assuming I'm right, he might be the only person who can fill in some of the missing pieces and tell me what my brother was investigating before he died.

Answering that question may help with everything else.

CHAPTER 5
WILLOW

I stare at Lucian's motionless body lying in his hospital bed.

An array of machines and tubes is attached to him, keeping him alive.

This is my fourth visit since I was allowed to walk around. Every time I walk into his room, I hope something will change, but nothing does. I've been here now for five days, and the doctors are talking about releasing me late next week. I was hoping Lucian would wake up before I leave, but it doesn't look like he is.

Part of me is terrified he never will; the other part is holding on to faith with everything I've got.

I guess I should be happy I'm getting the chance to see him. I worried Caspian would get on his high horse and stop me from visiting Lucian altogether, but he seemed to cave when I stopped talking to him.

Silence was better than arguing as I tried to get information from him and kept being met with the same mantra that things were being investigated. When I got tired of that, I'd take my medication a few minutes before I knew he was going to arrive so it would kick in on time and I'd drift off to sleep.

Admittedly, I was exhausted. I haven't been able to fall asleep on my own since waking and remembering my attack. I tend to sleep during the day after I'm given medication. Then I'm up for most of the night.

Hence why I'm here at this hour. It's barely seven in the morning. Visiting hours aren't until twelve, but the nurses have been nice enough to let me come and see Lucian at this time.

It's better this way because it's just the two of us. On my first visit his parents were here, and it was awkward.

I kept feeling guilty because I know Lucian is here because of me. I can't connect the parts that are supposed to fit and explain what happened, or why, but it's the only thing that makes sense. It might explain Dorian's presence in Lucian's apartment, too.

My anxiety has been substantially worse than before, accompanied by horrible nightmares of my attack. I also keep dreaming about Lucian and imagining him being shot and dying.

I shuffle in closer, sitting forward on the chair, and set my hands near his left, which is cold. That's not normally a good sign, but at least his cheeks have a slight bit of color in them against his olive skin.

What really happened to us?
Who tried to kill us?
Who tried to kill me?

I can't stop thinking about who it could be, and I can't stop the stifling fear that cripples me with trepidation.

I haven't done anything to anyone, so the only thing I can come up with is what benefits a person might gain from my death. When I think of that, my inheritance comes to mind, but I push the thought away because of the accusation that comes with it in relation to the judges.

Fuck, no wonder I can't sleep and I'm on edge.

There are guards stationed outside the door on this floor and on mine. They're some of the best guards in the Knights, but I still feel like I have to keep looking over my shoulder.

I should, because no matter who helps me, I'm in trouble. The fact that I'm alive and my attackers are still at large means trouble is something I need to have in the forefront of my mind.

I just don't know what the hell I'm supposed to do about it.

Escape?

I've thought about it and all the ways I could leave, followed by all the ways I'd be found. Escaping is not an option, and all the choices laid before me feel like doom.

I straighten as the door opens and the nurse walks in.

"Two more minutes. You both need your rest." She offers a kind smile and glances from me to Lucian.

"Okay, thank you."

Dipping her head, she backs away and closes the door with a soft click.

I push to my feet and run my fingers over Lucian's hand.

"Please wake up, Lucian. I miss you so much." It's strange. He feels more like a brother to me now than he ever did, and I pray he pulls through. "I hope you can hear me. I truly do. Please... don't die and leave me. Don't."

I leave before the tears come.

My heart lifts when Eilish walks through the door.

Although there's a bounce to her mid-length blonde waves and the sparkly gloss on her pink lips enhances her beauty, the dark shadows under her eyes are testament to the extent of her worry.

A little smile graces her lips when she sees I'm better than I was on her last visit. Better as in I'm more awake and likely to stay that way for longer than five minutes.

"Hi," she says, closing the door behind her.

"Thank you so much for coming to see me."

"Oh, Willow, of course I was going to come by."

She makes her way over and gives me a warm hug.

It's a good sign that things are okay between us, but I'm still cautious as we've yet to talk about Caspian. Now that I'm more lucid, today might be that day.

Once she sits in the chair beside my bed, she covers my hand with hers. "How are you feeling? You look better. Do you feel better?"

"Yes, I've been walking around, and my head doesn't feel like it's gonna fall off."

"That's really good. The nurses said you need your rest, so I won't stay too long. I just wanted to see how you were."

"I'm doing much better, and I've rested quite a lot today. It's good to talk, especially to you."

Her smile widens. "As long as we don't talk about anything that puts too much stress on you."

"Honestly, I think not talking will do that a lot quicker." I chuckle. "Everyone's being so careful with me, it's actually a little unnerving."

"We nearly lost you." Sorrow enters her eyes. "The same way we nearly lost Lucian."

"I know." I nod, trying to control my grief. I cried again this morning after seeing him. "I've seen him a few times. I went the moment they told me I could walk around."

"I keep expecting him to jump up out of that bed and tell me this is one of his pranks. But it's really happening."

I squeeze her hand. "Let's try to be strong. We need to be." I'm hoping if I say things like that enough times, I'll start believing it.

"I'm trying, but I'm scared." Her shoulders slump.

"Me too." The fear that Lucian could die is pulling me under, but I have to try and stay afloat. "I keep reminding myself that Lucian is one of the strongest guys I know. Knowing him, I'm sure he's fighting to come back to us."

"I pray so, Willow. I truly do." She dabs away a tear

with the heel of her hand. "It doesn't help that no one can find anything about who shot him. I heard there was no news on your attack either. I can't believe something like that happened on campus and no one can find out anything. Don't you think that's weird?"

"Of course, I do."

She holds my gaze. "I think the two incidents are related. It can't be a coincidence. I don't know why Dorian was in Lucian's apartment, but the whole thing is off."

"I completely agree." I pull in a breath. "Dorian being there is a mystery to me, too, but if the two incidents aren't a coincidence, I'm sure it has something to do with me. Something I don't know and might be the same reason someone wants me dead."

"Has anyone been able to figure that out yet?"

I shake my head.

"What about you?" She searches my eyes. "I'm sure you've thought about it."

"I have, but I can't come up with anything."

Given that Al, her foster father, is a judge and so is Adrian, I'm not going to talk about my inheritance yet, or at all. Thinking someone wants me dead because of it is a serious accusation to make. Especially when I have no evidence.

The only thing I have are the notes. Or rather, Caspian has the main note and Lucian the rest.

The past keeps ringing through my mind along with the warning of ending up like my sister. I believe the answers lie with what happened to Lillian, but I have no way of making the connection or figuring out what it all means.

I never got to show Eilish that last note because we weren't talking. When we were, I didn't want to burden her with my problems. That was also the night Lucian was shot.

More sadness shines in her eyes. "I feel terrible for how I behaved after what happened to you in town."

"Don't worry about that. There are other things I need to tell you. How much do you know?"

She bites the inside of her lip. "I heard about Caspian and the wedding. That's all. Everyone's drip-feeding information about the attack. I figured we'd talk about Caspian at some point, and you'd tell me how you were feeling about him."

Here we go. This is the moment I've been waiting for. I swallow past the lump in my throat and gear myself up to be open with her. She's the only person I have whom I can be real with, so I shouldn't shut her out.

"I'm sorry I never told you I was seeing him." My words come out in a hushed whisper.

I glance down at my lap for a moment, too embarrassed to look her in the eyes. When my gaze climbs back up to meet hers, I'm surprised by the understanding I see in them. It's understanding I never thought I would receive from her after the way Caspian used to treat us back in high school. He'd always start with Eilish first. *Always*. Maybe because he knew it would get to me more.

"Please don't think I didn't care about how he treated you in the past," I add with conviction.

"I won't lie. I was shocked when I realized you guys were together. I was hurt that you kept it from me. But with everything happening, I realized being upset was trivial. How could I be when I could have lost both my best friends forever?"

"So, you aren't mad at me?"

"No... I think in some ways I get it, in other ways I don't, but that's not for me to decide. Caspian has always had this fascination with you, and you with him, even when you didn't want to."

She's right. I can't even refute it, because it's true.

"Did Lucian know?" she asks.

"Yes, he knew. Caspian told him."

"How are you feeling about getting married to him? Is... that better?"

"No," I rasp out, almost afraid of the confession.

"Why?" Her brows wrinkle, and she levels her gaze with mine.

"I should tell you all the parts you don't know."

"Tell me. Tell me everything."

As my anxiety heightens, I draw in another breath to clear my head. I then tell her everything. Or maybe it's better to say I unleash and there is no off-switch to what I tell her.

The moment I mention what happened with my guardianship and Caspian's father, she understands perfectly what that will mean for me. Even though she doesn't voice her worries, I can also tell she's thinking about the same things I am regarding Caspian pleasing his father. Not to mention my grief over not investigating

Lillian's death and what will happen to me if I talk about her.

"My God, Willow." She brings her hands together. "What are you going to do?"

"I don't know. I'm trapped, Eilish, and I'm in danger. I already felt like my life wasn't my own. Now it's definitely not."

We're quiet for a few moments, both of us thinking, neither of us confirming how right I could be. I won't even bother to mention that I know I won't be the only woman in Caspian's life. That blonde girl from the other week evidences that perfectly.

"Is there anything I can do?"

"No, but just us talking helps."

She gives me a warm smile. "Well, I can at least do that. And... I believe you about Lillian."

"You do?" My spirits lift.

"Yes. I do, and that's why I want you to promise me you'll do what you have to, to keep yourself safe. Please promise me you will, Willow."

I nod, but I feel like I'm humoring her.

Keeping myself safe means accepting the protection I'm getting and Caspian's twisted obsession. I'd be foolish not to want to accept help where I can get it to save my life. By the same token, I'm scared of being right about him. And of what I feel for him.

That day in the meadow, he told me he took me there because it was the only place for him where the sky was still blue, my hair was still red, and my eyes still loved him. I knew even as he said those words that I did love him.

Love is my weakness.

It makes him dangerous to me because if I truly allow myself to fall for him, he'll hurt me worse than he did in the past when he declared us enemies and promised to destroy me.

So, I'm left trapped in a situation I can't get out of and the looming uncertainty of my future hanging over my head. That's assuming I still have a future.

My near-death experience wasn't my first brush with death. Next time, I might not be so lucky.

CHAPTER 6
CASPIAN

Willow is being released today.

I should feel better than I do because the doctors said the worst is over—even though we'd still need to be careful. Nevertheless, the tension of the situation is spiking my nerves, making me feel unhinged.

I'm in the same position I was when I was here twelve days ago. Nothing has happened with the investigation, and the more time slips away, the more difficult everything becomes.

I offered to collect Willow's pain meds while she went to see Lucian.

We could have done both things together, but she's still not talking to me. And while I've gone to see Lucian by myself quite a few times, I don't particularly want to see her with him.

I don't want to watch how she behaves around him. Or watch her love for him.

Both are just as bad as feeling the guilt riding my shoulders for my part in him being here.

Willow doesn't know anything about that, and I want to keep it that way.

Aside from wanting to keep my plans regarding Zak a secret, I fear if she knows why I asked Lucian to help me, it might drive us further apart. Because she'll blame me.

She'll blame me for getting him involved and for the fact he's fighting for his life.

When I first asked Lucian for his help, it was because of the note Willow got about Lillian. Then, when he found out Zak was the last person to access her father's files, things changed swiftly and turned into something that could help me.

Obviously, that's no longer the case. Now I'm left with the aftermath of shit not knowing which way to turn.

In a few weeks, the girl I tried to help will be forced to marry me, and I can't help but feel she hates the idea of that more than when she was going to marry Dorian.

More than anything, I wish I could go back to two weeks ago when Willow was truly mine.

Only two mere weeks ago, I woke with her in my arms and the promise of later in my mind. I had that crazy thought of not allowing anyone else to have her.

I never knew we'd be ripped apart the way we are now.

I'm snapped out of my thoughts when the nurse approaches me with a little white paper bag containing Willow's medication. The same wary smile I get from most people who are aware of who and what I am tips the red painted on her thin lips. I dip my head with a curt nod while I take the package, then make my way down to the second floor, where Lucian's room is.

As I get closer, my steps slow, which is unbecoming of me.

The normal version of me fears nothing, not even death, but this version of myself is what I become when things slip out of my control. And that always happens to me when it comes to Willow Raventhorn.

Willow Raventhorn, who will become Willow Ivanov, my wife.

When I reach Lucian's door, I notice it's slightly ajar, so I peek in to check out what I'm up against.

More guilt writhes through me the moment I see Willow's frail body doubled over with her head resting by Lucian's arm on the bed. Her shoulders are shaking as she sobs.

Guilt takes me, and so does jealousy in its most potent form.

I'm a fucking asshole for being jealous of a guy who's barely hanging on to life, but I can't help the way I feel.

As I stand here, invisible to them both, I'm forced to acknowledge the real reason for my jealousy.

It's not exactly because of the relationship they have, although I hate that. It's more to do with the fact that Lucian and I come from the same dark world but are not the same.

Yes, we're the same breed of ruthless, and the same

when it comes to taking what we want. Except, we're as opposite as darkness and light.

That's why he would be able to become a Knight and one of the most lethal members of the Bratva but still be able to offer her something as close as possible to a normal life.

I can't, and I'm sure that's something to do with what happened to me in Russia when I was a child. Witnessing the deaths of family members in the way I did and being beaten daily with the same weapon that killed them will do that to you.

The saying *"Monsters aren't born, they're made,"* rings true with me.

I'll never forget that last beating. It was the making of the monster I am now. I used to see the world in vivid colors, which I'd paint. But that last time, those men beat the colors out of my mind and replaced them with the darkness that still clings to me. The kind that fucks you up for life.

Like death, everything I touch decays, corrodes, and corrupts.

As I watch Willow, all I see is shades of black. I'm only aware that Willow's hair is red, her skin ivory, and her sundress green because my brain registers the names of those colors. But I'm blinded by the dark void still consuming my soul.

So, what's a girl like her supposed to do with a devil like me who wants her even though he knows she shouldn't be with him?

Like Hades, I'm greedy for the girl, and I can't control

the obsession riddling my mind, making me more insane than I already am.

"I need you," Willow mumbles through her tears, snapping me out of my thoughts. Her voice breaks, and she sobs a little louder. "You have to come back to me, Lucian. I don't know how to live in this world without you."

Rage rattles my mind, and I have to bite down hard on my back teeth to control myself.

I stare at Lucian wondering if hearing those words uttered by his dearly beloved *Red* will pull him back from the prison of his mind.

Will it be like in the movies when the guy wakes from a coma for his girl?

If he does, he still wouldn't be able to have her. My father wouldn't allow it.

And neither would I.

The dark thought infused with greed moves me, and I push the door open.

The creak interrupts my Malyshka in her heartfelt plea, and she straightens, wiping away her tears.

The look she gives me is a combination of annoyance and fear.

The annoyance is in response to the hard expression on my face that must look like I'm ready to kill. The fear is there for knowing I heard what she said and I'm not happy about it.

When I walk up to her, I harden my gaze, and for a fleeting moment, raw arousal pierces through her bright blue gaze.

She doesn't look at me the way she does at Lucian, but she doesn't look at him the way she looks at me. Even when she's furious, she still looks at me like she wants me. She knows it, feels it, knows I *know*, and she hates it.

She despises it because she can't control wanting me any more than I can wanting her, and she knows it's my way in.

"We're leaving now," I say in a cool, even tone, and she tries to school her emotions.

Wiping away more tears, she gathers herself but squeezes Lucian's hand before she lets go and comes closer to me.

I place my hand at the small of her back and guide her away, officially taking her back to my world to be mine.

Before we walk out the door, I glance back at Lucian Sokolov, willing him to wake up, too, because I need to know what he knows. It also hasn't escaped me that others might not want that to happen.

The moment we step out of the unit, we're joined by my father's personal guards who will be staying with her for the next three days in New York.

I wish she were going back to Raventhorn with me, but I agree spending time with Adrian and Elaine will probably help her and help mellow her defiance. I'm hoping they will talk some sense into her.

Despite the guards with us, my sense of protection kicks into overdrive when we step outside, and I find myself checking our surroundings for danger. I continue to do so even when we climb into my car because the hair on the back of my neck is reaching for the sky. Like when someone's watching.

Are they?

Why wouldn't they be?

I have to assume that they are and now they know Willow is leaving the confines of where she was perhaps safest.

I meet her cautious wide-eyed glare, knowing she senses my discomfort.

"Did you see something?" she asks in a trembling voice. Those are the most words she's said to me in days.

"No. I was just checking," I decide to say, forcing the eerie feeling away.

When I start up the car and pull out of the parking lot, she stares out the window, but I notice her doing something I've never seen her do before.

She seems to be counting silently but mouthing the number with each breath.

I don't know what that's about, but it looks like something to worry about.

"Are you okay?" I ask, brushing over her elbow.

"I'm fine." She doesn't look at me.

Resuming her coldness, she reaches into her bag to retrieve her iPod.

I smirk when she puts on her headphones, and she cuts me a glance.

"Not gonna talk to me on the long journey?" I already know the answer, but I'm forcing her to talk to me, even for her expressionless one- to two-worded answers.

"About what?" That sarcasm I hate laces through her tone.

"I don't know, maybe our wedding."

No answer this time. She presses play on the iPod deck, and the echo of her way-too-loud music filters through her headphones. She makes a point of turning away from me again, a clear indication she doesn't fucking want to talk about our wedding. *Ever.*

I squeeze my hand into a fist, once again willing the rage away, but it flares up again when I recognize the song she's blasting. It's that woo-hoo shit from weeks ago in the library. I hated the music then as much as I do now, but hearing it makes me remember that whole twenty-four-hour time frame.

That was when I lost my mind and decided to give in to my craving for Willow Raventhorn. That was the day that landed me in this mess, and that craving never left me. It's here now even in my angst-filled, ready-to-kill state, making me want to grab her and fuck her senseless, fuck that defiance from her mind and coax her to submit to me.

The thought makes my dick hard, and as I glance at those pouting lips illustrating her displeasure in breathing the same air I am, I remember them sucking me off and swallowing my cum.

My eyes flick to the soft swells of her breasts when she rests her head on the seat. Much as I try to keep my eyes on the road, I'm drawn to the memory of her tits in my mouth and her lithe body pressed up against mine while I was buried deep inside her.

Damn it, I'm my own worst enemy because I want that again.

I un-ball my fist and focus on the road, but she's in my periphery with her godawful music on repeat.

She falls asleep not long after, and I take the opportunity to switch off the music and take off her headphones. Thankfully, she doesn't stir.

For the next two hours of reprieve, I think of what I'm going to do about Willow and what I want. I want her. I've tried to un-want her but failed as badly as someone trying to un-see something.

I think of all the things I could do to make us better and go back to the way we were, but I know none of those will work because of my father.

As long as he has legal guardianship of her, it fucking emasculates me.

My father is a fucking savage. So am I. So, I know in order to conquer the devil at his own game, I'll have to fight back with something stronger that will crush him.

Whatever that *thing* is, is something I'll have to find.

I drag myself out of my turmoil when I pull up in front of the gates to Adrian and Elaine's home. This is the first time I will be using the front gates. Every other time I've been here saw me sneaking onto the property to get my fill of the princess touching herself.

The gates open, and my convoy of guards and I drive through. When I park up, I gently wake her. She mumbles something I can't quite hear, so I shake her shoulder slightly harder.

"Willow, we're here."

"*Lucian...*"

Fuck, really?

Now she's saying his name in her sleep. My hand stills, and I narrow my gaze as I seethe.

"Willow, it's me. Caspian."

"Lucian, no..." she replies in a breathy tone, and I'm not sure if it's the sort of sultry tenor her voice takes on when she's experiencing pleasure or if it's terror.

As my mind tells me it's the former, fury lights me up like the sky on the Fourth of July.

"Willow, wake up, now." The harsh command does the trick.

Her eyes snap open, and she's panting. Of course, my fucked-up mind tells me she's having some sex dream about her *friend,* and that just enrages me even more.

"We're here?" she breathes, looking around.

"What were you dreaming about?" I demand.

"What?"

"*What* were you dreaming about? You were saying Lucian's name. Why?" I raise my brows and give her a ruthless stare.

The don't-fuck-with-me look on my face should intimidate her, but on this occasion, it doesn't. The annoyance I saw at the hospital returns, and she grits her teeth.

"You are unbelievable."

"Why the fuck am I unbelievable? You were dreaming about some guy and calling his name. I'm within my right to ask you what the fuck you were dreaming about." Not even I can be in the wrong about this.

"Lucian isn't *some* guy."

"Oh, yeah? I'm sure you wouldn't like it if I were dreaming about someone else and calling their name in my sleep."

"I wouldn't give a shit," she snarls. "You can dream about whomever you want. I don't care!"

There it fucking is. The answer I never wanted confirmed.

She grabs her bag, tosses her iPod in along with the headphones, then bolts out of the car.

The wrath flaring inside me is a warning I should let her go. At the same time, it sends me after her.

Grabbing her arm, I yank her back to me the moment she steps onto the cobbled path leading up to the porch.

"Let go of me, you asshole!"

"Not before you tell me what you were dreaming."

"I'm not saying anything to you."

Wrong answer. Now I can't help but think she *was* having some fucking sex dream.

I tighten my grip on her arm. "Tell me what you were dreaming, Willow."

"Let go of me. You're crazy."

"Yes, I am, and you are making me more fucking insane with every second that passes. You were having some filthy dream about Lucian, weren't you?"

The accusation makes her snap. With her free hand, she raises her bag and hits me with it right across my chest. It does nothing to me but show how angry she is with me.

"You fucking asshole! How can you be such an idiot

at a time like this? Lucian is in a coma fighting for his life, and you're here talking shit."

"I'm not talking shit. His condition has nothing to do with what you feel for him."

"And what do I feel for him, Caspian? You seem to know so much about me you can read my mind, so you tell me."

I grab her other arm and pull her flush against me. She tries to break free, but I lock her in. It's time to give her a rude awakening and remind her of certain truths.

"You listen to me. You are *mine*. I don't fucking care what you feel for him or anybody else. It doesn't matter. Have your filthy dreams. It won't change a goddamn thing because I own you." When I see I have her undivided attention, I lean closer to her ear. "Your body belongs to me. Every part of you belongs to me. I was the first man to make your pussy bleed, and I will be your only. When I get back inside you, I'll give you the reminder that you'll always belong to me. I'll make you scream again like you did last time and beg me to fuck you."

She glares at me with a potent stare that would incinerate me if such a thing were possible. It intensifies when I give her a maddening smile that must make me look like a psycho.

Her eyes illustrate the wealth of her attempt to hate me, but the flush of color creeping down her elegant neck speaks of her arousal.

"Let me go," she grates out.

"Never, Malyshka. Never."

"Let her go, Caspian," calls an authoritative voice, which makes me look away from her.

It's Adrian.

He's standing on the porch. He wouldn't have heard what I said, but the way I'm holding Willow is enough to guess she's not pressed up against me of her own will.

"I said let her go," he repeats, staring me down.

When Elaine joins him, I release Willow, and she steps away.

With the air of menace still lurking inside me, I lean back toward her and give her a wicked smile that makes her shudder.

"Soon," I promise, riveting my gaze to hers. Taking a lock of her hair, I allow it to curl around my thumb then float back to her side. "See you in three days, Malyshka."

With that said, I give her an easy wink and walk away.

Before I leave, I glance back at her and make another promise to myself to break down her walls to *make* her want me again.

No matter what it takes.

CHAPTER 7
WILLOW

"Willow." Adrian mutters my name tentatively, turning my gaze away from Caspian's car speeding down the drive.

As my godfather approaches, I try to calm my rage, but my blood is still on fire from my heated exchange with the devil.

I'm enraged with Caspian for his accusations about my dream—which was another nightmare about Lucian—and I'm mad at myself for my treacherous body's attraction to him.

When Adrian reaches me, tears prick at the back of my eyes like the points of sharp pins.

I'm eighteen years old, but damn, do I ever feel like the lost little girl I was after my parents died.

The moment he touches me, I crumble and rush into his awaiting arms.

"Don't worry, sweet girl. You're home now," he whispers against my hair.

His words soothe me, and I find myself wishing everything were different. Maybe then my parents and Lillian would still be alive.

Sometimes I wonder if maybe they could be if I hadn't kept that secret.

Perhaps this is my penance.

When we pull apart, Elaine moves in and kisses my forehead. She then looks up at the convoy of guards who arrived with me and her brows furrow.

We already have guards on the property, but these guys will remain here for the duration of my stay. They will also be with me twenty-four seven when I return to campus.

I should feel grateful for the extra protection, but the sight of them distresses me further. They are a reminder that I'm the Pakhan's investment.

"Come, let's go inside," Elaine suggests.

I nod, and we head inside the house, where the soothing scent of home greets me.

The aroma of Elaine's freshly baked bread hangs in the air, mingling with the fragrance from the long-stemmed roses in the vase in the hallway.

We enter the living room, where we all sit.

"How are you feeling?" Adrian asks.

"I'm okay. I'm just unsettled by the situation. I wish I could spend more time with you guys."

"We do, too," Elaine replies.

As I take note of the sadness in her eyes, I remember what she said to me about wishing we could get in her car and drive away, escaping this life.

For the zillionth time I wish we could, but I know she can't. I know *we* can't go anywhere and everything is going to be harder from now on.

"I suppose I should be thankful I got to spend these few days with you. God knows what my life will be like when I leave here."

The three of us spoke at length about the situation, but in the end, it came to the same answers. No one can help me. And realistically, I landed myself in this mess.

There are a number of things Adrian and Elaine aren't happy about. The top of the list was me telling Caspian about Lillian, and not telling them about the notes.

Both placed me in a position where they couldn't help.

"We don't want you to worry while you're here." Adrian sits forward.

"It's hard not to." And I'm worried about this weird relationship I have with Caspian.

I left home a sensible virgin, went to college for a little over a month, then gave my body to the one guy I should have stayed away from. I can't even cast off my stupidity as a one-time-only mistake. I slept with Caspian countless times and didn't stop until I was made to.

I'll never forget the look of disgust and fury on his father's face when he walked in on us having sex. It made me feel like a slut.

"You know what Aleksander Ivanov is going to do to me, don't you?" I chance asking.

We've spoken about everything else besides the obvious—that Caspian's father wants Dynamic Corp.

Over the years, both Adrian and Elaine have been careful not to badmouth him in front of me. I've tried not to as well. However, I think the time has come to state things as they are.

"We just have to work hard so that doesn't happen." Adrian nods.

"I think that plan is already in motion. If I don't die first."

"Please don't say that." Elaine frowns. "That's not funny."

"I wasn't joking." I sulk.

"Willow, everyone is doing everything in their power to make sure your attackers are found and punished. We're all trying to keep you safe."

"I know." I swallow hard and sigh. "I'm scared. And my safety isn't the only thing I have to worry about. What if I get sent back to St. Jude's?"

"Don't worry about that." Adrian shakes his head. "I need you to trust that we're here if you need to talk."

"You can call us any time, sweetie," Elaine concedes.

"I know."

"I know you know, but we need you to believe that you can talk to us," Adrian cuts in. "That way, if you're feeling stressed, we can talk things through. We can be there for you when you think of Lillian."

My breath stills, and I try to pretend the way I normally do when my sister's name is mentioned—like I believe she ran away.

Adrian doesn't believe me. Elaine doesn't either, although she's never said anything one way or the other. Adrian, on the other hand, outrightly told me what I believed wasn't real.

"Okay. I will talk to you."

"You just have to remember that what you thought happened at Bluff Island never happened." He nods with conviction.

Words can't express how much my heart breaks on hearing him say that. It breaks a little more when I nod in agreement—*still pretending*.

"You're going to have to watch what you say and whom you say it to," he adds.

Nothing is truer than that, but it also unfortunately applies to them.

In the end, Adrian is a Knight and a judge. Above all else, he reports to Aleksander.

"Alright...no more talk of this." He takes my hand. "Let's not waste the time we have together as a family. Okay?"

"Yes."

Family. It will be nice to believe I have one. If only for the next three days.

I WAKE in the early hours of the morning, stirred by my nightmares, which seem to be getting worse.

I keep having the same reoccurring one about Lillian nearly every single night.

At least before, it was sporadic and happened at the end of days spent grieving.

I get off the bed and grab a drink of water from the jug Elaine left me earlier. As it's still cool, it soothes the dryness in my throat.

When I calm down, I sit on the edge of the bed. Almost instantly, Caspian's face enters my mind, pushing away the calm.

I have four days left here before he'll come to take me back to Raventhorn to start this crazy journey. I hate that I'm venturing into a situation I can't control, and I have no idea what shape the future will take.

I keep trying to come up with some grand plan to save myself and find out what happened to my sister, but there's nothing that will work besides what I'm already doing now. Which is going through the motions of doing what I'm told to do.

Is that really all I can do, though?

I was hoping the clarity of being home would help me come up with something more, but it hasn't.

I feel now that I've gotten to the point where I can't ignore the gravity of the situation. I don't want to die. I don't want anyone to kill me.

Staying alive then means doing what I have to do to weather the storm life has in store for me. The only way I can do that is by essentially trusting Caspian—the same devil who told me I couldn't talk about my sister anymore.

Just watching him try to keep me safe pushes me toward trusting him.

But does the devil become a good person just because he saves your life and is actively going out of his way to ensure your safety?

He's still the devil, and that's something I shouldn't overlook.

It's like that saying about the injured snake. You know what it is when you pick it up. So, when it bites and thereby poisons you, you have no right to be surprised or disappointed.

The same analogy can be applied to Caspian.

He's twisted, obsessive, and volatile. His temperament can change like the wind, catching me off-guard and throwing me out of sync. When we clash, it's like the rough waves of the sea smashing against jagged rock.

Yet all he has to do is look at me for my body to betray me.

Unwanted arousal heats my blood when I remember his promise to remind me that my body belongs to him.

Does wanting to survive mean allowing him to take me?

I'm being foolish for worrying about that because he's going to be my husband, and we've already slept together. It's just that things have changed in ways I never imagined.

Even with all that's happened, the part of me that has feelings for him is always alive, fueled by something I can't describe.

I feel it coursing through my veins thicker than blood. It's something wicked that only he does to me. It's always existed and is the thing that draws me to him.

So, no matter which lie I tell him, or myself, truth is truth, and it will always be the truth whether it's good for me or not.

One day, it's going to break me. And that's when he'll steal my soul.

That's when he'll hurt me the most. Like that viper tattooed on his neck, when he poisons me, it will be potent and lethal.

Only God knows what will happen to me then. I just pray I'll have strength to survive the battle when it comes.

The sound of something smashing has me bolting up.

It sounded like it came from downstairs in the living room. I listen for a few moments, waiting for something more, but nothing happens.

My heart starts racing, and the first thing I think is that someone's broken into the house. It seems near impossible with so many guards around.

But look what happened to me at Raventhorn. The whole campus is supposed to be secured, but two men almost succeeded in killing me.

My chest starts to tighten, a sign that my already heightened anxiety has been triggered. So, I immediately start breathing deeply and counting backwards.

As I calm, I slide off the bed and carefully pad across the floor to my door.

Adrian and Elaine's room is on the other side of the house.

Did they hear the noise, too?

I listen for the thud of Adrian's heavy footfalls but hear nothing.

Deciding to be brave, I open the door and make my way across the landing. I stop when raised voices filter up from downstairs—voices which belong to Adrian and Elaine.

Curiosity sends me down the stairs, taking my time so as not to alert anyone to my presence.

Their voices get louder when I make my way to the living room, and I realize they're arguing. I don't think I've ever heard them argue. Not in the whole time I've been living here, or even before.

Of course, all couples are prone to arguing, but I foolishly thought they were an exemption.

I can't quite hear what they're saying, so I move closer.

"It's out of our hands. You keep fucking doing what you're supposed to do," Adrian barks, shocking me further by the harsh tone he takes with Elaine. I would never have thought he'd speak to her like that.

Are they arguing about me?

"How can you say that?"

"I'm saying it. Now do what I tell you to do." Adrian's voice is so loud the walls tremble at the sound of it. "He's already furious enough as it is about the situation. I don't know what the hell to do to fix it. You will not make things worse."

As his footsteps move toward the door, I slip into the crevice between the wall and the bookshelf. I'm just in time to hide as the door flies open and Adrian marches out.

I expect him to go upstairs, but he heads to the front door and leaves the house.

Moments later, the roar of his car tearing down the driveway fills my ears and Elaine wanders out of the living room sobbing.

She moves down to the sitting room, and I'm left wondering what the heck just happened.

Who were they talking about?

Was it Aleksander?

Why is my gut telling me they weren't talking about him?

Maybe because they weren't. It didn't sound as if they were, and honestly, the only person who is happy right now about *the situation* is him.

So, who could make Adrian and Elaine argue like that?

CHAPTER 8
CASPIAN

Thorne and I decided to keep our usual meetup at the Verge tonight because we needed a break.

Today was one of those long fucking days when we seemed to do a lot but didn't accomplish much to move us forward.

We're sitting at one of the booths that overlook the raucous crowd of people who are either dancing, doing lines of coke off naked chicks, fucking, or talking.

Thorne managed to set up some elaborate spyware to keep tabs on all the information my father is receiving on the investigation. Essentially, whatever my father sees, we see, too.

So far, the only significant thing to happen is that my father has started an investigation on the judges. It stands to reason if we suspected they could be involved, he would, too. He did the same thing when Zak was killed. However, he found nothing incriminating on any of them.

I'm glad he's considering them on this occasion, too, but I imagine he's just doing all he can to protect his plans to take Dynamic Corp. He won't want to share anything with any of his peers if Willow died on his watch.

At least his extra eye on the judges will allow us a way to check out whatever he finds on Peter.

This situation requires patience, one quality I don't have and can't muster when I'm worried. I loathe feeling useless while time slips away.

The only thing helping me keep my shit together is knowing if I don't try to play the game the way it needs to be played, I'll blow all my hopes of unearthing the truths I seek and lose my mind, too.

So, I'm looking the part I'm supposed to assume by planning the wedding, going to classes, and pretending to be the little bitch my father wants me to be.

"Time to see Lizbet," Thorne states, glancing at his watch with a smirk.

"Have fun." I take a long drag on my joint as he stands.

"You know I will."

At least one of us will be having some form of a normal night.

"You gonna be okay?" He lifts his chin.

"Yeah. Don't worry about me. I'm gonna leave soon." I need some time to myself anyway to think.

"All right. I'll check in if I have anything. You do the same."

I dip my head, and he walks away.

Releasing a haggard breath, I return to my tempestuous thoughts as the music changes to one of the woo-hoo songs Willow likes.

I swear to Christ everything has been set up to either remind me of her or make me think of her. Much of the music tonight has been like that. At one point, I was sure I could have been listening to her playlist.

I pull out my phone and check for any updates from the guards who are with her.

There's nothing more since their last check-in three hours ago. I have them updating me morning and evening, but I keep listening out for some shit to happen.

Some damn thing that will occur while I'm hours away and can't reach her.

I'm trying not to worry, but it's hard. Harder when I know I'm the last person she'll want to save her.

After the heated way we parted, it's going to be interesting to see what shape our next meeting will take. I can just imagine how anxious she must be, thinking of what I'm going to do to her when I see her.

She'll be right to be anxious. I'll be doing everything she thinks of me doing to that body of hers. After all, she knows how I like to fuck.

The thought brings an uncanny smile to my lips and hardens my dick.

The first thing I'm going to do when I get her back to my place is fuck her senseless. I'm going to fuck every hole in her body and make her ache so badly she won't be able to walk for days.

I finish the joint, closing my eyes to savor the last dose of sinful delight.

At that moment, soft fingers flutter over my shoulders, pulling me from the daze, and I turn to find Becky Hawthorn standing behind me with the brightest smile on her face.

Her platinum hair looks like a halo in the club lights, and her bright blue eyes sparkle for seeing me.

The last time I stared into those eyes, she was on her knees sucking my dick. That was after my initiation and wasn't that long ago.

That night and most of the following day saw her in my bed with me buried balls deep inside her.

She's here now looking like she wants a replay.

"Caspian Ivanov," she coos in a seductive voice. "I was starting to think I was never going to see you again."

Sliding her hands over my shoulders, she makes her way around me and props herself onto my lap.

Of all the girls I've been with before Willow, Becky might have come the closest to becoming a possible girlfriend. I'm not sure why that is, and I can't explain my reasons for hooking up with her as much as I did.

Usually, when she'd do something like this, we'd head out to get high together and fuck. My body is set to do that by default, except I'm not that guy anymore.

When I feel myself lifting her off me, I realize just how hooked I am on Willow.

Hooked or screwed over—they might be the same thing.

"What's wrong with you?" Becky purrs with a smile. I

can see in her eyes, though, that she's hurt by my reaction. "I heard congratulations are in order."

"Then you know we can't hook up anymore."

She gives me an incredulous glare and chuckles. "Is that supposed to be some kind of joke? Come on, I miss fucking you."

"I don't joke." I stare back at her, my serious expression unwavering. She searches my eyes, and soon the smile recedes from her face.

She pouts and sets her hands on her hips, flicking her gaze up and down my body as if she's still trying to figure me out.

"I can't imagine that little princess actually does it for you."

I know I'm probably holding on to something with Willow that's dead, but part of me refuses to give up.

"Come back to my apartment." She runs a finger along my jaw. "I promise to show you a real good time."

"We're done here, Becky," I reply to her dismay. It's time to go. I'm in enough trouble as it is.

She smiles and leans closer, reminding me of a snake. "Somehow, I don't think so, Caspian. You and I are never done. I'll see you when you're ready for a real woman to ride your cock."

With that, she saunters away, her hips swaying. She glances back at me when she's paces away and winks with a promise in her eyes that she'll be back for me.

If and when that happens, I'll give her the same fucking answer. Along with the reminder of who I am so she doesn't think to come back a third time.

I sigh and turn away, but the slight movement of people on the balcony across from me catches my attention.

No, not people—*one person*.

In the mingle of bodies smashing together as the music changes once more, I spot a guy with longish shaggy black hair wearing a leather jacket. He's in the crevice between the bar and the stairwell, leaning against the pillar.

I thought he was looking at me, but now I'm not sure.

Since he's in the shadows and the club lights are bouncing around, I can't quite see his face. But there's something about him that seems off but familiar at the same time. I just don't know what.

Given the circumstances, I know I might be more prone to paranoia.

Nevertheless, I can't ignore the weight in my gut, which grows heavier the longer I stare at him.

It's the same unhinged feeling I've been getting for the last few days since I picked Willow up from the hospital and felt someone was watching me.

Fuck it. What am I even doing standing here questioning myself?

I'll go over there, look the guy in the eyes, and decide if I need to deal with him or not. If he's the type of enemy I've been searching for, I'll ram his teeth down his throat, get answers from his ass, then kill him.

I keep my gaze trained on him while I feel for my gun in my back pocket. I always carry it now, along with my knife. All fully initiated Knights are allowed to carry their weapons on campus. It's just unusual that they'd need to use them.

I quicken my pace along the rail, and the moment the guy straightens, I know why he looks fucking familiar.

The muscular build and height are what triggers my mind, and I start to run even before my brain processes the image of him wearing a hooded sweatshirt.

I never saw his face that night when he was on the bridge. I didn't see his face that first time weeks ago either, but I remember the rigid outline of his posture and the way his left shoulder slightly dips.

I know it's farfetched to take such minute details into consideration, but I've been trained to spot every single aspect about a person.

And right now, I believe I'm staring at the guy who attacked Willow on the bridge.

I believe it even more when the fucker runs when he notices me approaching.

"Hey!" I call out, but the fucking music is so loud no one can hear me.

Damn it to hell, I'm too far away again and not fast enough because he has a head start.

When he turns down the stairs, I jump down one flight and pull out my gun. The students who see me coming start screaming and scattering, which slows me down all the more.

Nevertheless, I can still see him. The motherfucker is on the ground floor, heading to the fucking door while I'm still stuck up here.

I won't get to him. I already know that even as I push past the people in my way and leap over the next barrier.

Just before he moves through the door, the lights flash on him, lighting him up when he looks back at me. That's the moment I see his face bright and clear.

Dark stubble lines his jaw, dark eyes glower back at me, and the scorpion tattooed on his cheek sticks to my memory.

He bolts forward through the door, and I'm too late. By the time I get outside the club, I have no idea which way he went.

Cursing myself, I throw a fist into the wall.

The motherfucker got away.

But... I now have something he never anticipated.

I know what he looks like.

Two hours later, Thorne and I sit in front of his computer running a drawing I made of the guy through his facial recognition software.

The only surveillance I'd managed to get from the club is a recording of the guy running to the left of the building once he got outside. He then disappeared around the corner, and no other cameras caught him or captured a full view of his face. What was captured wasn't enough to work with because of the angle.

So, the only image of his fucking face is what's in my mind.

It's a good thing I can draw so well. Thorne has been

using what I did to look through the profiles of the students and staff who visit the campus.

It's mostly students who attend the Verge, but sometimes they have contractors and associates who might be there. Even so, they need permission to be here and would have passed through security.

"I got nothing," Thorne announces, resting his fists on the table with a heavy sigh. "So, if your drawing is right, which I don't doubt it is, the guy is not anyone authorized to be here."

"And if that's true, he could have only come through the secret passages."

Thorne sighs. "I guess we're probably not going to hear from your father tonight."

"Or at all."

I had to tell my father what happened. It would have been foolish not to. I also sent him my drawing. He said he'd get back to me. I'm not holding my breath, which is why I'm here.

"Leave it with me. I have a few more ideas, and I'll keep tabs on what your father might find."

"You'll tell me first if you find anything, right?" I check.

"Of course, I will."

"Thanks, man. Sorry to ruin your date with Lizbet."

"Don't worry about that. I can reschedule." He nods. "They're following you, Caspian. This is not good."

"No. It means they're checking on me. Maybe I'm close to figuring out what's going on. You need to watch your back, too."

"I know."

"He was in my grasp, Thorne. Right there in front of me. I don't want to bring Willow back to this. It means she's not safe here."

"We'll keep looking," he promises, but that's the best he can do.

No one can do any more than what they're already doing, but it's still not enough.

I need to keep Willow safe, but how safe can she be if this guy is bold enough to follow me?

Who is he?

Who the fuck is he?

Damn it, I need to find out.

CHAPTER 9
WILLOW

C *aspian is here.*
And just like that, the three days spent with my godparents are over.

As I stare through my bedroom window at Caspian's black Ferrari coming down the driveway, my heartbeat triples.

This is it. He's here to pick me up.

I'm going to live with him.

Later tonight, I'll be in his apartment, and it will be another start to the rest of my life.

A quiet knock on my opened door pulls me from my daze. I turn to acknowledge Adrian and Elaine as they walk in.

Although they've tried to act normal, I know something has been up with them since their argument nights ago.

Adrian returned home early the following morning,

and they both fell into their routine of the perfect couple. It made me realize nothing is as perfect as it seems.

I'm still trying to figure out what their argument was about. I hoped Elaine might have spoken to me about it because I sensed she knew I'd heard them. But she didn't say anything.

"I guess you know Caspian is here." Adrian sighs.

Worry lines appear on his face when I nod.

"I heard the car before I saw it." I smirk, picking up my little bag.

"Do you have everything you need?" Elaine asks.

"Yes." The majority of my things is already at Raven-thorn. I'm only taking a few of the clothes and novels I left behind weeks ago.

Adrian rests his hands on my shoulders. "Remember to call us any time you need to talk."

"I will," I assure him. "Thank you for having me here. I appreciate it."

I do. They're no longer responsible for me, so it was nice to have this respite.

"You can't thank us for that." He taps the top of my head like he used to when I was little. "This will always be your home, and we will always be your godparents. Nothing will change that."

"Thank you."

"I'll see you next week to pick out your dress," Elaine promises with a hopeful smile. "That will be a nice thing to do together."

She'll be helping to organize the wedding. As well as teaching me how to be the *wife* of a Knight. Although it will be great to see her, I'm not going to enjoy any of that.

I smile a smile I don't feel and decide to humor her. "Yes, it will."

"Ready?" Adrian asks, biting the inside of his lip.

As I'll ever be. My stomach twitches like I'm going to vomit. I pray I don't.

"I'm ready," I answer in a small voice.

He dips his head. "You're stronger than you think. You can do this."

"Thanks, I appreciate that." It's nice to hear those words even if I'm having difficulty believing them.

We head outside, where we find Caspian waiting, leaning against his car.

Dressed in full black with a cigarette slinked to the side of his mouth, he looks like the perfect depiction of the guy you should never take home to meet your parents.

Smoke wafts around him in a mysterious haze as he continues showing off his badass attitude by blowing out more fumes, uncaring of what anyone thinks.

His spiky hair looks messy, like he just got out of bed. On him, though, of course it looks sexy, like everything else. And I'm almost inclined to think the ooze of smoldering sex appeal might make your parents forgive you if you did bring him home.

Pushing away from the car, he strides toward us, looking taller, if that's possible.

My cheeks burn when his eyes lock with mine and he gives me a seductive stare. The effect scatters my nerves.

When he reaches us, he nods at Adrian and Elaine then slips a strong arm around me, whisking me away from them.

As he ushers me away, I force my mind to think of survival so I can take this leap of faith. Except it feels like I'm falling off that cliff again. This time when I land, I just hope I'll be in a better position than where I am now.

As the car drives through the gates and we speed down the road with our convoy, I resist the urge to look back at the only real place I can call home.

Instead, I look at the Viper as he cuts me a glance and try to steady my erratic thoughts.

"Are there any updates on the investigation?" I ask. I practiced this conversation earlier hoping if I stick to business, I'll be okay.

"No. There's nothing for you to worry about." Caspian's grip tightens on the steering wheel.

"What does that mean exactly?"

He gives me a hard stare. "It means exactly what I said. There's nothing for you to worry about."

So, he does have updates. He's just not telling me what they are. I get that he might not want me to worry, but anyone in my position would want to know everything that's going on.

I know Adrian would have been told if anything was found. I was just hoping Caspian might be able to tell me something more since his father is taking care of the investigation.

"It's been nearly three weeks, and that's all you can tell me?"

"Yeah. That's it. Did you miss me, Printsessa?" He grins, changing the subject.

"No," I answer nonchalantly, pretending I never thought of him at all.

He laughs, and the sound seeps into me. "You always were a terrible liar. Lies don't work on people like me. We see straight through bullshit."

"It's not bullshit."

"Well, I missed you, Malyshka." He glances over at me again. "Certain parts of you more than others."

His gaze drops to my breasts, and I glower at him.

"Don't worry," he adds. "There's plenty of time later to get reacquainted."

"I'd rather not."

"Somehow, I don't believe you." His voice deepens. "I think you did miss me, and you thought of all the ways I was going to own your body in that refresher session I promised you."

The scandalous look the ruthless devil gives me makes me shiver with heat. He smiles when I blush, clearly knowing what he's stirring within me.

I don't have the energy to battle with him yet, so instead of searching for my non-existent comeback, I reach for my iPod and put my headphones on.

I know listening to music when I'm with him irritates the hell out of him and he can't stand my music, but he's still smiling because he knows he won this round.

I turn up the volume when an old Collective Soul song wafts into my ears, and we travel in silence for the next three hours. Our only exchanges are the occasional glances we give each other.

Night falls by the time we reach Boston, then we get stuck in heavy traffic for over an hour. The extra time increases the tension between us, but it doesn't escape me that Caspian would have been driving all day. Days ago, he hand-delivered me to Adrian and Elaine and drove back to Boston.

The acknowledgement makes me recall what I thought about him keeping me safe, and strangely, it warms something inside me.

Curious to know what he's thinking, I steal a glance at his sharp profile when my music stops.

I still think he carries a beauty that is almost suffo-cated by his permanent poker face. He always looks like that, and his jaw is constantly clenched into a hard line, like he's gearing up for a fight. It makes him look older than his nineteen years.

I suppose it's the look of a leader in the making—the leader he will be one day, and I will be his wife. The thought of being the wife of a Pakhan terrifies the life out of me.

I will be like my mother. Will I suffer the same fate she did from being with a man who falls out of love with you?

The older I get, the more I think of how hurt she

must have been when she found out about my father's affair.

There's no reason I should think I won't suffer the same fate since the man I'm about to marry already holds some hatred in his heart for me.

That pang of guilt pierces my heart once more when I think of our ugly past, and I try to push it to the back of my mind.

"What is it?" Caspian's voice cuts through the thick silence like a razor blade.

He faces me, searching my eyes.

"Nothing."

The dimple in his left cheek deepens as he smiles, highlighting how ridiculously gorgeous he is. "Looked like you had plenty to think about while you bore holes into my head. Why not talk it out?"

"There's nothing to talk about." That's technically not a lie. I just prefer to keep those types of thoughts about our future to myself.

He grins and looks like he's gearing up to continue pressing me for an answer, but I'm grateful when he doesn't.

Moments later, we turn onto a country road, and I straighten.

I'm thoroughly surprised when we drive into the parking lot of a diner called Roberta's and park.

"We're stopping here?" I ask.

"Yeah. Don't tell me you don't like diners."

"I do. I just never imagined you in one."

His father owns several Michelin-starred restaurants.

When we were children, those were the sorts of places our parents would take us to, even though my parents were more down to earth when we were just hanging out as a family. His family, however, was always elaborate.

Now that I think of it, I have no idea what kind of places he likes to eat at anymore because we've never been on a date. The most we've eaten together is pasta in his apartment or pizza we ordered in.

"I'm here nearly every week," he states with a sexy half-smile. "Don't worry. When I take you on that date we're supposed to go on, it will be somewhere I can show you off."

Of all the things I expected him to say, it wasn't that.

The comment stuns me, throwing me off kilter in a way that pushes me toward that fantasy of us—the alternate version of us I haven't conjured in weeks. Not since we got together.

The fantasy makes me wonder if we'd ever go on such a date, where I'd get dressed up and he'd show me off, proud that I was his wife.

"Come on, let's go eat." He gives me a wide toothy grin, giving me his trademark wink. He then points at my iPod and shakes his head. "Leave that here."

I don't protest. If he was trying to butter me up, it's worked—a little, just a little—so, I put my headphones and iPod back in my bag and we get out of the car.

Two guards escort us into the diner, but they stay at the door. I'm grateful they do as it's less overbearing.

Once Caspian and I are seated in a booth, the waitress walks over to take our orders. Since Elaine fed me enough food to last a lifetime, I order a salad, while Caspian requests the biggest meal they have.

His phone starts buzzing the moment the waitress leaves, and his brows knit when he retrieves it and looks at the home screen.

Instantly, I worry it's something to do with the investigation, but I know if I ask, he won't tell me.

"Stay here," he says.

I tilt my head and give him a cold, measured stare. "Where do you think I'm going to go?"

"Nowhere I can't find you, Malyshka," he promises with a smile. "I'm just not in the mood to chase you tonight."

He stands and answers the phone, walking away as I process the sordid reminder of my captivity. I watch him until he walks through the door before I release the breath I'm holding.

"Wow, your boss man is real uptight," comes a voice from behind me with a hint of a Southern twang.

I don't recognize who it's coming from until I turn and see the guy they call *Jack* on campus. It's not his real name, but he was nicknamed such because if you want to get *jacked-up* with whatever drug you desire, he's the guy to speak to.

He gave me my first joint free of charge just because I smiled at him. I'm not used to how people like him work, but I know to be wary, especially since he knows who I am.

He moves to sit in Caspian's seat, and instantly, the bodyguard at the door comes over with his hand raised.

"Whoa," Jack says, mimicking the guard by putting his hand up, too. "Princess Raventhorn knows me, don't you, darlin'?" He winks at me, and I nod.

"It's okay. I know him from Raventhorn." I'm almost certain everything I said there was wrong. I don't know this guy, and I'm pretty sure from the way he looks at me that he wants to get in my pants more than he wants to sell me my next fix.

At the same time, there's something oddly comforting in speaking to someone who isn't Caspian. Someone neutral who isn't part of the shit show that is my life.

"I'm watching you," the guard says.

"Okay." Jack nods. "Watch away, buckeroo. I swear I won't bite her unless she wants me to."

The guard looks him up and down, giving him a scathing glare. When he backs away, he doesn't go far.

Jack proceeds to sit, and his smile brightens as he looks at me.

"You shouldn't joke around like that if you want to speak to me," I state.

"Who said I was joking, Princess?"

"Please don't call me that." I can't stand it. *Princess, Printsessa.* It's the same fucking endearment.

He chuckles. "I just wanted to see how you were. I heard what happened. Everyone did."

Relaxing my shoulders, I pull in a slow breath and wonder what I can say.

Before I say anything more, I assess him, studying his athletic frame as I try to figure out if he could have been one of my attackers. Jack's athletic, but he doesn't have the muscle those guys were packing. They were there to kill me that night, and they weren't supposed to fail.

"I'm okay," I decide to say.

"How's Lucian doing?"

"He's not so good. We're praying."

"I'll pray with you, sweetheart." He leans closer, pulls out a little roll-up, and holds it up so that only I can see. "Did you know the good Lord helps those who help themselves? Want this, baby? It will take the edge off. Once again, it will be on me."

"Why do you keep giving me free things?"

"Because I like you, and I know you can't pay with a blowjob."

I was right. He does want to get in my pants. "No, I can't, and I shouldn't accept your *generous* offer either."

"Shouldn't." He pushes it closer. "Baby, that means you want it and you're of two minds. Don't take this the wrong way, but you look like you've seen better days, which is perfectly understandable with the Viper breathing down your neck and Daddy Dearest at the helm. Life won't get much better than this. A little escape is worth its weight in gold."

I'm thrown off balance by how right he is. I'm sure he wouldn't know my entire situation with Caspian's father, but he's saying all the right things. I haven't taken any drugs in weeks, and it was just that one time. Quite honestly, things were so crazy after that, I'd hoped to see him again at the next party.

He's here now, so why am I turning him away?

Perhaps it's because I know I'm walking on the edge and having a joint might push me right over.

"I can't," I amend, and he closes his hand, removing the roll-up from my sight. "There's a party at Lapetus House on Monday. The offer stands until then. If you find you need a break, come and find me. I'll be waiting for you."

The heavy thud of footsteps has us straightening. We both look up to see Caspian walking toward us. His eyes are fixed on Jack's, and he looks like he's ready to beat the life out of him.

"Get the fuck up!" Caspian barks.

Thankfully, Jack stands.

"I was just—"

"Nothing," Caspian cuts him off. "You don't speak to my girl, *ever*."

"I'm sure she can be friends with whomever she wants." Jack narrows his eyes.

"Not with you. Now get the fuck out of my sight before I remove you myself."

My mouth drops, and I glare at Caspian.

"All right, Viper, leaving now." Jack makes a show of bowing.

He then walks away, but not before glancing back and giving me a secret smile.

He leaves the diner. When I look back at Caspian, I shudder when he's already glaring at me with that contemptuous stare.

Great, here we go. I'm sure he's going to lay down the law on me now even though I did nothing wrong.

"Did you have to be so rude?" I ask.

His eyes widen. "Tell me you don't know that guy for the reasons I think." He drops into the seat before me and balls his hands into tight fists.

I clench my jaw so hard I fear my back teeth might snap. I want to deny his implied accusation and tell him to fuck off. Except, since his accusation isn't exactly false, I stall, not knowing what to say.

I dare not lie. He wouldn't need to use his creepy special powers to see through my bullshit because everyone knows Jack only speaks to you if you're a customer or about to become one.

"He was just checking to see how I was." I try to steer the conversation away from my sometimes-secret drug habits.

"You are not to speak to that guy ever again."

"You can't tell me what to do," I argue, folding my arms.

"I just did."

"There was nothing wrong with asking me how I was."

His brows furrow into a deep line, and he tightens his left fist until the bones in his knuckles crack. "You know that's not all he was fucking doing, so don't fuck with me and give me bullshit. Did you take anything from him?"

His eyes never leave mine, and I realize this is something more than his obsessive disposition. The fury in his expression is different. It's laced with worry and tells me to pick my battles wisely, especially since Caspian knows Jack a lot better than I do.

"Willow, answer me." His voice rises, eliciting curious stares from people in the nearby booths.

Even the waitress, who was on her way with our food, stops by the counter and observes my embarrassing interaction with my soon-to-be husband.

"No," I answer, lifting my chin. "I didn't take anything from him."

"Let's keep it that way."

On hearing the condescending air of his tone, my temper flares. I can't help it. I hate it when he speaks to me like I'm a child.

"Is this how it's going to be?" I snap. "You telling me what to do and who I can speak to?"

"He's dangerous."

"You're dangerous."

He doesn't like that comment one bit.

Caspian's nostrils flare, and the flash of fire in those emerald eyes confirms I just pushed all the wrong buttons.

"Willow, for the love of God, do not cross me on this. Do it, and you will not like what happens."

My God, I really do have my very own monster.

And we're just getting started.

This is just day one.

CHAPTER 10
CASPIAN

J esus Christ, I'm going to have a fucking aneurysm.

This girl is going to kill me, whether by natural causes or physical forces.

I cut Willow a hard glance as we get back in my car and she looks away.

She resumed that irritating-as-fuck stupor of silence after I threatened her about Jack.

She's even more pissed at me than before, and she can stay that way.

Willow doesn't know shit about Jack, and she's the lost little lamb again if she thinks he's a good guy.

It's fucking bad enough I have to worry about these assholes who want her dead, but now I have the possibility of her taking drugs to contend with.

Possibility?

Who the hell am I kidding?

If she was talking to Jack, it means she's taken something from him before. And once he has his eyes set on you, he'll find ways of getting you hooked.

When the hell did she meet him?

It would have been at a party.

Which one? And what drug did he give her?

Fuck. I saw him leaning over to her with his hand out, which means he was offering her the hard stuff.

The problem with that motherfucker is that he's dirty and sneaky. He'll mix his own blend of shit with other shit that can fuck you up.

I'd be the pot calling the kettle black if I got on some moral high ground with her because I get high at least once a week. But Jack is the kind of dangerous asshole you don't see coming until it's too late.

Jack is in the same year as me and one of the heirs who were drafted into the Knights through his mother's marriage to one of my father's brigadiers.

Willow didn't seem to mind him. I fucking hate that.

Sure, she didn't seem overly thrilled to see him, but she certainly didn't look as put out as when she's talking to me.

No matter, I was serious about my threat. His ass is as good as dead if he goes near her.

As for any tolerance she might have for him, I'll be sure to eradicate that by the end of the night when I make her remember who she belongs to.

When I'm done with her, my poor Malyshka won't know what to do with herself. I'll drive her as mad with desire as I am for her and break down every brick in the walls she's built up to keep me out.

We leave in that silent angst and reach Raventhorn University thirty minutes later.

As we drive onto campus, Willow goes rigid with fear, and it's clear the realization that she's back at the place she nearly died is truly hitting home.

If I had my way, I wouldn't bring her anywhere near here until everything is resolved, but Father Dearest wanted her back. He felt the extra security would be sufficient. I did not.

That call earlier was from Thorne. He hasn't found anything on the guy yet but was just checking in.

No way in hell am I going to tell Willow about that guy. Not until I have to.

If I tell her the guy is following me, it will give her more reason not to feel safe with me. Not only that, hearing he's still around will terrify her even more. I don't want to do that.

When we park at my apartment, the air between us shifts as attraction steps in and Willow looks cautious for other reasons. The fear entrenched in the outline of her beautiful face is not about the looming threat. What she's afraid of now is herself and what she might feel for me.

It's almost fascinating to watch her fight. At the same time, I want her to give in willingly. So, when I usher her inside my apartment, I make a point of being too close, and I make sure she knows what I'm doing.

I place my hand to the small of her back when we walk into the hallway, and she glances over her shoulder at me.

"We're going upstairs to the bedroom, Printsessa," I husk, and her cheeks turn pink.

Leaning closer to the shell of her ear, I inhale her scent as I brush my lips over her skin. Of course, she pulls away, but I return my hand to her back and guide her upstairs.

Thankfully, she doesn't complain. Perhaps she's learned that it's fruitless to do so.

When we enter the bedroom, she walks to the window bay, where I've placed one of her T-shirts.

While she picks it up, I pull my shirt off. The color in her cheeks then deepens when her eyes dart back to me.

There is no mistake in the arousal darkening her blue gaze as she looks over the tattoos inked on the rigid muscles of my chest. Except, once again, she hates that she wants me.

It's evident in the manner she schools her expression and the way she fails to hide her body's natural reaction.

Her nipples have already started hardening, and I'd be willing to bet my left nut that her sweet pussy is growing wet for me.

"When did this get here?" Her voice comes out uneven.

"I got your clothes the other day." When I saw the amount she owns, I was glad I had more than enough space for her.

I thought she would appreciate me doing so, but the flare of her nostrils suggests otherwise.

"I would have preferred to get my things myself." She pouts.

"I left your books. You can get those when you're ready."

Her annoyance seems to lessen somewhat. That's good for me.

"What about classes, and my work at the magazine? I feel well enough to go back."

"You're signed off classes until after the wedding. So, no to classes."

"But I said I'm fine."

"I'm following the doctor's orders, Willow." She's not to have any external stress. The only thing she's able to do right now is exercise—that includes fucking. I won't tell her that. I'd rather show her. "You can go to the library and the magazine for a few days a week. But I don't want you to spend any more than two hours there. Maybe three at a max. The guards will accompany you at all times. Understood?"

She looks like she wants to protest but holds back. "Yes. Can I see my friends, too?" she asks tentatively. "Or are you going to act like the dick you were at the diner?"

"Jack is not your friend."

She lifts her chin in defiance. "How do you know that?"

I lean closer, smiling wider as she flinches.

"Don't push me, Malyshka. If I say he's not a friend, he's not. We're not talking about Jack anymore." I hope this will be the end of any conversation to do with him.

"Fine. I just want to be able to see Eilish and Lucian."

There's no problem with her seeing Eilish. Just

113

hearing Lucian's name, however, rubs me the wrong way, and it shouldn't.

I'd be an evil asshole if I told her she couldn't see him, and she'd be right to hate me for it. But that doesn't mean I can't attach certain stipulations.

"You can see Eilish whenever you want, but I will take you to see Lucian."

Her lips part and she sighs with frustration. "What if I just want to see him with Eilish, or by myself?"

So she can tell him how much she needs him? Or how she can't live in this world without him? I don't think so.

Besides, there's always the threat of the enemy watching for Lucian to wake up. I don't want her in danger if that happens.

"That's how it's going to be, Printsessa. Take it or leave it."

She rolls her eyes at me and sighs in an exaggerated manner. "I guess I'll have to take it, won't I, *sir*?"

Fuck, she has no idea that her calling me sir, in that tone, hardens my dick.

Like the lost little lamb again, the poor thing just entered the Viper's Lair, and it's time to play.

I give her a sinful smile that makes her square off with me.

"Malyshka, you can call me sir any time you feel like it. I forgot you're the perfect sub."

The instant I say that, I know she's thinking of the threesome she saw at her first campus party. The girl was tied up. The way Willow watched the trio in open fascination made me think she was curious about all of it—to be shared and tied up while being shared.

"I'm still not sharing you," I inform her, repeating what I said that night. "I'm definitely tying you up, though. The dom in me won't be able to resist."

Her cheeks redden fiercely. "You're crazy."

We've had this *crazy* conversation too many times before, and we both know the answer. But I'll play—harder.

"How about you put that mouth of yours to better uses? My dick misses those lips."

"Fuck you."

"No, but I'll happily fuck you."

Scowling, she makes the mistake of trying to walk away. I allow her one step before I reach for her and hoist her over my shoulder.

She shrieks and starts pounding my back with her little fists. As if that will

help set her free.

"Put me down, you asshole!"

"No, I haven't started to get nasty with you yet."

I set her down on the bed and pin her arms above her head, locking her in with my body pressed against hers so she can't move. Or rather, she does move, but it's against me, and I'm sure she can feel the length of my arousal poking into her belly.

"You're being a complete dick!"

I widen my smile. "And you're wet for me, Malyshka. I can smell your sweet cunt."

She looks at me like I've lost my mind. "I'm not wet."

I might believe her if raw desire weren't raging in her eyes like wildfire, begging me to take her. Like a moth to a flame, it draws me closer to her lips.

The scent of her arousal is making my mouth water, and I can almost taste her delicious nectar.

"What did I tell you about lying to me? I know you're wet for me, Willow. Are you aching for me to touch you the way I did last time? Are you aching to have my cock inside you?"

The blood drains from her cheeks, and her lips part. Before she can protest, I take full advantage of the flimsy dress she's wearing and push it up to her waist so I can find her panties.

I cup her pussy and press into her mound, making her moan. With the flick of a finger, I move the lace away and push inside her slick, wet opening.

Holy fuck, she's soaked.

I want to gloat and bask in the triumph of feeling her wet pussy, but fuck, the joke's on me because her desire is intoxicating. I'm addicted to it, and I want more.

She gasps when I push deeper, starting a slow thrust as a reminder of how good my dick will feel inside her.

"Are you ready to tell me how badly you want me yet?" I kiss her cheek, driving my finger into her tight pussy faster and harder. "Right now, I'm contemplating whether I should bend you over and fuck you into submission, or watch you try to resist your desire for me until you lose."

"*Bas...tard...*" She cries out a loud moan of pleasure,

arching her back and pressing her breasts into my hard chest.

Her tight little nipples feel like razor-sharp peaks, begging to be sucked. I plan to do just that, but I need to play with her pussy first.

"It's okay to want me, Willow. You're mine. Now give yourself to me."

With that, I crush my lips to hers and kiss her hard.

It takes nanoseconds to screw myself over as the kiss becomes all-consuming and I feast on her like I'm devouring an exquisite meal.

My poor Malyshka tries to hold on to that willpower of hers. I give her credit for her attempt, but the effects of the kiss capture her, too. I feel the moment her resolve weakens and she kisses me back with the same hunger I feel, giving herself to me.

Sweeping my tongue over hers, I explore her sweet mouth, relishing the taste I've longed for, for what's felt like eons.

But I want to see her eyes, the windows to her soul. So, I pull out of the kiss and gaze into them, feeling triumph surge through me when I see exactly what I want to see—*it's her*. The no-holds-barred version of her who gave herself to me.

I have her back. Back to where we were when we were last in this bed.

"More?" I ask, finger-fucking her. "Do you want me to give you more, Willow?"

I want to hear her say it.

"Yes..." Her breath hitches. "*More.*"

CHAPTER 11
WILLOW

"Say it again," Caspian demands, thrusting his fingers mercilessly in and out of my pussy. "Tell me you want more."

As his eyes roam down my body, the intensity of lust in his gaze sets me on fire.

"More...*please*. I want more." I hear the voice that sounds like mine plead.

Each word is spoken loud and clear, filled with desire. Except I'm having difficulty believing I'm actually saying those things, and in that sultry voice which makes me sound like I'm begging.

Am I begging?

Begging is what you do when you desperately need something. Since *desperate* is exactly how I feel, I think I can agree I'm begging.

Shame fills me at the confirmation. Even if I were to lie to myself, the growing wetness between my legs is testament that I want him to fuck me.

Damn it to hell.

I hate him for this feeling and his control over me.

I fucking *hate* him for weakening me to this pitiful state, yet I want him so badly it hurts.

Staring back at him, I want to scream, *I hate you, but I love you!*

And that makes no damn sense. Nothing fucking does.

It's like I'm two different people. One version is the girl from earlier who was looking for a way out of this mess. The other doesn't want him to stop touching her.

That's the dangerous side of me weakening the other to cave to temptation.

It doesn't take much for me to go tumbling into the arms of temptation when he presses his massive erection harder into my belly and thrusts another finger into my pussy.

As he pumps deeper inside me, raw pleasure crashes into my body. It unlocks more desire, which pours out of me on a tidal wave of bliss.

When I arch my back again, rubbing my pussy against his hand, he releases my arms.

This is the moment when I should do something to get away from him. I should move or try to push him off me. But I don't.

I don't fucking do anything besides shock myself further by staying where I am, locked in the pleasure he's giving me.

I would have bet all I owned that I would flee out of his arms the first chance I got. Good thing I didn't because I would have lost all my possessions the same way I'm losing my mind.

Just as I'm about to savor the elation from his thrusts, he catches my throat,

exerting his dominance once more, reminding me he owns my body. Just like his promise.

That was the goal all along, wasn't it?

Well, message received, loud and clear. He has me right where he wants me—caught in his trap, unable to free myself.

Thoughts of freedom are torn from my mind when his thumb strokes along my skin, trailing down to my cleavage. There he caresses the swells of my breasts and lowers his head to take my left nipple into his mouth through the fabric of my dress.

The fiery combination of his lips nibbling on my nipple and his fingers in my pussy heats up my body with vicious energy. It tightens my nipples painfully and makes my pussy ache with need.

With a feral look in his eyes, he gives me a sinful grin and tugs at my dress. "Take this off for me, so I can suck your tits."

At that moment, it's scary how the desperation he's created inside me has made me agreeable to do what he tells me.

I lift myself up onto my elbows and pull off my dress, leaving just my panties on.

As he looks at my breasts and takes note of how hard and swollen with arousal my nipples are, the look in his eyes shifts to hunger. The way a predator would look at its prey before consuming it.

I barely catch a sip of air before his mouth closes over my right nipple.

He sucks hard and moves to the left with the same wild suckle that has me arching into him and weaving my fingers into his hair, encouraging him to give me more.

He does just that, knowing exactly what to do to make me come undone in his arms.

Relishing the attention he's giving my body, I tilt my head back and allow myself to truly let go.

I know I shouldn't give in, but God, I never want this moment to end.

Shuddery gasps leave my lips as he moves down to my pussy, parts my legs, and buries his face between my thighs. Keeping my panties pushed aside, he pushes his tongue into me and sucks on my swollen clit.

A desperate, uncontrollable cry of ecstasy rips from my throat, and I'm lost to him.

His clever tongue thrashes inside my passage, giving me what I need to forget everything that's not him. The potent rise of my orgasm climbs, and one hard tug of my clit pushes me over the edge. My orgasm comes, hot and scathing, sending streaks of untamed pleasure coursing through my body.

I brace myself by grabbing his shoulders, crying out from the undiluted luxuriating sensation flowing through me.

Caspian consumes my release, lapping the flow of my juices until he's taken it all. When he straightens, a wicked smirk appears on his face.

"I'm going to fuck you," he husks in my ear. "I want to bury myself deep inside you and fuck you hard, Willow. Let me."

I knew even before he said the words that I was going to let him take me.

"Let me fuck you, Printsessa. You want this. I know you do. So, say yes to me," he adds, and I nod. "Say the words, Willow. Tell me to fuck you."

"Fuck... *me*." This time, I recognize my voice, and I feel worse that I'm so desperate for him.

The smile on his face now is one of victory for making me bend to his will.

"Take off your panties and get on your hands and knees."

While I drag off my panties, Caspian pushes his pants down his long athletic legs, showing off the vast array of Bratva tattoos and runes as he frees his massive cock.

He's perfectly erect, ready to claim me. The thick, bulbous head of his cock already has pre-cum coating the tip with more leaking out in a clear pearly bead.

He guides me to settle onto my hands and knees. When he positions himself behind me, he gives my ass a firm squeeze and smacks it, jolting my body forward. Running a warm hand down to my pussy, he strokes my outer lips.

I just came, but I'm wet again. So wet for him it's embarrassing.

"You're fucking soaked for me, Willow. I love it."

All I can do is moan in response to his touch.

"I'm going to make you feel so good," he promises. Then I feel his cock press against my entrance.

My mind short-circuits as he slams into me with one brutal thrust that fills me up.

I cry out from the maddening cacophony of pain and pleasure. The twisted part of me savors the sensation of feeling his cock inside me and my pussy contracting around his thickness.

He grabs my hips and moves his as he hammers into me, every thrust bringing a new wave of pleasure that pushes me into that blissful state I crave.

When he starts fucking me harder, I dig my fingers into the mattress so I can take his vicious pounds. I climax again within seconds and the impact makes us both cry out as we give ourselves over to pleasure.

"Fuck, Willow, I need to fuck you harder," he growls like a savage beast. Then

he does exactly what he said he would and ruts into me.

It hurts. He's too big and too rough, but I take it as the pain blends into pleasure.

His pace, although hard and relentless, becomes more rhythmic and surer.

As if he wants to guarantee giving me the hard fuck he promised while hitting my sweet spot with every powerful thrust.

Suddenly, I can't get enough of him, just like when he was tasting me, and I fall into the precipice of carnal ecstasy.

I lose track of how many times I come while his stamina is unwavering.

Time scrambles around me. I'm not sure if it feels like it stands still or speeds up. All I know is we stay like this for a long time—*fucking*.

Relentless, merciless fucking. It makes every nerve in my body delirious, like I've just dosed myself with a powerful drug.

It's utter possession, and I feel like I've been waiting for this moment forever. All that is left is the circle of pleasure cocooning me in this state of unbending delight. The force is so strong it drains me.

That's when Caspian comes, too, climaxing inside me with a primal masculine roar which pours from his chest.

Pleasure explodes through every nerve in my body as I come one last time.

Breathing raggedly, we both collapse in a sweaty heap. The air around us is permeated by the scent of sex and the sound of my heart thrashing in my ears.

The sound beats reality into my mind with the realization that I gave myself to him again.

I lift my head when he caresses my belly. As our eyes lock, I know what we just did strengthened our connection. It's left me feeling like I'm being held captive in other ways I'll never be free from. The scary thing is, I'm not sure I want to be free.

So, when he turns me to face him and plants a possessive kiss on my lips, I let him. I allow him to kiss me.

By the same token, I take what my body craves from the ruthless devil.

CHAPTER 12
WILLOW

I stir from the fog surrounding my mind, fighting the urge to fall into the nightmare.

It's like a monster outside my door waiting for me to succumb to weakness so it can lock its fingers into my soul and devour me.

When I open my eyes, I'm momentarily disorientated until I realize I'm naked.

Naked and pressed against Caspian's equally naked body with my head and my hands resting on his chest, as if we're young lovers who always fall asleep like this.

The sight of him fills my mind with memories of last night and all the ways he took me.

We had sex all night. I barely remember falling asleep, but I know it was in the early hours of the morning when we did.

He's out cold and doesn't even stir when I move out of his embrace.

I swallow hard and stare at him. In the glow of the

126

morning light, he has that fairytale prince look again, but I know not to be fooled by what I'm seeing or what I'm feeling.

Which is what?

Confused?

In love?

Hatred?

Desire...?

Shit. I don't know which emotion is more prevalent, and like the lost little lamb he keeps calling me, I fell asleep in the beast's bed, wrapped in his arms.

Forcing the thoughts from my mind, I slip off the bed and put my dress and panties back on.

I then pad over to the window bay, where I left my bag to retrieve my phone from inside. Maybe some sense of normalcy will help.

There are messages from Adrian and Elaine letting me know they're a phone call away if I need to talk. There's also one from Eilish that lifts my spirits. It came through a little over an hour ago.

It says:

Guessing you're back on campus now. Let me know when His Royal Highness will allow me to see you. It's crazy here. Misha has a zit the size of Texas and is taking the week off until it goes away. That should make you laugh. I also accidentally overheard Kelly planning ways of snaring Professor Lansky. As if she could. Miss you.

I smile, missing her like crazy.

Caspian shuffles, and my breath stills. Relief washes over me, however, when he doesn't get up. I decide to sneak out of the room with my phone in hand so I can message Eilish back.

I need a break from him.

His slumber is possibly the only chance I'll get for that break, so I'll take it.

I walk down the hallway and fire off a message to Eilish letting her know I'm back. I suggest meeting later for lunch and grabbing the rest of my stuff from my apartment.

In what seems like two seconds, she messages back agreeing and sends me a heart and rose emoji, which means she's thinking of me.

I do miss her, and I can't help but wonder what life is going to be like when Caspian and I are married. I can't believe our wedding day is next Saturday.

For what it's worth, it was nice to live next to Eilish for those few short weeks. I suppose it was hardly any different to staying in a hotel on vacation, but at least we did it.

Now I'll be here with Caspian for the next four years. Or maybe it will be three since he's a year ahead of me? I don't know if he's staying for grad school or anything like that. Chances are he won't if he's going to be working at Ivanov Tech.

Until then, it will be him, me, and a whole fraternity of guys for neighbors. Including Thorne, his sidekick cousin who is the same type of bully as Caspian.

My mind hasn't accepted any of this yet.

Or that Caspian and I devoured each other like animals last night. It was like we both went crazy.

My cheeks burn as the sinful memories flow into my mind, and I quicken my pace down the hall. I don't have a destination in mind; I just don't want to see any of the guards yet.

They didn't come inside the apartment last night, but I was told they would be here when Caspian's away, or sometimes through the night.

I've been here enough to know the place, but I didn't exactly spend time checking it out when I was last here. I might have probably seen three or four rooms at most.

I reach the end of the hall ending up on the other side of the apartment.

There's a staircase that looks like it might lead back to the living room, and a wooden door in the wall that looks out of place.

Since it's ajar, I decide to peek in.

What I see inside makes me freeze and my skin crawl.

A dim light illuminates the room enough to see paintings and drawings on the stone wall of what I can only describe as nightmares.

Horrific shadowy images fill every single one of them in huge black swirls that depict the dead or dying.

There are dead faces, dead bodies, dead animals, dead things.

Everything is death, the antithesis to life and living —*surviving*. The macabre vibe inside the room weighs me down, and I feel like taking another step closer would poison my soul.

My instinct tells me to leave, but something else compels me to enter.

So, I do.

I take careful steps toward the first painting that looks like a tortured soul with their head on the ground. I think it could be a woman because the figure seems to have long hair, or it could be wisps of smoke. I'm not sure.

While the person's body is still standing upright, the head has been painted with her mouth open in a scream and her eyes like hollows. Nails protrude from the top of her head and neck.

Feeling bile rise in my throat, I move to the other paintings, which are just as bad, if not worse.

Who created these paintings?

It could never be Caspian. His artwork is full of color.

Well, from what I remember anyway. He stopped showing his drawings to me after he returned from Russia. Thinking back now, what I saw before was genius for an eight-year-old. I remember his mother being so proud of his work and showing it off.

I wasn't as talented as that.

These look nothing like what I'd expect from someone who used to see the world in so many colors.

They must belong to him, though, if they're here.

What happened to him?

What happened in Russia?

He said he couldn't talk about it. Is this why?

"Are you lost again, little lamb?" Caspian's voice nearly makes me jump out of my skin.

I whirl around to face him, my heart beating wildly in my chest. When I catch my breath, I'm embarrassed for being caught in here, although the room wasn't off-limits. It just feels like it should be.

He walks in, and my nerves disseminate from the combination of his presence and the paintings. I realize at that moment that they're both giving off the same soulless vibe.

When he stops a breath away, I notice for the first time in eleven years that something is missing when I look at him.

He's hidden it so well, though, that I think I'm only noticing now because we're in here.

It's so hard to believe he's the boy from my childhood I have so many fond memories of. But it is him. He's just different, and deadlier.

I always thought the deadly side was spurred on by his mother's death, but I don't think it was. The darkness was there before.

"I'm sorry," I stutter as his eyes roam over my body. Arousal spirals through me again, but I try to steady my thoughts and emotions. "The door was open, and I was just looking around."

"Have you started doing Psych 101 on me yet?"

I study his handsome face and search those green eyes, which appear paler today. I don't know what I'm looking for, but what I see amidst the darkness is the boy I used to know.

"I don't remember you painting like this. You used to like painting the things you saw around you."

"I still do," he replies, and my stomach knots.

Glancing around me at the images, I realize what he's telling me and what I'm seeing is what he witnessed in Russia. Bile churns my stomach when I glance at the painting of the woman again. In my vague memory, I try to remember what his aunt and cousin looked like. That would have been Thorne's mother and sister—Anushka and Evangeline.

Staring back at the painting now, I'm convinced it's a woman.

Is that what happened to one of them? Which one?

"These are things you see?" I mutter.

"Things I saw, and still see."

"Death?"

"Yes." He holds my gaze for one long moment, and deep sadness enters his eyes.

"This is about Russia, isn't it?"

Instead of answering, he leans forward and kisses me lightly. Like a whisper of memories from last night. "No more talk of darkness, Printsessa," he whispers against my lips. "It's not part of your world."

"But it is."

"Not like mine, baby girl." He brushes his nose along mine and cups my face, caressing the edge of my cheek.

The touch is far too tender for him. It does something to me I can't quite describe, other than the fact that it draws me deeper into him.

He moves to my lips, and I close the space between us, moving to him, too. When he kisses me, I'm left breathless and dizzy with pleasure.

The spellbinding effect makes me lose myself again. Losing control over my mind, my body, my heart.

"I need you again. Need your body again, Willow." He repeats the same words in Russian, sounding sexier, if possible, and God help me, I crumble.

He surprises me by scooping me up. Then he returns to my lips and carries me out of the room of death. As the door closes behind us, the vibe vanishes along with it. In the back of my mind, however, I know Russia is something he'll only ever talk about when he's ready. If that day ever comes.

He takes me to the En suite bathroom, where we only stop kissing to take off our clothes.

When we stand in the shower, he turns on a light sprinkle and pushes me against the smooth granite wall, where he continues devouring my lips.

He squeezes my breasts, kneading the huge swells and rolling my nipples until they're tight with arousal.

His fingers flutter down to my pussy, where he massages my clit until I'm crying out, aching for release.

With a devilish smile on his face, he holds my face, and I wonder what wicked ideas he has up his sleeves for me next.

"Seeing as how I spent all night pleasing your pussy, it's your turn to pleasure me now. Get on your knees and suck my dick."

That's supposed to give him pleasure, but the thought of having his cock in my mouth sends arousal clawing through me.

He pushes me down to my knees, and I take the base

of his thick cock in my hand, running my fingers down the length.

"Suck," he orders, and I take his hard cock into my mouth.

I glide my tongue over the smooth skin, then I start sucking. His fingers lace through the strands of my hair, encouraging me to deep throat him and suck faster.

I do, and damn me, there's something about hearing and seeing him in the height of pleasure that exhilarates me.

I suck his cock until it pulses and his balls tighten when I massage them.

HE THEN REACHES for my arms and pulls me to my feet.

I'M TURNED to face the wall, and just like last night, he plunges into my pussy with such a brutal force I see stars. He starts pounding into me, hammering hard so our wet bodies slap together and the sound of us fills the room.

My mind splinters when I come, and I'm caught in the eye of pleasure, riding the wave of the tempestuous storm it stirs in my soul.

Just when I think I couldn't feel any better, he traces his finger down to my asshole and circles the tight rosette, pushing his finger inside.

I'm stunned by how good that feels, and a little shocked at myself.

He slows his pumps and slips his hand around my waist to bring me closer.

"Let me take you here," he mutters. "I want to own every part of you."

Own?

There's that word again.

Yesterday, it sounded toxic to my ears. Today, it stirs passion.

He pushes his finger deeper into my asshole, and the combined pleasure of him filling up both my holes weakens me.

"Give yourself to me." He tightens his grip on my left hip, and I nod.

"Yes."

"Good girl."

He pulls his cock out of my pussy, and I stay there obediently, allowing him to rub my juices into my asshole. Him touching me there is weird, but a forbidden sensation tempts me to allow him to do whatever he wants to me.

When he rubs the head of his cock over the tight rosette, I flinch. He then grabs my hips and pushes his cock into my asshole.

I gasp from the filling sensation of his cock stretching me, wincing from the pain.

"Steady, Malyshka. It will feel good soon."

I remember him saying similar words to me when he took my virginity, and he was right. So, I believe again.

Caspian pushes deeper and harder until he's fully seated and buried to the hilt.

Fuck, it hurts. It really hurts, but... it also feels amazing.

Then, suddenly, he's pumping, and I forget the pain. He starts slow then speeds up and starts fucking me.

I lose my awareness as pleasure scorches me relentlessly. I come, but there's no build-up. It just happens, and I feel it everywhere—inside and outside my body.

He growls, and his cock feels impossibly huge inside me as he roars his release. I cry out my own, feeling wiped out and utterly spent.

My knees buckle. I try to hold on to the wall but miss. Thankfully, he catches me.

Caspian pulls out of me, and I feel the warmth of his cum running down the backs of my thighs. It's the warmth of his strong hands, however, that makes me feel like I could crawl up inside him and stay there forever.

He turns me to face him with a smile on his handsome face.

Just as he's about to kiss me, there's a knock on the door and we both still at the intrusion.

"Caspian, your father is here," says a hard, gravelly voice. I recognize it as the guard who came inside the restaurant with us.

Embarrassment attempts to flood my mind because I know he must have heard us having sex, but I know I have bigger things to worry about because of what he said.

Caspian's face hardens with fury, and he stares at the

bathroom door. "Tell him I'll be down in five minutes," he calls back.

"He's here to see the girl."

Me.

My eyes widen, and the fantasy bubble shatters before my eyes.

CHAPTER 13
WILLOW

Like the king in his courtyard, Aleksander Ivanov squares his shoulders and raises his chin as Caspian and I walk into the living room.

The moment he looks at me, my stomach knots so tightly the constriction thrusts all the way up to my throat and shuts off my airways like an invisible hand is choking the life out of me.

The similarities between father and son seem more prominent today.

Maybe that's because I feel vastly outnumbered— two to one. *Me* the only one. The only Raventhorn left without power. The two men in this room with me have taken that power, and the weight of their dominance makes me feel microscopic.

It wouldn't take much for either of them to crush me, wiping me out of existence. The sordid thought reminds me I'm little more than a thing, and the night I spent with Caspian with all those untamed emotions fades from my mind.

Like it never happened.

Caspian's hand has been at the small of my back since we walked down the stairs. His touch is supposed to be soothing. Instead, it feels more like he's pushing me toward my destroyer, who is now looking at me with disgust.

The way you would look at a disgusting slut. He thinks of me as the slut who shouldn't be with his son but is because I'm a benefit to him—to *them*.

It's written in his hawk eyes and that flinty gaze he's casting my way.

I suppose, too, our wet hair is a dead giveaway that we were showering together and he's caught us again. Except this time, he didn't witness the act.

Jesus. What am I going to do?

Things are in motion now, and they're just going to keep moving along, taking me in whichever direction I'm pulled. And I'll just have to go along with it.

"Good to see you back on your feet, Willow Raventhorn," Aleksander states in that insincere tenor that grates on my nerves.

"Thank you," I mumble, doing my best to hide the storm of trepidation brewing within me.

A mocking smirk graces his stony face. "You almost look like the vivacious girl you were at Raventhorn Hall who disrespected me in front of the council."

I knew I was going to get roasted for that, but the darkness in his glare tells me I'm lucky his words are all he's issuing me for the moment. I have a feeling death would be the result if not for that luck.

"I didn't know you were going to be stopping by so soon, *Father*," Caspian cuts in, drawing Aleksander's attention away from me.

"Because I didn't tell you, and I'm not *here* to see you. So, you are dismissed from this conversation."

Caspian's hand stiffens at my back. "I'm sure the stipulations of our oath entitle me to be in this meeting, so I'm staying."

The word *oath* stabs at my mind, and I wonder what exactly Caspian signed up for.

He's only loosely spoken about what he had to do to save me from his father, but this is the first time he's used that word.

All oaths I know of are signed in blood and binding by the same.

I chance looking at him for a moment and note how tense he appears. It's not a good sign for either of us.

"Very well, then, take a seat. Maybe you should hear what I have to say." Aleksander smiles, motioning toward the sofa before him.

Caspian ushers me over, my legs shaking with every step I take, and they don't stop even when I sit.

Aleksander sits in front of us on the armchair, and there's a noticeable shift in the air when he fixes his gaze on me.

"I'm here to tell you that I've arranged with the team at St. Jude's to take over your psychiatric care."

As the words fall from his lips, the room feels like it's closing in on me, and my heart stops beating.

"What?" The little voice that squeaks from me is barely audible.

"You heard me. One of your previous psychiatrists will be meeting us tomorrow afternoon."

"*Us?*"

"You and me," he answers with a little smile. "As your legal guardian I want to be there to hear what is discussed. The psychiatrist will do a re-evaluation of you. Following his recommendations, I will then decide what to do with you."

Oh God. All is lost.

"Why did you need to do this?" Caspian snaps.

"Let's not pussyfoot around shit." Aleksander's nostrils flare. "I have informed them that she lied to get herself out of hospital. The truth is the truth, and lie is what Willow did. It's a serious fallacy, and now she must deal with the repercussions and consequences."

"You can't do this to me!" My voice is louder, but I hate the emotion laced in my tone. It shows he's affecting me.

"My dear, I can do whatever I want to you, and there's not a goddamn thing either of you can do about it. Do not cross me *again*. That is a warning you'd be wise to remember."

"But—"

"Willow." Caspian grips my arm.

When I look at him and he shakes his head, all my fears push to the forefront of my mind.

I was right, and everything I worried about is happening.

Caspian is going to allow his father to hurt me. It's happening right in front of my eyes, and there is nothing I can do.

My throat closes, but I want to scream and tear my skin off.

As I return my attention to Aleksander, I want to lash out and attack because I know what he's up to.

But... I hold back. I'm playing with fire again, but this time, I won't just get burned. If I say anything, anything at all, it's going to accelerate my demise.

On noting my submission, Aleksander smiles and rises. "My dear, if I were you, I wouldn't piss me off again. You need to calm the fuck down and do as you are told."

He switches his gaze to Caspian but doesn't say anything to him. He just walks out, leaving me to process the bomb he just landed on my soul.

Caspian touches the top of my thighs when we hear the front door close.

"Willow, look at me."

I do, but I can't stand to look at him, so I get up and bring my hands to my cheeks.

"You need to stay calm." He tries to reach for me, but I step away.

"Are you kidding me?"

"You have to listen to me and stay calm," he says with more force.

"He's going to find a way to send me back to St. Jude's. You know it."

He pulls in a breath, presses his lips together, and leans closer. "We don't know anything yet, so just do what he says."

There it is. The perfect illustration of his loyalty to his father. That connection binding father and son is the thing that will always be against me.

"What other choice do I have?" I shake my head at him and walk away before the tears come.

"There's no way he can send you back to St. Jude's," Eilish scoffs, glaring at me as we step into my former bedroom at Myrddin House—the place where I nearly died.

I release an exasperated sigh, and my shoulders slump in defeat.

"He can, Eilish." I nod.

Once I'd cried and took time to allow the gravity of this new turn of events to sink in, I accepted the hard truth. At least now I know what I'm up against instead of it being something that's looming in my mind. It's real.

"He can," I mutter again. "Even if the psychiatrists tell him I'm fine. He's Aleksander Ivanov. What he says is law. And it doesn't help that I did actually lie."

Sympathy enters her eyes. "You were just doing what you felt was right. I would have done the same thing.

When you think about it, what else were you supposed to do? You shouldn't have been in that place."

"No, but it's clear Caspian's father thinks I need to go right back there."

I've been thinking about what could happen and trying to figure out his next move. That man is a ruthless bastard, but he'll want to look legit. At least I hope so. I'm just considering the lesser of his evil options so I don't have a full-blown anxiety attack. One that will likely last for days, like it would when I was at St. Jude's.

I'm on the verge again, but this time, I feel like counting backwards or listening to music won't help me. If that happens, I fear I might actually go crazy.

Just being here in this apartment is hard right now. I've just arrived. I left Caspian at his place half an hour ago, and I was glad he didn't make things more awkward than they were by talking to me.

After everything that happened with his father, and last night with him, I just wanted to see Eilish.

When I met her here with my entourage of guards, it was refreshing to see her, but the place felt like death to me. It had the soul-stealing vibe, similar to Caspian's room of deathly paintings.

I glance around the bedroom, remembering how happy I was to have a place for myself. But it was quickly tainted.

Glancing out the door, I look at the archway leading to the living room where I was attacked.

I was supposed to die that night. That man was here

waiting to kill me, and the one on the bridge wanted to make sure the job got done.

Eilish moves closer and rests her hands on my shoulders. "You're remembering stuff, aren't you?"

I nod and dab away a tear as it rolls down my cheek. "I just want a moment's peace. Just a break, but it's not going to happen. Every time I get close, there's always something waiting around the corner to screw with me."

She sighs. "Try not to worry. I know that sounds ridiculous to even say, but sometimes it's the little things that help."

"I'll try."

"How about we go see Lucian together sometime next week? As he would say, he might not be talking, but he's listening." Her smile doesn't quite reach her eyes.

I can see she's trying to be positive, but it's taking great effort.

"Lucian would say that, and yes, I'd love to go together." I nod, then I remember the stipulations on me seeing Lucian. "If you don't mind Caspian tagging along," I add sourly.

Her eyes widen and her brows snap together. "Are you serious?"

"Unfortunately, yes. He wants to take me to the hospital when I want to see Lucian."

"But the guards will be with you."

I bring my hands together, deciding to tell her the truth even though it might bother her since she nearly got as crazy with me over Lucian as Caspian did.

"He doesn't like my friendship with Lucian," I reply.

Understanding forms in her expression, along with embarrassment.

"Oh, but he knows you're friends, right?"

"It doesn't matter. I could conjure up some weird channel to make Lucian my brother legally, and Caspian would still have something to say against it."

She dips her head briefly, and when her gaze climbs back up to meet mine, she presses her lips together.

"I guess I kind of treated you the same not that long ago. I'm sorry."

I shake my head. "It's fine. I should have been more careful. I relied on him too much, and Lucian is the kind of guy who will be there for you when you need him. My neediness made us look like something we aren't."

"And I... got jealous."

"There was never anything to be jealous about. I pray you believe me now."

"I do. I just want him to wake up, regardless of what I feel. Let's go see him, even if Caspian is there, too. That part doesn't matter." She nods and offers a little smile. "I saw them talking on the quad the day before Lucian was shot. They went off together, and for one moment, they didn't look like the enemies they were in high school. It made me remember the old days. So, maybe it won't be so bad."

I get the gist of what she's saying, but *what* she said registers in my mind and raises my suspicions.

To my knowledge, Caspian only spoke to Lucian after his father caught us together. Lucian told me it was Caspian who informed him we were together. I assumed it must have been that same day. That evening, Lucian was shot.

I can't imagine why Caspian would have spoken to Lucian before then and not look like they were at war.

"Do you know what they were talking about?" I ask.

"No. I was watching from the bleachers. I thought it was weird, but I suppose stranger things have happened."

I'm not really sure about that, but I have a sinking feeling that little encounter was important, and I'm going to ask my dearly beloved about it.

WHEN I RETURN to the place I'm supposed to call home, Caspian isn't there.

I have no idea where he went, and neither do the guards—or if they do, they aren't sharing.

When he eventually gets in, it's late.

I'm dressed for bed, but I'm not in the bedroom and won't be going up there tonight. I've rooted myself in the sitting room by the window with my book which Caspian looks at with distaste because it's *The Bell Jar*. He always scowls like that when he sees me reading anything by Sylvia Plath or everything to do with her.

That's fine by me because I don't care. Reading is the only thing on my side right now, so I'll read whatever the fuck I want.

Especially since the sight of him tightens my stomach and throat like this morning.

"Let's go to bed," he says, seeming to guess my plans.

"I'm reading."

"It's late."

"It's part of my therapy. I'm sure you don't want to disrupt that now, do you? Or maybe you do."

His eyes blaze. "What the fuck is that supposed to mean?"

"You know what it means." I don't care what I'm saying or how I sound. Until now, he hasn't said one way or the other if he still believes me about Lillian.

That tells me he's just as dangerous as anyone else who doesn't believe me, no matter how much he's trying to protect me.

"What happened this morning wasn't my fault."

"No, I know that, but you still had a part to play in it, and there's nothing you can do at the end of the day."

"I'm not arguing with you tonight." He balls his hands. "If you want to sulk down here and read that depressing-as-fuck book, do it."

I will, but I'm not allowing him to leave before I ask him what I need to.

"What were you talking to Lucian about the day before he got shot?" I blurt.

He was about to walk away but freezes mid-stride and appears to contemplate his next words.

When he turns to face me, I can see I was right to be suspicious.

Sure, this guy is no open book, and he masks his emotions incredibly well to the point where one might wonder if he ever feels anything.

But I can read his emotions. And that's perhaps because my curse is to be as obsessed with him as he is with me. Except, I came by my obsession to stop the predator from trapping me in his snare.

I am still afraid of him, and I'm terrified of my feelings for him. None of those have changed, nevertheless, there's something about knowing your enemy can't kill you because they need you that gives you some element of bravado—even in moments like these.

"Are you going to tell me?" I push, intensifying my stare.

"It was Knights' business. I'm not at liberty to discuss that with you."

He's lying. Oh God, he's lying to me. I know he is. There's a shift in his eyes that so slight you'd miss it, but I see it crystal clear.

"You never spoke about Knight business before with Lucian. It's odd that you would suddenly do so."

"It is what it is, and like I said, I'm not at liberty to discuss it with you. Don't let me have to repeat myself." His eyes hold me in place for a few labored moments before he turns and leaves.

The little ounce of bravado I felt evaporates and is replaced by more suspicion and worry.

That ominous feeling worsens, and I wonder if there's more to why Lucian was shot than what I think.

I have no theories because nothing makes sense— Dorian in Lucian's apartment, both of them getting shot.

Before Caspian used me as an alibi, everyone thought he was responsible for what happened to them. There was an obvious connection; even I would have suspected him.

What if there still was a connection?

If so, what was it?

What else are you hiding from me, Caspian?

CHAPTER 14
CASPIAN

My heart shrinks as I gaze at my soon-to-be wife asleep on the sofa. The tartan-patterned blanket she brought from home is draped over her and she's curled in on herself, looking younger—*vulnerable*.

I crouch down next to her, thankful she doesn't stir. It looks like I'll only have these moments of peace with her when she's asleep.

Every other time sees us arguing in some way. Yesterday, though, was a real bitch, and I'm sure today will be the same after the re-evaluation meeting. My father really dealt one hell of a blow.

That whole St. Jude's thing was twofold—the first to punish Willow for her defiance in front of the council, and the second must be part of his plan.

I can't keep on like this. It's no way to live. Control like that over Willow and me will destroy us both.

Things have never been so bad with my father. This

is the first time I've landed myself in conflict with him that I can't seem to get out of.

That's why I allowed her to sleep down here last night. It was an allowance of a break I knew she needed.

Being around her when I'm fuming also wasn't a good idea. I'd come home filled with wrath because I'd spent the whole day split between trying to reach my father and tracking down that guy with Thorne. Both to no avail.

I also found out later in the night that my father was going to be in Boston until after the wedding. I guessed to keep an eye on things, or me.

By the time I arrived home, I was ready to snap. So, when Willow looked at me like she believed I was just like my father, it angered me even more.

But when she started asking about Lucian, I didn't know what to say.

I guess it must have been Eilish who told her she saw me speaking to Lucian the day before the shooting. She was the only person Willow went to see yesterday, and I remember Eilish watching Lucian and me that day on the quad. I just never knew such a minor encounter would come back to bite me.

I still need to keep what I'm doing regarding Zak a secret along with my knowledge about him looking at her father's files.

With that aside, I still wouldn't know what answer to give her when I don't even know what happened myself.

All I know is that I dragged Lucian into this shit. Being responsible in some way for her precious friend's life-threatening injury will fuck me over even more. I blame myself enough as it is.

I straighten and walk away. It's best I leave and get started on the day.

My first agenda is going to see my father.

We need to talk.

My father gives me a devilish smile when I walk into his office in Raventhorn Hall.

The last time I was here, we made the pact and blood was spilled to seal the vow.

I knew even as I sliced my palm and saw the wealth of crimson flowing from my skin that he was going to find a way to fuck with me.

I didn't even bother to hope he wouldn't. I just knew to be ready.

"I didn't expect to see you so soon, son." His smile brightens with menace. "Not playing with your new toy today? Or are you bored already? That would be interesting."

The taunting air of his words is supposed to anger me, but I tamp down my rage. Unleashing it will be fruitless. We'll be like wild beasts fighting to the death.

The thought conjures that question in my mind once more—could I kill my father?

Each time that question floats into my mind, I get closer to pulling the trigger. I think what I'd worry about is how I'd feel after. While my mother is no longer on earth, I don't think she'd want me to take his life in such a way.

However, she left him in the only way she knew she could by seeking refuge in another man's bed. I don't want my girl to do that.

"You could have shared your plans with me about Willow," I say in an even tone.

"Oh, I see, so she's still of interest to you? At one point, I thought you'd come to your senses. You hated her enough to. I know you still do. I'm sure when you fuck her, it's the barrier that stops you from feeling more than you could."

I don't want to talk about that, and I don't want him to be right. Although I hate that he...is. My feelings are my own, and I don't want to share them with him to give him more ammunition against me. I'll work out my demons by myself.

"Answer the question, old man. From where I'm standing, it looks like you're working your magic to usurp what we agreed to."

"I'm doing nothing of the sort, son. It's my duty of care to make sure I do what's right for my legal charge."

"Bullshit. Don't bullshit me, Father."

"I'm not." He leans forward and steeples his fingers. "I exercised the same duty of care when I contacted the board at Dynamic Corp and informed them that we might need to look into making other arrangements for transfer of ownership."

Cynical laughter falls from my lips, and I shake my head at him. "You are one nasty motherfucker."

"Mne povezlo, I raised one hell of a fucker, too."

That's it. I've had enough. I rush to the table, whip out my knife, and growl as I ram it into his fucking shiny desk.

He flinches, moving back, something he wouldn't have done before. He would have second-guessed me, but just now, I lost my mind a little and gave in to madness. Just for a moment I did it to see how it would feel.

With my knife in the desk and my hand on the hilt, I glare at him, and he looks back at me—*shocked*.

"She's not going back to St. Jude's. Don't you fucking dare put her back there."

He smiles again and taps my hand holding the knife, showing the moment of trepidation is gone.

"That's not your decision. It's mine. She doesn't get to be happy with my son while my girl is six feet under. I will do whatever I see fit with her life until I think she's paid, and you will not stand in my way."

"Paid? That is against our agreement." He's fucking insane if he thinks I'm going to stand by and allow him to hurt Willow. What kind of man would I be if I allowed that?

"Our agreement is you get to marry her instead of me. I was also kind enough to agree to her safety. However, as long as I hold her legal guardianship, what I choose to do with her is my business." He chuckles. "So, fuck with me, and I will only do the same to you. Like I said before, there are other ways of taking her away from you."

This is fruitless. He can't be reasoned with in any shape or form. Violence and deceit are the only things he understands.

The only way to unravel his claws is to find something to use against him. A man like my father is going to have all kinds of heavily guarded fucked-up secrets.

I just have to find one of them that's dark and weighty enough to destroy him.

The task of finding such a secret might be something I have to do on my own. I have no idea where to start looking, but I will find something.

On that thought, I yank my knife out of the desk and walk out. I don't even close his door. I just leave.

When I reach the foyer, my gaze connects with Peter Belkov's as if fate drew me to look in his direction.

Hello, motherfucker number two.

He's standing on the second floor talking to his secretary who takes care of his Knights duties. I've forgotten her name.

While she's talking it up, Peter is staring me down like he wants to kill me. I guess that's answer enough of how he feels about me.

Dorian's funeral was three days ago. It was a private ceremony for the family only. Understandable. I wouldn't have gone anyway if it were open to me because I had every intention of killing Dorian when we fought during training.

Peter knows that. The murderous look he's giving me expresses his displeasure that I'm taking the fortune he would have gotten had his son married my girl.

No one else would dare look at the Pakhan's son in such a manner, no matter how much you hated him. Yet here he is.

Here I am, too, and the question in my eyes as I walk by is, is he guilty?

What is his part in this mess?

Was it him who wiped Timofey's files?

Did he kill my brother?

That last question flares my temper, and I almost unleash the beast inside again.

He looks away first, which snaps the rage from erupting.

I continue walking until I find myself by the river.

When my phone rings, I almost think to ignore it, but I don't. These days, I know I need to answer when I'm called, no matter what mood I'm in.

Thank God it's Thorne.

"Hey," I say.

"Hi, I got a name, Caspian. I got the guy's name."

I sigh with relief. Thank fuck, this is something we can work with.

"Who is he?"

"Raphael Torriano. From what I've seen, he's an associate from the De Marco family, but he's got hookups all over, which explains how he's on our turf. Looks like he also gets hired mostly to get intel and when someone wants to make a hit look clever."

What a motherfucker. Who I need to get my hands on, though, is the guy who hired him.

"Thanks, Thorne." He was so right; I couldn't have

done this alone. There are way too many moving parts to handle.

"Don't mention it."

"Does my father's team know about him?"

"No, I had to dig deep underground for this intel."

"Let's keep this to ourselves for the moment."

"You got it."

I want to talk to this guy first before my father gets to him. Of everyone investigating, I'm the only person who's looking at the series of fucked-up events holistically and trying to make connections. Anything that can push me ahead might give me answers to how everything else fits.

"I got some ideas on where to find him. Meet me later."

"Will do."

CHAPTER 15
WILLOW

I t's colder today.

I'm not sure if it's just me, or if the room we're in really is that chilly.

Since I'm the one whose sanity is being interrogated, I'll play devil's advocate and assume I'm the one at fault.

Then again, the icy temperature I'm feeling could have everything to do with the people whose company I'm in for my re-evaluation.

Aleksander and I are sitting next to each other on the soft leather sofas in the student council room while Dr. Taylor has taken the armchair in front of us.

He was the Henry Cavil look-alike at St. Jude's. He still looks like him, more so as the years have gone by.

He was responsible for a lot of my care while I was at St. Jude's, so it seems fitting that he should see me today.

There's that, and I always suspected he might have some affiliation to the Knights. Although there's nothing to mark him as such.

It seems he might also have a different position now. I haven't been told this, but I have a feeling from the authoritative way he's carried himself. I don't like it, but maybe it's because I have a problem with people who have any kind of authority over me.

Like the man sitting next to me with that smug-as-fuck expression on his face.

The room we're in is used by the guidance counselors and other student therapists for career planning and therapy sessions.

I remember noticing the building during my tour of the campus on my first day. At the time, I didn't even want to hear the words *therapy* or *counsellor*. Now look at me.

I'm here for a session.

Caspian is in the waiting room outside. He wasn't allowed to come in with me. Part of me feels some comfort for knowing he's here, but since things are far from good between us, I feel alone and exposed.

"Well, unless you have any questions, I think we can get started," Dr. Taylor says, glancing from Aleksander to me.

"The questions might be best placed after the meeting," Aleksander suggests.

"Of course." Dr. Taylor focuses on me and gives me a fake smile. He might be gorgeous, but his façade of looking like he cares about my wellbeing makes him ugly to me. "Willow, do you understand why we're here today?"

"Yes, I do."

"Good, the aim of today is to talk about a few important things regarding your mental health care. Once that's done, I'll recommend what I think we should do next. I will tell you now that you mustn't feel pressured or stressed in any way. People like me exist to help you. Do you understand that?"

"Yes, I do," I mutter the words with the same taciturn undertone and maintain my jaded appearance.

If he remembers what I'm like—and I'm sure he does—he'll know why I look this way.

It's because I'm not buying his bullshit. What he should have asked me is if I believe him.

I don't because he's not here to help me.

I remember with perfect clarity what he's like. He was one of the worst of the doctors at the hospital because he didn't care. In my catatonic states, he'd let things slip and I'd hear things I shouldn't.

Like him telling the nurses to up this one's medication just when they'd started to get better so they would stay in the hospital longer. Or him ordering some fucking shit for another patient so they'd get worse and die.

He was fucking that nurse, too, who couldn't keep her eyes off him, and he fucked the patients as well—the rich ones who could get him ahead in his career.

So, he's here to see what he can get from me.

I'm the girl who lied her way out of a mental hospital. People like me pay the bills and fill his pockets. We keep people like him in work, and right now, I'm one hell of a case.

Everything he says next will be for Aleksander's benefit, not mine.

The moment I saw him, my hopes of this meeting going any way in favor of what I want died.

He rests his hands on his lap and keeps his gaze riveted to mine.

"Willow, the first thing I want to ask you is why you felt the need to lie about your sister. Why did you do that?"

Why do you think? That's what I want to say, but I hold my tongue.

"I don't know." It's not the best answer, but I think anything other than that won't bode well for me.

"Okay, well, that's a start. I'm going to ask you a series of questions, and I want you to answer to the best of your ability. I also want you to answer what you're most comfortable with."

As if he's been programmed to do so, he pulls out those godawful psych evaluation ink blob images.

Just the sight makes me feel like I have gone crazy.

He then proceeds to ask me what I see when I look at each one. I'm tempted to resurrect my jokes from the past, but I don't because I don't want to damn myself any more than I already am.

An hour passes during which I'm asked a host of questions to which he writes down my answers in his notebook.

When he places his pen back in his pocket, I take that as a signal that the meeting is over and he's come to a decision on what to do with me next.

"I think that's enough for today. Willow, you display the abilities and skills of an intellect. While your answers are impressive and you have grown up to be one fascinating scholar, I'm concerned about your beliefs about your sister. It doesn't sit well with me that you don't seem willing to talk about her."

"Nor I," Aleksander concedes.

I cut him a sharp glance then return my focus to Dr. Taylor. "I don't want to talk about her. When last I checked, that wasn't a crime."

"No, it's not a crime, but it's important." He straightens. "As long as you believe Lillian died at Bluff Island in the manner you said, we have a problem."

That doesn't sound good, but I can't say his words surprise me. Nevertheless, I have to try and save myself somehow. I can't just sit here.

"I'm sure you have seen various reports of my evaluations and treatment plans over the last few years. I'm living a normal life and am going to school. I'm different to what I was when you last saw me."

"Be that as it may, there are concerns, and we can't overlook the fact that you lied while you were in our care. We believed you and set you free. Essentially, you manipulated us into getting your way out. That can't be overlooked."

"It shouldn't be," Aleksander states boldly.

The cold weight of his stare forces me to look at him. He looked smug-as-fuck because I'm sure he already knew the outcome of this meeting—which I'm yet to hear.

"Dr. Taylor, I'm sure you are aware that Willow Raventhorn is heir to an immeasurable empire, one that I am bound by." Aleksander breaks our stare and looks at Dr. Taylor.

"I am aware of that."

"As her legal guardian, I think it would be a gross error on my part to overlook what she did, too. From a business standpoint, I believe she lacks the capacity to run the multibillion-dollar company her father left her, and I don't believe she is well enough to take on the responsibilities entrusted to her."

"I am well." I know I'm to shut the hell up and do as I'm told, but I can't allow him to talk that way about me.

"Remember my warning, my dear." He gives me a blunt smile.

This time, I pipe down because I know I've already lost.

"With all that said, here is my recommendation," Dr. Taylor states. "I think you would benefit from a full psychiatric evaluation."

I swallow hard past the lump in my throat. "What would that entail?"

"If your guardian agrees, it would mean going to St. Jude's and staying with us for a duration of three weeks."

Oh no. No, no, no.

Please, God, no.

"No, I don't want to go. I don't want to do that." Three weeks at St. Jude's. Jesus. I don't want to think about what that truly means.

"I am in full agreement," Aleksander declares. His words sound like knives in my ears.

"I'm not. How could this be okay?" I direct the question at Dr. Taylor.

"Willow, it's not as bad as what it appears to be. I can't just ascertain your mental state from this one little meeting, but what I'm certain of is that you need something. Honestly, given everything that's happened to you, I think it would be beneficial and therapeutic if you were with us. A three-week stay would allow the

team to observe you properly."

I shake my head. "I don't want to go."

"I'm sorry, Willow, but that is my recommendation. I understand you are getting married next weekend, so I'll make arrangements for you to stay with us after the wedding. That should give you some time with your husband and to wrap your head around things."

"Wonderful. I'll need a report of today's meeting, if that's okay with you," Aleksander states.

"Of course. I'll have it ready for you by tomorrow morning." Dr. Taylor focuses on me again. "We're finished now, but if you have any questions, call me."

I don't answer him. Instead, I bite down hard on my back teeth, willing my tears away.

I can't believe this is happening to me.

Again.

CHAPTER 16
CASPIAN

There, I did it.

I'm in my father's secret accounts.

I'm not Thorne, not anything close, but I can do a thing or two with equipment I already have at my disposal.

I've set Thorne's spyware to watch my father's secret email address and phone number he doesn't know I have.

It was Zak who found them when he was snooping around, so I can't take full credit. In the past, the phone had been used to arrange meetups with high-end prostitutes and drug dealers. I thought it was for shit like that until I saw messages from people I knew to be U.S. government officials.

I've set the system to notify me when the phone is in use and record incoming and outgoing calls, too.

I open the inbox and find a lot of messages from undisclosed recipients.

The last email came in six months ago, and the others look like they were received in a similar time frame, which means he only uses this email address for certain things. I'm willing to bet the phone's call log will show the same.

All the men in the Knights have their secret contact details. This is one of my father's, and I'm going to use it to my full advantage.

After Willow's re-evaluation earlier today, I had to do something fast.

I can see things being blown out of proportion and becoming something they shouldn't be. There is no way she needs three fucking weeks at St. Jude's for anything. Being there is going to destroy her.

And yes—once again, I realize my part in this mess. I was the one who made my father aware that Willow still believed Lillian died at Bluff Island, so it followed that she lied to get herself out of St. Jude's.

It's my fault, so I have to find a fucking way to fix it. At this point, I'll sell my tainted soul to the devil, prepped and ready for Hell to get anything that will help me free Willow from my father's control.

Then I'll find a way to fix us.

This setup I have here is risky because it's uncertain and might not work for when I need it. But it's something.

She's asleep now. All day, she carried a soulless look in her eyes. The moment she stepped out of that office with my father and Dr. Taylor earlier, I knew it was bad news.

She told me what happened and hasn't spoken since. She didn't eat dinner either or drink anything.

It's now late, nearly ten. I have to go out to meet Thorne in an hour, but I don't want to leave her.

I'll have to, however, to take care of our other problem.

Here's hoping this all works.

At least I have a name for this guy who tried to kill her. Thorne has a list of places we can search for him, but the list is based on the places the De Marco family runs, which means we could be looking for a while. Tonight, we're seeing a lead who'll hopefully narrow down the search.

I start looking through my father's emails but find nothing I can work with.

They're all what I expect, though—brief messages alerting him of something being done but not saying what.

The sender also either leaves an initial at the end of the message or a number. Neither tells me anything, and they're too old for me to try to decipher anything.

They are all like that, so I know I'm going to have to keep a close watch if I want to find something.

Realizing I won't find anything tonight, I quickly switch into my father's usual files—the ones we're keeping track of for the investigation.

I checked them about two hours ago. I can see he's made a file since for the judges.

I open it to check what he's put in there. There's not a lot to see, but it looks like he's making each judge go through a rigorous investigation with his team. Every single one of them has the same files, and it looks like he has them supervised, too, so they're being watched.

I'm sure they're going to know they're being watched and act accordingly.

The frustrating thing is, apart from Peter, I can't think of anybody else who could be guilty.

I click out of the folder then notice another file at the bottom labeled *Zak*.

I open that and I find pictures. Pictures of my parents and Zak together.

It's sad, not because there's nothing there of me and I suppose it looks like I don't exist, but it's sad because my father is clearly still grieving. I would hate to be a man in his shoes with so much power and no way of knowing who killed my son.

I close the file and glance at the clock. It's time to go.

Better to fill my head with the things that are within my control than what's not.

No magic on earth can make my father love me the way I wish he could. It's odd, though, because my last memory of him looking anything close to human was when he rescued me from the bottom of the well in Russia. He was the only person who looked human in my childhood nightmare.

"THIS IS OUR GUY," Thorne states, motioning to the tall, muscular guy across the road who just walked into the mechanics' shop.

The guy is Latino and has a black bandana around his head. He looks like he's in his mid- to late twenties.

"Let's go." I move away from the wall, and we both make our way over.

We've been waiting for this guy to show for close to an hour. He's supposed to have some intel for us. I hope it's something useful.

He's speaking Spanish to one of the guys opposite him working on a Mustang. When he sees us, the conversation trails off and he straightens.

The first thing his eyes go to is the tattoos on our wrist that mark us as Knights. Not everyone knows what runes mean, but those who do, automatically become as wary and guarded as this guy.

He knows that while we might look like teenagers, we're not, by the usual standards. The runes mark us as killers, and if you don't want to die, then don't fuck with us.

"You're late," I state. His jaw clenches.

"I had family business to tend to. Let's go out the back." He cocks his head to the side, toward a door.

He leads, and we follow him through the door, which takes us down to a garage area with a lineup of cars that look like they were pulled from the set of *Fast and Furious*.

Thorne and I exchange glances but give no thoughts

away. The cars are hot, but that's not what we're here for.

The guy stops by a Lamborghini and leans on the hood, staring at us both.

"You got a name? I like working with names," I state.

He gives me a measured stare before his expression loosens and he nods.

"It's Hector. I'm ready to talk, but the bills won't pay themselves." He chuckles.

I pull out the two thousand I promised and hand it to him.

He straightens, and I raise my brows when he starts counting the money in front of me.

"Alright, looks like we're good to go. Your boy Raphael is going to be hard to find."

"I didn't just pay you two thousand Gs to be told what I already know."

"I know, that's why I'm going to give you some tips on how to find him and maybe some intel. Which do you want first?"

"Tell me how to find him." That's the most important thing and what I'm desperate to hear.

"Raphael runs a drug circuit down by the clubs around the harbor. The problem is, no one ever knows which club he's going to be at."

"What about a home address?"

"Nah." Hector laughs. "Unless you have big tits and a wet pussy, you're not gonna get anywhere near that guy's house. The best place to start looking is the circuit. Chances are he'll be there one night."

"All right." I guess that narrows things down a little. "What about the intel?"

He sighs and bites the inside of his lip. "About eighteen months ago, there were whispers of your kind down here setting up connections with Raphael. It was to organize a hit. I believe he's been working on his target ever since."

My stomach tightens. The pieces of the puzzle are falling into place, and now I see my hunch was right. Eighteen months ago, Willow would have still been in high school, and I was just finishing up. I feel that is the point at which something significant happened.

I know I can think of one thing for myself.

Eighteen months ago is also pretty damn close to when Zak was killed, and if I know one thing, it's that there are no coincidences.

"Anything else?"

"Nah, that's it."

I pull out another two thousand dollars, and his eyes widen when I hand it to him.

"If you see anything."

"I'll call you."

CHAPTER 17
WILLOW

Jesus, I'm not going to last if I already feel like this—like the world is ending, and as it dies, I will die, too.

I know the world is fully capable of surviving long after I've left it, but that sense of impending doom is how I start to think when everything is out of my control, and the full-blown anxiety attacks I used to get strike.

The buildup was with me all through yesterday and last night, and I couldn't shake it. I kept thinking about going to St. Jude's.

The fear of what's going to happen to me flourished into this monster stifling my soul.

The moment I woke and saw Caspian was nowhere to be found, I felt worse.

I still think he's hiding something from me in relation to Lucian. Nevertheless, I'd like to know where he is.

The only thing I'm holding on to now is seeing Elaine and Adrian tomorrow.

It was initially just supposed to be Elaine to finalize everything with my dress, but after I called them last night and told them what was happening, Adrian decided to join us, too.

As I didn't want to stay in the house all day with the guards, I've decided to venture to the library. It's always quiet at this time on a Saturday. The silence and scent of old books are most welcoming and just what I need right now.

As is the sight of Nina's familiar face beaming at me over the counter.

"Oh, my gosh," she gasps, bringing her hands to her cheeks.

She opens the little gate and comes out to meet me. We then hug like we're old friends even though we've only known each other since I started college.

"Hey, there," I say weakly when we part.

"I was hoping to see you, but are you okay to be out and about? Please don't tell me you're here to study." She shakes her dark head at me, and her long curls bounce.

"No. No studying." I'm glad Caspian followed the doctor's orders on that one because going back to classes would have been too much for me. "I just had to get out of the house. I'm doing a lot better, though."

"I'm so glad. I was worried. I know we haven't hung out much or anything like that, but I think we bonded enough for me to worry when I heard what happened to you."

"Thank you for worrying about me."

I genuinely mean that. Nina has been super nice to

me, and honestly, her company has given me a lot of comfort at times when I couldn't speak to my friends.

It was nice to just talk about books when I was seeing Caspian in secret and didn't even know how to wrap my head around it. It was also nice to talk about books when Eilish wasn't speaking to me.

"Of course. Are you here for anything specific?"

I shake my head. "I just thought I'd get here then see what took my interest. I should be around for about three hours." Points to me for making that sound like I choose the time limit. If it were up to me, I'd spend the whole day here.

Nina smiles, and her eyes sparkle with an idea. "Well, if you're up for it, how about we hang out now? It just so happens that I'm writing a paper on Sylvia Plath. I'd love to run some ideas past you."

For the first time in weeks, I find myself smiling sincerely. "That would be great. I would really love that."

"You can tell her no, you know," comes a voice from our left. It's Ilya. He's just come out of Nina's office with Oleg. Both gaze at me with amused expressions.

"Shouldn't you be still resting?" Oleg asks. Concern fills his eyes.

"Honestly, I'm okay. I figured if I can get married next Saturday, I can go to the library." I sound a lot more lighthearted than I could possibly feel. The smile I plaster on my face must also seem convincing because Oleg chuckles.

"Fair point." He dips his head. "Don't overdo it. We'll see you next Saturday."

"Yes, Saturday."

Everyone who's anyone is going to be there.

Because Caspian and I are heirs to two senior descendants and such a union has never happened before in the entire Knights' history, we will be married at Raventhorn Hall.

We'll also have a handfast ceremony, something I've always thought was so beautiful. It won't be on this occasion because I'll be made to feel like the sacrificial lamb.

Oleg turns to Nina and speaks to her in Old Norse. I'm used to hearing them speak Russian because we all swap between it and English, so hearing the secret language uttered piques my interest. I'm even more intrigued when Nina replies.

Not a lot of women know the language, hence why I don't know it. Although I'm sure my father would have taught it to me and Lillian if he were alive.

I'm guessing Oleg knows I don't speak the language and was telling her off again and didn't want me to hear.

"Yes, Father," she says, rolling her eyes at him.

He smirks, then he and Ilya leave us.

"I didn't know you spoke Old Norse," I say.

"Yes, and if you guessed that he was telling me off, he was." She laughs. "He basically said I shouldn't keep you out too long or bore you."

"I could never be bored."

"I thought so. Come on, let's go out back. I have muffins and donuts and tons of chocolate."

"That sounds perfect."

We head to her little office and spend the next few hours talking about not just her paper but classic literature. Since I've never had a friend like her to do this with, hanging out with her does the trick of mellowing me out.

When the time runs out, my heart shrinks away, and I wish I could stay a little longer—escape reality for just a few more hours.

But I have to go.

Nina walks me back to the front counter, where I can see the guards already waiting for me by the door.

"I'll see you next Saturday, but don't hesitate to come by if you want to chat or just hang out," Nina says.

"Thank you." If I can, I might come by tomorrow evening.

"Take this. It's something new to add to your reading list." She hands me a copy of the *Complete Poems of Emily Dickinson*, another of my favorites.

"I'll enjoy reading this," I tell her.

"Perfect." She gives me a quick hug, then we part.

She heads back to her office, and I turn to go the other way, however, I'm not paying attention, so I accidentally stumble into someone and nearly fall over.

I drop the book Nina just gave me and my purse, so I bend down to pick them up.

A flutter of giggles greets me as I lift my head, meeting Misha's stuck-up bitch face and two of my other sorority sisters.

I also see that the girl I bumped into is the pretty blonde who came to Caspian's apartment weeks ago.

While the others laugh, her haughty glare pours over me like acid.

I straighten and prepare to apologize, although I don't want to. That's so unlike me. I'm usually the first person to accept my faults. Just now was undoubtedly mine, but as I look at this girl with her patronizing stare, I want to be a bitch, too, and say nothing.

But that wouldn't be me. And the only reason I'm thinking of acting that way is because I'm jealous.

She's been with Caspian. She's slept with him, and I know she's not going to be the only girl on campus who would have. She's just the only one I know about because she made it seem so obvious when we first met. And, of course, she's not just pretty. With that platinum hair and boobs that literally look like melons—and I'm sure are fake—she looks like a young Pamela Anderson getting ready to run across the beach on the set of *Baywatch*.

Realizing that I'm staring her down and verging on the side of rudeness, I decide to speak.

"I'm sorry. I wasn't looking where I was going," I apologize and instantly regret it when she gives me a condescending smirk.

"That's fine, sweetheart." She looks me up and down. "You do look like the lost little princess."

"Excuse me?" I raise my brows. The stab of awareness pulling at my senses tells me I should just walk away. But I'm so tired of being treated like shit that I stay right where I am and gear up for whatever this turns out to be.

"I suppose your presence at the library days before your wedding suggests Caspian is probably either bored or tired of you."

"I couldn't just be at the library?" I counter, hugging my bag to my chest.

"Sorry, sweetheart, I believe that even less than the prospect of you being able to keep a guy like Caspian Ivanov in your bed."

All the girls laugh again, Misha the loudest—which doesn't surprise me. After all, didn't I catch her having sex with Dorian weeks before he died?

I'm the joke—the idiot—and I can't say anything because I don't believe I can keep a guy like Caspian Ivanov in my bed either.

"He knows where to find me when he's ready," the bitch says. "My bed is still warm, so tell him Becky sends her love."

She saunters away, and the girls follow, giggling.

The heat of humiliation flushes through my body as I watch them go.

I didn't know I could feel any worse than I do about Caspian.

I was wrong.

I'm about to shrink into the gloom of despair when a warm hand grips the edge of my waist and splays across my belly. I'm pulled toward a hard chest, and I lift my head to find myself staring into Jack's silver-gray eyes.

The seductive smile on his face grips at my insides. It's not arousal I feel, however. It's fear.

It heightens when he dips low to my ear. "She wasn't

lying, you know, darlin." I pull out of his grasp. "Which part wasn't she lying about?"

"All of it." He leans in and smiles wider. "And yes, her bed is still warm for Caspian Ivanov. I don't think it ever got cold. Sometimes, they didn't even use a bed. They'd fuck right out in the open for everyone to see."

The pulsing knot in my throat tightens when I conjure the image of Caspian having sex with Becky, and the coldness of the truth squeezes my heart. Hurt is just the beginning of what I feel. All my fears are coming to life. Every single one of them.

This one, however, seems to injure me the most.

On seeing my obvious trepidation and disappointment, Jack takes my hand, presses something small and hard into my palms, then closes my fingers around it.

"A present for you, Princess. If you want more, come and see me at the party, and I'll take care of all your needs."

He glances over my shoulder as the guards approach, then he tips his head politely the way a Southern gentleman would. Before they can reach us, he walks away.

I haven't looked at what he's given me, but I don't need to. I can feel that it's the same small vial of drugs I've seen him give people.

This is the hard stuff, and I didn't refuse it.

As we leave the library, I slip it into my purse.

CHAPTER 18
WILLOW

Adrian and Elaine sit together on the sofa opposite me.

We're seated in the wedding boutique at Nordstrom, waiting for the seamstress to join us.

We're a good half an hour early, but that was arranged purposely so we could spend some time together.

They also needed to go over a list of shit Aleksander wants Caspian and me to do after the wedding ceremony. It's all the meet and greet crap with the Bratva elite and other business associates. But realistically, everything on that list is designed to showcase me as an emblem of victory over my father, even after his death.

As usual, Adrian and Elaine are trying for their normal perfect selves, but sometimes, like now, I hate it.

Our meeting began with them telling me about the arrangements that have been made for St. Jude's. On the Friday after the wedding, I'm supposed to report there at midday. I will then be there for the next three weeks, after which I'll know if they're going to keep me for a longer period of time.

I just love how Dr. Taylor made it seem like I'd *only* be going there for the three weeks for a full evaluation. It sounded like I could leave at the end of that time, but I can't.

Things aren't looking good for me at all, so I don't want to act like everything is fine when it isn't. And I don't want to be here to pick up a fucking wedding dress when I know Caspian will cheat on me the first chance he gets—if he's not doing so already.

After yesterday's encounter with the bitch squad, I just want a black hole to swallow me.

I can't get Jack and Becky's words out of my head, and it didn't help that Caspian didn't come home last night.

I haven't seen him since the re-evaluation meeting with Dr. Taylor. Of course, after yesterday, the first thing I'm going to wonder is if he was with Becky.

In the early hours of the morning, I found myself looking at my purse and contemplating reaching for the vial Jack gave me.

I have no idea what stopped me and persuaded me to put my head back down on my pillow and go back to sleep.

The only thing that soothed me somewhat was getting the chance to see Lucian this morning. When I woke, the guards informed me that Caspian had granted me permission to go to the hospital with

Eilish, so I called her straightaway and we went to see Lucian.

I assumed Caspian allowed me the visit because he was trying to smooth things over between us. It was a nice gesture, but the road our relationship is traveling on is still fragmented. Nothing will be smooth until I trust him, and I don't.

"Willow, you look like you're about to burst into flames," Adrian observes.

I can see he's trying his best to sound lighthearted. Unfortunately, nothing of the sort is going to work with me today.

"I don't want to do any of this," I confess, although he already knows. "And I'm worried about going to St. Jude's."

They've both been as supportive as they could be, but no one can put me at ease because I know what's going to happen. That full evaluation is a bullshit formality. I know the decision has already been made. It was a done deal even before that shitty re-evaluation.

Adrian releases a labored breath. "Willow, worrying is only going to make everything worse."

"I don't want to go back to St. Jude's for anything. I'll die if they kept me in."

"We don't want you to be kept in either, so it's important you focus." He bites the inside of his lip. "I just wish you'd exercised more care when you confided in Caspian. I know you've explained yourself before, but I still can't fathom why you didn't speak to us. Of all the people in your life, we should have been the ones to know what was going on with you—mentally and physically. You told him about Lillian, and you told him about the notes. Those were both serious things we should have known."

"I'm sorry." I've apologized many times before, and it's all I can do now for my stupidity as I'm reminded that I got myself into this mess.

I've begged them to help me multiple times, but desperation stabs at me once more to ask again. More so because accepting everything as it is feels like lying down in the middle of a busy highway, waiting for a truck to run over me.

"Is there really nothing you guys can do?" I plead.

"My dear girl, we've been through this several times. You know there isn't. It's out of our hands. All we can do now is support you. My advice is to focus on what's fact and what's not before your evaluation. All you have to do is remember what you reported about Lillian wasn't real. That will be your starting point."

Those words twist a knife in my heart all over again. I've heard him say them repeatedly over the last few weeks, and the same hurt pierces through me each time.

After Lillian was killed, Adrian and Elaine were two of the first people to hear my testimony. I poured out my soul, thinking they believed me. Even when I changed my story, I still hoped they believed, but they didn't.

The contemplative stare Adrian is giving me suggests he wants me to be as agreeable as I always am, but my poor soul is so tired of lying.

I'm exhausted, and every time I lie, it feels like I'm

spitting on my sister's sacrifice. I just wish with all my heart they could believe me.

Of all the things I could have said, why the hell would anyone think I made *that* up? Surely, it would be more believable for me to have made up some story that Lillian ran away over her dying.

"Willow, are you listening to me?" Adrian prods.

"Yes... I'm listening."

"You do still maintain that what you said happened at Bluff Island wasn't real, right? You do believe Lillian ran away, don't you?"

I search his eyes for understanding but find none. When I switch my focus to Elaine, however, the look in her eyes pleads with me to say yes.

Normally when we have this talk, she has an unreadable expression on her face. Always.

She's so neutral sometimes, I wondered if she felt anything, which I knew was unfair to think.

The pleading look in her warm brown eyes opens the door to her emotions, and just for one brief moment, there's a flicker of something that whispers she believes me.

At that same moment, hope sparks in my heart and I dare to believe that I might have found an ally in her. Someone other than my friends.

However, that look in her eyes begs me to conform, and I remember who Adrian is and whom he answers to.

"Yes," I say and nod through the ache in my heart. "Yes, I still believe that."

Adrian offers a warm smile. "That's a healthy start."

His phone rings, and when he looks at it, his brows furrow. "I have to take this call."

"Okay."

He leaves us, and once the door clicks shut, I return my gaze to Elaine. We stare at each other for a few seconds before she stands, too.

"I have... a call I need to make before the seamstress sees us. I'll be about five minutes," she says in a weary voice.

She starts walking toward the door, and I take in the shudder in her shoulders.

I can't forget that connection we just had, nor the countless times she's been there for me when I've thought I was alone.

Her actions so far, even before someone tried to kill me, make me wonder if she has thought of ways to get me out of this mess but hasn't done so because of her duties.

The urge to find out screams at me, riding on the wave of my desperation.

"Elaine," I call out, but she doesn't stop. "Elaine—"

"No," she says, stopping now with her back still turned to me.

"But Elaine—"

"No, Willow." She continues to march toward the door.

I stand, and in my hopelessness, I think of anything I can do to speak to her.

"Mom," I cry in such an anguished tone I sound injured. That stops her once more.

I don't know what made me call her that, but it felt right. She's not my mother and never will be, but she has tried to be.

Slowly, she turns to face me with tears streaming down her cheeks, and she looks like a woman who's always wanted to be called Mom.

I almost feel bad for giving her the special moment that isn't quite real, but it's real to me.

"What did you just call me?" she mutters, stalking back to me.

"I said, Mom. You've been my mother nearly as long as my real mother has, so why not?"

She sits me back down and crouches before me, taking both my hands into hers.

"You know... I was one of the first people to hold you after you were born. Your mother was kind to me in so many ways. Not many people know this because Adrian and I don't talk about it, but, um... just after we finished college, we had a daughter."

My lips part, and I stare back at her, astounded and sad in equal parts.

"You did?"

"Yes... we had her for two weeks." Remorse fills her eyes, along with tears. "She had a rare birth defect in her heart that wasn't picked up on the prenatal scans. When she was born, we found out and the doctors prepared us for the worst. But nothing can prepare you for a loss like that. As I held her that one last time, your mother sat with me and..." Her voice trails off, but then she rights herself and releases my hands to dry her tears.

"I'm so sorry, Elaine," I say.

"No, I'm not telling you this for you to be sad for me. I'm telling you because I love you the same way I loved and still love that little baby. When she died, we found out the birth defect was hereditary from Adrian's side, and it would likely affect all our children. I wanted to adopt, but he didn't. Then we got you and Lillian, and it felt different somehow, as if you belonged to us." She nods. "That last day I got to hold my baby, I imagined living a life where I got to see her grow up. She'd go to school, meet a boy, fall in love, get married, and live her life in happiness. None of those things were meant to be, but I got to experience some of those things through you. You will never know what it meant to me to hear you call me Mom. I swear to you I have thought of a million different ways to move the moon and the stars to save you from this disaster, but every plan I come up with fails."

She holds on to my hands tighter, and I take the moment to really look at her. I think of Lillian and know if I was ever going to ask what she truly thought, now would be the time.

"You believe me, don't you?" I whisper. "About Lillian."

When she nods, I feel some sense of reprieve.

"I believe you, but I can't accept it." She lowers her voice. "It means I failed. It was easier for me to believe Lillian could be living somewhere in her own happily ever after than to accept someone killed her."

"Why didn't you tell me that before?"

She drags in a slow breath. "Because we have nothing, Willow. We have nothing that hasn't been investigated already, and there is nothing we can do."

"If you believe me, how can you be okay with accepting there's nothing we can do?"

"Because there are things you don't understand that are out of my control."

My interest and suspicion pique. "Like what?"

She shakes her head. "I can't talk about those things."

"Why not? If they involve me and my sister, then you should." I hold her stare. "I heard you arguing with Adrian while I was home. It sounded like you were arguing about something to do with me."

She looks thrown, so I know I'm right.

"That argument doesn't matter. Right now, I need you to focus on your safety and your mental health. I know what Aleksander Ivanov is like, so please don't do anything foolish. That man won't hesitate to keep you locked away in St. Jude's for life. You hear me?"

As my heart takes in what she's saying, my insides twist into knots and my stomach churns.

Fuck. It seems like there's more to this disaster than what I know, and as usual, I'm being fed information in dribs and drabs.

"Tell me you understand," she insists.

"I do," I mutter.

The moment for questions is over because Adrian opens the door and walks back in with the seamstress.

Elaine quickly assumes her usual elegance and poise, while I sink deeper into despair.

~

I STAY in that funk for the whole afternoon and can't shake it.

Knowing it will only get worse if I return to the apartment, I head to the magazine instead. The only other place I know which will comfort me apart from the library.

I was hoping to work a few hours next week and finish that paper of mine even though I'm not supposed to be doing anything to stress myself out. I also thought it would be a nice distraction as the wedding is on Saturday and God knows what will happen next week.

Going tonight, though, might take the edge off the last few days, especially since no one should be here on a Sunday night. It should just be me getting lost in the silence.

I'm going to review what I've done so far and bring myself up to speed on what's been happening since I was away.

I leave the guards at the door. Walking into the building is refreshing, although the sad thought hits me that when I go to St. Jude's, these parts of my life will be over.

My hopes of working for *Real Magazine* will die, and the only writing I'll be doing is within the confined walls of my room at the hospital.

I don't want to believe that could be how my life ends, but right now, I feel that it's a real possibility I need to factor in.

I'm pulled from my thoughts when I arrive at the floor I work on and notice the light in Caspian's office is on.

He's in there. I can hear his voice.

But... he's not alone. I can hear a familiar female voice, too.

Curiosity draws me closer, and as his door is slightly ajar, I creep up to it and take a peek inside.

The moment I look, I wish I didn't. I truly wish I didn't, because inside his office is a topless Becky sitting in his lap with her arms around his neck.

Yeah, that's why the voice sounded familiar.

It's her, and I suppose this means Caspian is either bored or tired of me.

She has the brightest smile on her beautiful, model-perfect face as she strokes his beard and begs him to fuck her.

I don't wait for his answer. I turn and walk away, feeling the dull ache in my heart shatter the last fiber of hope.

CHAPTER 19
CASPIAN

"Come on, you know you want to." Becky brushes her lips over my cheek and runs her fingers down my chest.

I catch her hand before she can grab my dick and rise with her, removing her from my lap.

She tries to push her breasts into me and wrap her legs around my waist, but I stop her and set her down on the ground.

The lascivious smile is still on her face and stays there until I shake my head.

"Get your clothes back on and leave." I'm surprised by how calm I sound given how stressed out I am.

She was the last person I wanted to see tonight. She followed me into the building, and we ended up like this.

"Caspian, this is ridiculous. You and I make sense. You and *that girl* don't."

"This is the last time I'm going to tell you to get your clothes back on."

Her nostrils flare. "You're going to regret this."

"I won't, so don't come looking for me anymore. I mean it, Becky. I fucking mean it. I am done with you. You and I were just fucking around, and we are done." I won't bother to explain anything further and waste my breath.

She might have been the closest thing I had to a girlfriend, but we were only interested in each other because it suited us. There was no love then and none lost now that I'm with Willow. I know what girls like Becky are like. She probably just wants to fuck me so she can rub it in Willow's face and make her feel like shit.

The weird thing is, the old me would have bent her over my desk and fucked her already, not caring one way or another.

"Get your clothes on, Becky."

Grudgingly, she does, and when she's fully clothed, she leaves. As I watch her go, I sense that was her last attempt.

I came here because I can work in peace in this office. After spending the last couple of days and nights on the street looking for Raphael, I needed to catch up on a few things I didn't want to take into next week.

Although I've been given time off to be with Willow and organize the wedding, I have outstanding coursework and all manner of shit to catch up on.

I'm on the streets tonight again, hoping to either find Raphael or get closer to finding him.

Then there's Willow.

She'll be at home wondering what's going on. We

haven't seen each other in days. I didn't purposely plan for that to happen; it just did.

The more I come up with nothing, the harder it becomes to see her and either lie or try to stave off her questions.

I thought seeing her godparents today would help, but I don't think anything can help now other than finding something that will either solve this grand mystery of shit or give her back her freedom.

My phone rings in my back pocket, so I reach for it and answer when I recognize the number calling as Hector's.

"Hey," I say.

"Your boy Raphael is going to be around tonight in the circuit. He has some clients coming in. He should be in the area around nine thirty."

I straighten, feeling a surge of hope fill me. "Where?"

"I don't have a specific location, but it's going to be at one of the clubs around the harbor."

That could be anywhere, but at least we know to look in the clubs.

"Thanks."

"No problem. If I hear anything else, I'll let you know."

We hang up, and I grab my things. It's eight thirty now.

≈

Iᴛ's nine fifteen when Thorne and I meet at Boston Harbor. We head to the back streets where the clubs and brothels are.

I stop and gaze down the road. There are four clubs in this area. They're the biggest with a more affluent clientele, so these are a good place to start.

If they are a bust, we can hit up the smaller clubs further along the circuit.

"I think we should split up," I suggest. "We might get through the area a little quicker, and if there's trouble, we won't be too far apart."

"All right."

"You take the two clubs over there, and I'll check out the others. We can meet back here in an hour."

Thorne dips his head and heads to the left while I go right. The first club I want to check out is next to a pawnshop in a business complex, so I head over there.

The rancid stench of piss and something putrid hits me as I reach the stairwell, but the shrill sound of a woman's scream stops me in my tracks.

The woman screams like she's being beaten up. I might be the devil, but if I'm right, there's no way I could walk by and leave something like that alone.

A man's voice mixes with her screams. They sound like they're coming from the alleyway to my right, so I make my way over there.

"You little bitch! I'll teach you a lesson you'll never forget," the man snarls with a hint of a foreign accent that sounds Italian. "You think you're too good for the likes of me? I'll fuck your brains out and show you just how good I am."

Another scream rips from the woman's throat as I reach them and realize there are two men and a woman.

The streetlight shines down on them, allowing me to see the woman on the ground with her clothes ripped. One guy is holding her down with a gun held to her head. The other fucker, who looks like the Hulk, is on top of her, unzipping his pants.

As Hulk grabs the woman's face and she thrashes, I freeze when I recognize her.

It's Eilish.

CHAPTER 20
CASPIAN

My brain switches into action, and I pull out my gun.

I use the element of surprise and shoot the guy holding Eilish down right in the middle of his head while he was smiling at his friend's taunts.

Blood splatters everywhere when the bullet connects. He doesn't even realize he's dead until it happens, and I'm not sure, neither do I care, if he did before the life left his body.

The Hulk-ish beast on top of Eilish has his dick out, and the motherfucker is caught off guard by his friend's sudden death.

He reaches for his gun, but he's too late. I end him in the same manner I finished his friend before he can stand, and in seconds, I have his blood splattered all over my jacket.

Eilish scrambles against the wall just as two guys I didn't notice before rush me.

One knocks my gun out of my hand, but it doesn't faze me. I thrust the same knife I rammed into my father's desk into the taller guy's chest, then whip it out and slice the other guy's neck.

In the space of two minutes, they're all dead. That is how a Knight works.

We're trained to eliminate a threat as quickly as possible. Men like these only get to keep their lives if they're of use, and they weren't to me.

I check to see if more are coming before I rush over to Eilish, who is shaking and crying against the wall.

I know her face is bruised, but she's covered in the blood from the first guy I killed.

When I crouch down next to her, she reaches with trembling hands toward me but pulls back when apprehension enters her eyes. Of course, she would. Of all the people in our friendship circle, I picked on her the most. No way would she believe that I'd save her like this.

But she's also afraid of me now for another reason. I'm not just the bully anymore. I'm the killer.

She just saw me slaughter four men, and I have their blood on me, too.

Now she knows with certainty that I'm dangerous.

"Come here. I got you." I reach for her, not giving her a chance to finish figuring me out.

What I want to know is why she's here.

I TAKE her to a Chinese medicine shop run by a doctor I use when I want to keep things hidden from everyone else.

His name is Dr. Lim. He works with a lot of Bratva and Italian Mafia guys but is neutral, owing no allegiance to anyone. That makes him good for keeping secrets.

The vet who took care of the guys I killed is of that same cloth. He would have cleaned up the gory mess I left behind and cremated their bodies by now. He would have also rid the area of any other evidence that placed me in that alley.

I pay both guys well, so I know tonight's services will be listed as one of the things that never happened.

Thorne is still checking things out on the streets. When Dr. Lim finishes examining Eilish, I'll talk to her.

I'm waiting outside the treatment room. We haven't been here long, but I don't know how hurt Eilish is.

I should have probably taken her to an actual hospital, but this was quicker.

After twenty minutes, the door opens, and Dr. Lim walks out.

"She's alright. Nothing's broken," he says in a cultured accent. "She has a few bruised ribs, though, so I gave her some painkillers."

"Thank you. Can I see her?"

"Sure."

As I walk into the room, the first traces of nervousness and embarrassment flit across Eilish's face.

Dr. Lim has given her an oversized T-shirt to wear,

which is swallowing her tiny frame. With her face clear of blood, I can see the bruise under her eye, her split lip, and the fear of God still making her tremble.

She's sitting on the little chair with an icepack held under her left rib.

I managed to get cleaned up somewhat when Dr. Lim took her in here, but I know I still have blood on me.

"How are you feeling?"

"Better and alive. Thank you for saving me," she says. Those are the first words Eilish has said to me in nearly seven years.

All those times I teased her; she never had a come-back. It was always Lucian who fought her battles. I'm sure I was no different from some of the demons who darkened her past.

"Don't mention it."

"If you hadn't walked by, I'd be dead." She glances down at her lap and sets the ice pack down before looking back at me with tear-filled eyes. "It's so strange. You're the least likely person I would have expected to save me."

"What were you doing out there, Eilish?"

I have a couple of theories, and they all revolve around drugs. The caution that fills her eyes tells me I might be right.

"It's probably best I don't talk about it."

When she wipes away tears with the heel of her hand, I reach for some tissues from the Kleenex box on the table to give to her.

She takes them and cleans off her face.

"You know not telling me isn't an option, right?"

"I was stupid. This is just one of my stupid *pill-popping* mistakes."

I was right. Drugs led her here. However, the *pill-popping* comment is one that's a double-edged dig at herself, and me, because of what I called her back in high school.

"What are you taking?" I ask.

She shakes her head. "I wasn't taking anything tonight, but it led me out here. With everything that's been going on, I was just trying to do something to help."

That piques my interest. "What do you mean? How could being out here help?"

She sighs and presses her lips together. "There was a guy at the first party we went to on campus," she begins in a meek voice. "It was that party at the Verge. I was supposed to meet Lucian and Willow there. I got there early, and this guy approached me. He said he was a contractor the club used, and he was there to check the setup for the party. I don't know how he knew I was into drugs, but he asked me if I wanted some of the best E money could buy for free. At the time, I hadn't taken anything for weeks, but being back in Boston was already getting to me. That was just day one."

When she grimaces as if she's witnessing some sort of trauma, I understand.

Sometimes when I look at her, I see a reflection of the darkness imprinted on my soul. The same way Russia changed everything for me, Boston is like that for her.

Nevertheless, she's braver than she thinks because she's here. I, on the other hand, avoid Russia.

"What else happened?"

"He told me I had to go somewhere with him. So, we left campus and went to a club called Brisk. It's just behind where you found me with those guys. The guy gave me the drugs like he promised. But when we got talking, he started asking me all these questions about my life, and my friends. It was weird."

Something churns my gut because that sounds off to me, too. "He was asking about your friends?" I straighten.

She nods. "He was interested to hear about Willow and Lucian, and I was so high I remember telling him everything."

"What kind of questions did he ask about them?"

"Things about what they were studying and what they did on a daily basis. I know it was incredibly stupid of me to tell him anything, but I didn't think he meant any harm. I'm still not sure, but I wanted to find out. I saw him a number of times after that first night, and we did the same thing. The club first, then his place after. It was all about the drugs, but I thought he was interested in me."

Her voice trails off, and I wonder what happened between her and this mystery guy.

"Did you get involved with him?"

"No, but I wanted to." Her cheeks flush. "I promised myself that when I started college, I'd move on and stop hoping Lucian and I would get together, but it didn't work. I couldn't forget how I felt about him. At the same time, I was still my own worst enemy because I couldn't stop comparing myself to everyone else...including Willow."

I bite down hard on my bottom lip at the confirmation that I'm not the only one who's not crazy about Willow and Lucian's relationship.

She takes a quick breath then continues. "I stopped seeing the guy. Then it wasn't until Lucian was shot that I wondered if maybe he had something to do with it. Those questions made me suspicious. Maybe I'm paranoid, but I felt it was someone off campus who might have shot Lucian. I've been coming out here nearly every night since the shooting to see if I could find the guy, but I haven't seen him, and he's never at his apartment. Tonight, I was just unluckier."

Since I'm suspicious of anyone asking too many questions and everything is still so vague, I think this is something I should look into.

"What's the guy's name?"

"Gio, but I don't think that's his real name."

"What does he look like?"

"Italian with longish hair, well built, and he has a tattoo of a scorpion on his left cheek."

Jesus Christ. I bring a hand to my head and glare at her.

Fucking hell. This is unreal.

That's the same guy—Raphael.

It has to be him. How many guys have tattoos of scorpions on their cheeks?

I pull the picture of him I've been showing people from my pocket and hold it out to her.

"Is this him?"

Her eyes go wide and her head bobs. "Yes, that's him."

"Fuck." I straighten, feeling like I'm caught in some kind of maze from hell.

This guy was tracking Willow and her friends from day one. So, the assumption that everything was in motion before they stepped on campus was completely correct. The asshole must have known a few things about each of them before they got to Raventhorn, and that's why he picked Eilish to get close to the rest of them. She was the easiest because of her drug habits.

I need to find this guy and find out who he's working for. Whoever it is wanted all of us watched, and they took steps to kill those who saw too much.

"Why do you have a picture of him, Caspian? What's going on?"

"I've been tracking him. He's the guy who threw Willow off the bridge."

Her skin turns alabaster, and her hands fly up to her cheeks. "Oh my God! What? It was him?"

"Yes. I came out here to look for him after I saw him watching me at the Verge."

"Jesus."

"What else do you know about this guy?"

"Not a lot more. Just where he lives, or was living, and that Brisk club he hung out at. But like I said, he hasn't been to either in weeks now, and everyone I speak to hasn't seen him."

Of course, they haven't. Either my new friend would have probably paid them to keep quiet, or if they're scared of him enough they'll know not to tell her anything.

Eilish wouldn't have known how to torture a guy into giving over information, but I do.

"Did he have roommates at his apartment?"

"Yes, three of them."

That's where I'll start. "I need the address."

"Of course." She nods vigorously. "I'll write it down for you."

"Good. Now listen to me. You are not to come back down here. This guy is dangerous. Do you hear me?" I give her a hard stare.

"Yes, believe me, I hear you. After what happened tonight, I don't want to ever come back here again. I just…" She sighs with exasperation and bites back more tears. "I was just feeling so helpless and guilty. Now I feel worse because that asshole used me to get close to my friends."

"It seems like he had a plan for us all."

"But he used me because I was the easiest target. What's going on, Caspian? No one will tell me anything. Willow doesn't know anything either. But if you're here, you must know something."

I can't tell her anything. Not because what I know is so vague, but it could blow my plans to hell if she tells anyone.

There was no way I would believe that I could break Willow's trust, but I had to. I had to hurt her to save her. There are no certainties in life, only eventualities, so I have to keep what I know close to my heart until the right time.

"It's best you don't get involved, Eilish. The less you know, the better."

"But—"

"No. That's final. Just know I'm working on it. So do not come back down here, and don't interfere. You are also not to tell anyone, not even Willow, that you saw me here tonight. Understood?"

"I understand. I won't say anything. Please don't tell her about me either. She doesn't know about the drugs. Well... she doesn't know how bad it can get. I don't want her to worry about me."

Eilish and I will probably never be the friends we were when we were kids, but that doesn't mean I can't tap into what little remains of my humanity.

"How bad are the drugs, Eilish?"

Her breath catches, and she stares back at me with more tears filling her eyes. "I'm trying to do better. Like with everything else. Just please don't say anything to Willow."

"I won't."

"Thank you. I truly appreciate it." Her eyes cloud as she holds my gaze. "I know things are crazy and they've always been that way, but I can only assume you must be here with me and tracking this guy because you care about Willow. Please don't hurt her. She never meant to hurt you. We're all broken in our own ways, but she's the only one who's ever looked past the damaged person I am and set aside her own problems to help me. Weeks ago, I forgot that. I hope she can get the version of *normal* she wants so badly. I think you could give it to her."

The hope-filled expression on her face directed toward me throws my heart out of cadence.

She's looking at me as if she truly believes what she's saying. As if she can see something inside the darkness in me.

It makes me wonder if a devil like me could really be normal.

Right now, everything with Willow feels like a lost cause.

But love may make me try for *normal* if it doesn't drive me insane first.

CHAPTER 21
WILLOW

Did he sleep with her?

That's the question that's raced through my poor mind all night.

Did Caspian sleep with Becky?

Did he have sex with her at the office then go back to her place?

Is that what happened?

Caspian didn't come home again last night.

I hang my head, pressing my hands against the granite walls of the shower as I allow the heavy spray of water to blast over me.

Although I have the temperature set to cold, I'm still on fire and my head feels like it might explode. The moment I felt that, I jumped off the bed and ran in here with my clothes on.

Water is the only thing that could stave off the ravenous anxiety attack that was heading my way.

I was awake for most of the night worrying, and

when I eventually fell asleep, I kept having nightmares about Lillian, Lucian, being back at St. Jude's, and walking in on Caspian having sex with Becky.

My mind kept telling me he was with her.

I kept wondering if I should have stayed at the office to find out what he did next, then I felt foolish because what do I think he did?

She was topless on his lap. He looked like he was getting ready to kiss her and devour her.

That's probably exactly what he did.

Jesus, I hate this.

I'm a fucking mess, and the wedding is now five days away.

Five freaking days.

In five days' time, I will no longer be Willow Raventhorn. I'll be Willow Ivanov.

I will be the first Raventhorn in our history to lose the surname because of the Ivanovs' senior rank.

While I count backwards in my mind, I pray these sickening symptoms of my anxiety will go away, but they're not budging.

My heart is still galloping a million miles an hour, my chest so tight it feels it's going to snap, and I'm shaking like I'm gonna die—die like I nearly did that night on the bridge.

When I start feeling like I'm going to faint, I turn up the water pressure. Instantly, the impact of coldness explodes against my skin, forcing my focus on the intensity of the water.

The distraction of feeling something else besides my

fears seems to do the trick, and the tension begins to unravel from my body.

Soon my chest releases and my heart slows to what can pass for normal for me, but I have to stay here for a long time before I feel like I might be able to get out.

The last time this happened, I had to be sedated. I woke from a nightmare about Lillian dying then realized my waking state was the real nightmare.

I'm at that point again, and I fear it won't take much to push me right over the edge.

The blast of water slows until it's flowing at a steady rate, but I didn't do that. Someone else is in here with me.

"Willow, are you okay?" The deep timbre of Caspian's voice raises my head.

I push my hair out of my face so I can look at him.

He's opened the shower door and is standing there looking foreboding in a white tank top and black slacks. He's dressed like he does when he's home, so I wonder when he got back.

I search his eyes for some tell-tale signs that he was cheating but find none. What are the signs, though?

I just thought there might be something that would tell me he's not mine anymore. But then he never was.

"I'm fine," I grate out.

"You're in the shower with your clothes on. That doesn't say fine to me." His brows knit as he allows his gaze to roam over my body. "Are you having a panic attack?"

"I said I'm fine." The last thing I want him to do is to report to Father Dearest.

He hardens his gaze, and those green eyes bore into me, challenging me to fight. But he knows I won't do shit because I can't.

"Get ready and come downstairs. I have something to give you."

That's strange. "What is it?"

"Get out of the shower, and you'll see." He walks away, and I watch his tattooed back until he leaves through the door.

At this point, I don't want anything from him. All I want is my freedom and to be rid of the Ivanovs.

Drawing in a deep breath, I find the strength to get out of the shower and get dressed. I leave my hair wet so it can continue to keep my head cool.

When I get downstairs, I see Caspian's made an actual breakfast. The table is set with a delicious spread of French toast, bacon, scrambled eggs, and pastries that look like they came from the bakery I like.

This is the first meal we would have had here together since I came back to Raventhorn.

"How come you made breakfast?" I have to ask because this is weird.

"It's an attempt at normal."

"We're not normal," I point out. I don't know who he's trying to fool, but it's not me.

"Sit."

I lower myself into the awaiting chair, holding back the urge to tell him I'm not a dog.

He grabs the plate before me and fills it with a decent selection of everything on the table, then he serves himself. It's too much, and I know I won't eat a quarter of it because my appetite is nonexistent.

"Where were you last night?" I ask the dreaded question when he sits.

My inquisitive tone makes him square his shoulders and stare back at me with contempt.

"Tending to business."

"Whose business?"

"Why?" He keeps his gaze trained on me, and I realize this is one of those times he's going to be a complete dick.

"Becky sends her love." My voice is overflowing with the dissonance of anger and angst that's been tormenting me. "She said her bed is still warm and you know where to find her. When I went to the magazine and saw her sitting on your lap half naked, I realized *she* must have found you."

I'm sick of treading softly and being careful with my words. I'm also so pissed off at him and myself I no longer care I might be pushing the wrong buttons or spoiling whatever this is he's set up for me.

"I think if you're sleeping in someone else's bed, I should at least know so I can protect myself," I add sourly and watch his gaze darken.

"Protect yourself from what, Malyshka?"

"That's all you can ask me?"

"Yes." He gives me a crude smile.

Bastard. He's not even going to explain what I saw, or

fuck, lie to me. Of all the times I wished he would lie, why couldn't he do it now?

"I just told you I saw you with some girl sitting naked on your lap, and you aren't even going to try and explain yourself?"

"No, because I shouldn't have to." A flicker of menace brightens his eyes. "You think I'm cheating on you?"

"Why wouldn't you? I expect you to."

"Do you now."

"Yes."

"All right."

My scalp tightens with the fury surging through me at his vagueness, and I want to tell him he can go fuck himself and whoever he wants. I want to tell him I don't care—except the tears stinging the backs of my eyes say I do. They also tell me I want to know the answer to the real question on my mind. So, I ask it.

"You slept with her, didn't you?"

"What do you think?" he spits back, venomously, like the viper on his neck.

Suddenly, he looks like the nasty bully he was in high school who wanted to hurt me, and I realize when he promised to destroy me, he had more than one way of doing so. This perhaps hurt me the most.

The air expels from my lungs, and a tear rolls down my cheek.

I can't answer the question, but I don't need to. He knows what I think, and clearly, I'm right.

"You know what? Fuck this. All of it." He picks up the

plate and throws it into the wall then walks out as it smashes.

I stare after him and shudder when the front door slams shut so hard the walls shake.

I allow the tears to fall and feel like shit as I cry.

I STAYED in the house all day. As night fell, I sunk into a deep ominous depression and found myself in the bedroom on the floor sitting against the wall with my eyes glued to the purse I took to the library the other day.

The vial Jack gave me is still in there.

Why haven't I used it yet?

So much has happened over the last few days, weeks, months, years.

Which person in my shoes wouldn't seek some reprieve from the pain?

I remember the first time I tried a joint from Lillian's stash. I knew it was bad for me and I shouldn't have it, but I took it because she did.

Lillian was the sensible, cool, older sister who knew how to handle herself.

She was smart, beautiful, and carried this light with her that you couldn't help but fall in love with.

Everyone, including me, loved her. I felt that if she was using drugs, then it couldn't be so bad. I felt if she was coping that way, then it might help me.

This is different. I have no one here besides myself to base my decisions on, and I've been through hell.

I think, though, I know what stopped me from taking drugs the other night. I still had some hope that what I shared with Caspian was real.

He's not telling me anything about the investigation, I don't know if he still believes my story about Lillian, and I know he carries this hatred for me for his mother's death.

However, I was basing everything on what happens to us when we come together. When we're together, I'm not damaged. I feel whole because he wants me.

This morning was the first time I didn't feel that. The connection severed, but it was also the moment I realized I'd fallen in love with him, and everything I thought I could do to stop loving him was a lost cause.

But we are lost if I can't even trust him. He answered the question and left me feeling like the villain for asking it, so I don't know what to think besides the obvious.

It's seven thirty now, so I'm assuming it's going to be another night like last night, and maybe he'll be with her.

I enraged him, so maybe he'll sleep with her to hurt me, and I'll be punished for my accusation.

Jack's words replay in my mind, and I imagine Caspian having sex with Becky in public. He would have done that to show everyone she's his.

The thought moves me to my purse. The image of them together in my creative mind and back at the office snaps my strength, and I reach for the vial sitting at the bottom of my purse.

I open the little top carefully then pour the white

powder contents into the palm of my hand. There's not a lot, just as much as you would get in one of those salt and pepper sachets.

Parts of it sparkle almost like glitter, and the rest looks like sugar, but the grains are powderier. I've heard Jack mixes his own stuff. I'm sure this is something like that guaranteed to jack you up.

I've never done this before, but I've seen people do it at parties, so I bend my head toward the powder and inhale deeply.

The moment I do, I see stars, then a blanket of happiness settles over me and I feel so good I can't remember why I was ever sad.

I laugh and rest my head back on the wall, lolling it from side to side as tingles ripple down my body then all over me. I moan from the pleasure, feeling like I'm having an orgasm.

Fuck, this feels amazing. Jack is amazing. When something that feels like reality tugs on me, I force it away and realize I must need more. More powder.

Jack has more.

Today is Monday. He's going to be at Lapetus House. He said I should go to him if I needed more.

I get up and go downstairs to grab my jacket. The moment I shrug into it, Maksim walks into the hall. I realize he's not going to allow me to go to the party. He'll probably call Caspian and tell him I want Jack.

"Where are you going?" he asks, looking me over.

Think fast, Willow. Think. You need more powder.

I think hard, searching through my mind for what I

can say. Then it comes to me. An answer in the form of the library. I remember something Nina said to me when I was last there.

She said she sometimes uses the maintenance access to sneak away from work and get cookies from the bakery. That bakery isn't that far from Lapetus House.

I almost laugh at my ingenuity. How resourceful to think of something so clever. This meathead thinks I'm a nerd. I heard him say so to the other guard and that he thought I'd live at the library if I could.

He won't notice me gone if I escape from there. Then I don't care what happens to me or him after.

"The library," I say. "I want to go to the library."

He rolls his eyes at me. "At this late hour? I was just about to eat."

"I want to go to the library right now. You can order something to eat while you wait."

He sighs with frustration, mumbles something under his breath—but loud enough for me to hear—about me being a stuck-up bitch.

When he turns, I follow, biting back the smile on my face.

We reach the library in fifteen minutes, and just like I thought he would, he leaves me inside and goes outside to smoke.

Perfect.

When I walk down the corridor and disappear from his view, I don't even bother to go upstairs; I head straight to the maintenance entrance and leave through the door.

Freedom hits me when I'm back outside and running across the path toward Lapetus.

When I get there, the music envelopes me and I'm pulled into the bodies dancing and the sight of two guys sucking a drunk girl's tits.

I smile at the sight like it's the best thing ever and continue my search for Jack.

I find him by the window, and the moment he spots me, he stops talking to the little blonde girl with the pixie cut and makes his way over to me.

He cups my face when he reaches me, and I take note of how good he smells.

"You had my present, didn't you, princess?" he asks, and I nod.

"Thank you so much for being so kind to me," I coo. My voice sounds overly grateful, as if he just offered me everything I could possibly want in life. I know that's weird because he hasn't, but I don't care. I'll say anything to get more powder. "I need more."

"Yeah, I thought so. Come with me, and like I said, darlin', I'll take care of all your needs. Maybe you can take care of some of mine, too."

I nod.

CHAPTER 22
CASPIAN

I knock back some more vodka and pop open the little blue velvet box I keep in my back pocket.

I set it on my desk so I can look at the beautiful engagement ring inside.

It's a princess cut diamond with a sparkle of pink I thought Willow would like because she loves pink, and I like how it looks on her.

That's what I wanted to give to her this morning. Now I'm wondering if I should. Maybe I should take it back to the store, ask for a refund, and get my sanity back because I'm crazy, and this ring is a testament of that.

I keep saying I know I'm a fucking psycho, but this love thing has brought out a new level of insanity in me.

The insanity stayed with me all day, but at least I put it to good use and managed a breakthrough on where Raphael will be tomorrow night.

The addresses Eilish gave me came through. Earlier, I went to Raphael's apartment. He wasn't there, but I beat the shit out of several guys to get the intel on a drug drop he's been hired to do at the docks. All I have to do is show up and take him out.

I got back to Raventhorn a little over an hour ago and decided to go to the magazine to do some work.

I needed some time to myself before going home. It's getting late, but I still feel like I need more time to cool off. The fury from this morning has stayed with me.

I just couldn't believe that after all we've been through and all I've done for her, Willow could look at me and think I cheated.

Yes, I'll fucking agree that seeing a topless Becky on my lap is reason enough to think something happened between us. Becky also fanned the flames by feeding Willow intel I would rather she not know.

I could have answered Willow's question and told her I didn't sleep with Becky. It would have been that simple. I could have cleared it up right there, except part of me wanted her to look at me and know I would never do that to her.

The same way I can look at her and know what she feels for me, I wanted her to look into my eyes and believe that I was the guy who was true to his girl.

That's what I am, and it counted for shit because she doesn't trust me.

I don't know what the hell I'm supposed to do to fix things between us. I've tried. Fuck knows when last I slept properly, and in the meantime, I can't fucking stop my feelings for her.

But damn, would I have looked like the fool if I had

given her this ring. She probably would have thrown it back in my face.

I didn't exactly have a plan on how I was going to give it to her. I thought we would eat breakfast and I'd know when to do it.

It wouldn't have been on bended knee like the fairy-tale prince she deserves because that's not me and trying to be one makes everything worse.

I got the ring in my attempt at normal. Eilish's words stayed with me.

I already decided on the breakfast, so I made sure Eilish got home safe before I went to the bakery I know Willow likes. It was while I was there that my eyes landed on that ring in the jewelry shop window. It felt like it was calling to me.

The thing looked like it was made for Willow, and all I needed to do was give it to her.

I'm looking at it now, and I still want to give it to her, but I feel like I'm beating my head against the wall.

A beeping noise cuts into my thoughts, and I snap my gaze to my phone.

It's a notification from the spyware I have set up on my father's secret email account.

Quickly, I log in from my computer and notice an email has come through from an undisclosed recipient.

I watch as my father opens it and sends back a response before I open both emails.

The incoming email simply says:

Are there any updates on the contract?

My father's response is:

Yes. Call me on the usual number.

My hands work lightning fast to connect to that number, and as the call comes through, I listen in.

When I hear my father's voice, I hit the record button.

A man with a deep Russian accent answers him, then Father says in a low voice, "I told you to wait to hear from me."

"Aleksander, you know I'm not a patient man. Patience is not something I can muster when we could lose the deal with Tobias Rivera and his bastard Camorra friends."

The infamous Tobias Rivera and his Camorra Syndicate are enemies to the Knights. Any deal with them sounds exactly like the dirt I need to fuck my father over and gain Willow's freedom.

"My son is about to marry the girl and the board is meeting with me in a few days about the current leadership. Let's talk more in depth and go over the figures in two weeks at the same time. Everything should be finalized by then, and I'll have control of Dynamic Corp."

"Okay, boss, messaged received."

Father hangs up, and the call ends. I take a moment to process what I just heard.

Father, what the fuck are you up to?

He thinks he's going to have control of the company in two weeks and is meeting with the board again. No doubt because Willow is going to St. Jude's.

The other day, he said he met with the board, so I'm

assuming his infiltration into Dynamic Corp has begun and he's talking about restructuring the roles.

I know the people who work there aren't going to be okay with that. Especially Adrian, who is the CEO, and Elaine his assistant. Fucking Peter also has business there, although he's predominantly based at Ivanov Tech.

Father also mentioned my marriage to Willow, so everything about that call was about her inheritance.

And he's in cahoots with Tobias?

What the hell is he up to?

I'm going to find out, and what will be finalized in two weeks.

Waiting until then, however, still means Willow has to endure the evaluation at St. Jude's. And it's not like she's going to come back out.

I know she's right to fear they'll keep her in. That's the kind of bastard my father is.

If I'm too late and they do keep her, I'll fight tooth and nail to get her back.

My phone starts ringing. It's Kensei, one of the guys in my unit.

I answer the call, wondering what he could want.

"What's up?" I ask.

"Hey, Viper, I don't know if you know this—I'd say you didn't—but your girl is here at the party."

I bolt to my feet at the same time my eyes bulge. "What fucking party?"

"At Lapetus. She's with Jack."

Jack!

Motherfucking hell no. That fucking bastard. I grab the ring, shove it in my pocket, and head through the door like I have hellfire on my ass.

"What is she doing?"

"She, um... just went up to his room."

Fuck.

"Are my guards with her?" I can't imagine that Maksim would take Willow to a party without calling me.

"No, no guards are here. She came in about half an hour ago looking like she was high."

Jesus. High?

How is that possible? I don't have any drugs in the house. I don't think Eilish would have given her any, or her godparents, so it must have been the asshole Jack himself. But when?

"I'll be there in a minute."

I hang up and run, allowing the beast inside to take over my thoughts.

Jack is fucking dead, and so are the guards. How the hell did Willow give them the slip?

Damn it.

I run faster and reach Lapetus in record time.

Moving forcefully through the boisterous crowd, I soon spot Kensei by the DJ stand. He nods at me and points upstairs toward the apartments.

The last time I was here, I came to see Dorian. I didn't know I'd be back again with the same vengeance in my heart.

I rush up the stairs and find Jack's apartment. I went

up there a few times in freshman year to buy shit from him until he mixed a bad batch for me that had me on the roof of the English building thinking I could fly.

I just hope he hasn't mixed the same recipe of shit for Willow.

I don't knock. I kick the door in, and there I find him half-naked on the sofa, pounding into a blonde girl from behind while Willow sits opposite in her bra, watching them.

Jack's eyes nearly pop out of his head when he sees me charging in, roaring like a wild animal.

He pulls out of the girl, who grabs her clothes and runs out the door, leaving Willow laughing.

The moment I hear that off-balanced laughter, I know she's high. One look at her eyes, and I see it. Then I see the drugs on the table next to her.

"You fucking dog!" I rush Jack and land a punch straight in his face before he can think to talk.

"I swear I wasn't going to touch her," he yelps. "I wasn't going to touch her."

"You expect me to believe that?" He must think I was born yesterday.

I throw several more punches in his face, lift him up, then ram him into the window, smashing it.

"What did you give her?" I demand as blood pours from his nose.

"Heroin... and E."

"You fucking piece of shit! How much?"

"I don't know. I just gave her the bowl and lost track while I was with Amy."

"And you were going to fuck my girl next, weren't you?" When his eyes go wide, I get my answer. "I told you to stay away from her, but you had to find some way of drugging her so you can fuck her! You're done." When I truly think of what he was going to do to Willow, it fuels my rage and I want to end him.

"Stop, don't." Jack holds up his hands. "I'm sorry, man. I'm sorry."

I whip out my knife and get it ready to slice his throat.

"Caspian, don't!" calls a voice. It's Kensei.

He knows me. *Everyone* knows me, and that's why Jack shouldn't mess with what's mine.

If I kill him now, I'm dead, too. I'd get the death sentence for killing another Knight.

It would be a repeat of weeks ago when everyone thought I killed Dorian. Except this time, it would be real, and I wouldn't have an alibi to save me.

If I die, she dies.

The thought floats into my mind, and I choose to live so I can save my girl again.

I tamp down my rage, but only by a fraction. Jack can still learn a well-deserved lesson, so I push him hard through the window.

When he goes backward, the fear of God writhes over his face. He cries out. It's clear he thinks he's going to die. He must fall a good ten feet but lands in the pool below.

As he surfaces and looks up at me, I stand there so he can see me and know that tonight, he nearly lost his life.

I was serious as fuck about killing him, and I would have done it, too.

I was just following the *rules* within reason. He won't cross me again. At the very least, I'm going to get him out of this school because he would have raped Willow.

I turn away and face her, seeing now that she's lying on the bed.

I pick her up and cover her with my jacket, then the crowd parts like the Red Sea did for Moses to let me through.

"You smell so good," Willow bubbles. "Why do you smell so good?"

She curls into my chest, burying her head into me.

She then starts singing that godawful song from her iPod mix I hate as I carry her back to my apartment.

Maksim meets me halfway with his fucking mouth hanging open like the dumb fucker he is.

"She gave me the slip. We went to the library—"

"You're fired! Get your shit and leave!" I cut him off and continue into the house.

When I get to the bedroom, I set Willow down, and she stumbles onto the bed.

I taught Jack a lesson, but she needs one, too.

"Why am I back here? Why are you here? Aren't you busy with Becky?"

"Willow, damn it. I told you to stay away from Jack."

"All you do is bully me and treat me like shit. You tell me nothing about the investigation and keep me locked up like an animal. I'm sick of being left in the dark, and sick of worrying that you'll cheat on me with fucking

Becky. So, I'm leaving you. I want more powder. Jack said he had more powder. Where is he? That liar." She gets off the bed then falls over and starts stroking the carpet.

I move toward her and crouch down, but she swats my hands away and shakes her head.

I pull her into my lap and allow her to pound her little fists into my chest.

"Hit me all you want. You're still mine."

"I'm not yours."

"Yes, you are."

"I don't want to be."

"Yes, you do." I crush my lips to hers, and she kisses me back. "You do, don't you, Willow?"

"Yes... I want you."

I know she does, and I wish I could bend her over my knee, spank her ass as punishment for tonight, then fuck her.

But I couldn't be with her in this drug-induced state where I don't have all of her: heart, mind, body, and soul. That would make me no better than Jack

"I need you to trust me," I whisper into her ear.

"I can't. You'll hurt me. You always find some way to hurt me. Always."

When her shoulders slump, I pull her into my chest and hold her. I don't want what she said to be true, but it is.

"I don't mean to."

"You do." Her voice is hushed and barely there, as if on the edge of a rustling wind. "You told me you'd destroy me. We used to be friends. How could you look at

228

me and say that? You told me you would destroy me, and now people want me dead."

Guilt grates on my insides as if attached to tiny pieces of blades. Each blade cuts into me, slicing into the remnants of my soul.

"I shouldn't have said that to you."

I hold her closer when she starts crying.

"I just want to live a normal life." Her shoulders wrack as the sobs come harder. "I ... don't want to die."

I wish I could promise her the safety I effortlessly offered weeks ago, but I can't. I would be a fool to make such a promise to her when everything is so vague and out of control.

She sobs quietly against my chest for some time, then I don't know what the hell happens, but she trips out. It's like whatever the fuck Jack gave her kicks in and she loses control.

Nothing she says makes sense, and it infuriates me even more when she starts begging me to take her back to Jack for more fucking powder.

I'm pissed as fuck she defied me, but I accept this is my fault.

Everything she said is right. I kept her in the dark, locked her away, and gave her reason to think I would cheat on her.

Those are the things that would destroy a person.

I hold her until I can't. When I find myself restraining her, I know tomorrow will be another interesting day once she climbs down from her high.

CHAPTER 23
WILLOW

My head feels like someone hit me with a baseball bat.

I've never been hit with one of those before, so I don't actually know what that feels like. I've just always imagined it to be terrible.

I heard once about this guy who had brain damage after being hit by a bat.

That's how I feel now. Like my brain has been mutilated.

What the hell happened to me?

God, I'm so sick of waking up like this and asking myself the same question.

But seriously, I can't remember anything, and I have a sinking feeling something else isn't right.

I try to lift my hand to my head, but my hand won't move—*both* my hands won't move!

My eyes fly open. I can see I'm in Caspian's bedroom,

but when I look to my left and then my right, I see my hands are restrained with ropes. So are my feet.

And I'm naked.

Jesus, I'm tied to the bed, naked.

Frantically, I look around the room and shuffle against the sheet, trying to break free.

"Caspian!" I call out because only he could have done this to me.

That bastard.

The door opens, and sure enough, he walks in, but when I look at his face, the events of last night come rushing back to my mind and I remember what I did.

Oh God.

I went to Jack, then I lost my mind when he gave me more drugs. I'd never had so much drugs in my life. Or those types of drugs.

It was like I lost control of everything that made me, me.

My God, I was watching Jack have sex with that girl.

I think he would have tried to do something to me, too.

God, I lost it, and Caspian knows. And he knows what could have happened to me.

Shit.

He walks closer to me and runs a finger across my belly.

His face is void of emotion as he stares back at me in silence and a deadly calm. The silence is eerie, and I have a feeling that this is the side of him I should be wary of.

Not the version of him who always has a snappy comeback.

"Cas...pian," I stammer.

"I told you to stay away from Jack, Willow."

"I'm sorry. I shouldn't have done what I did."

"Do you know what could have happened to you last night?" When he drills his gaze into me, a shudder runs through my body.

"Yes... I know. But I wasn't thinking."

"You were high when you got to the party. That means you saw Jack before. When was that?"

"The library. After I ran into Becky."

I can't even be angry about the whole Becky thing now because last night, I was in Jack's room practically half naked.

"You know, there are some animals who form bonds for life through mating." His fingers run down to my waist, glide over to my sex, and stroke over my slit.

"Why are you talking about that?" I'm afraid to get the answer. When he starts talking about things that are out of context, it's never a good sign.

"Because of its relevance to me and you."

"I don't know what you mean." I pull against the ropes.

"You'll see, baby girl."

"Caspian, untie me. This is ridiculous. You can't do this to me. Untie me now."

"No," he answers, coldly. "Not until I'm done with you."

"What are you going to do to me?"

"Like I said, you'll see. The animals that bond by fucking are mated for life. *Fated* for life. My theory is this: you and I were never friends."

A pang of hurt pulls at my insides. "Why are you saying that?"

"Because I've *never* looked at you and not wanted you," he states, and something inside me goes still. "When you look at your friends, you're not supposed to want them. You're not supposed to wonder what they'd sound like if you gave them pleasure, or what they'd taste like. You're not supposed to fantasize about them or jerk off to thoughts of them. So no, I don't believe we were *friends*."

"Then what were we?"

He doesn't answer. Instead, he shoves his joggers down his hips and takes out his cock, which is already erect.

My mouth goes dry, and I wonder if he's going to take me like this. I struggle against my bonds and try to free myself once more. It's a lost cause. The ropes are too tight.

"Caspian, let me go."

He starts stroking his cock, and the sight of him doing so is so hot I can't look away. When he starts fisting himself, I'm hooked.

"Does the sight of me pleasuring myself make you ache, Malyshka? Watching you watching me, turns me on."

Embarrassed, I blush and swallow hard, but I keep watching him fist himself until pre-cum beads on the fat head of his cock.

He gets on the bed and hovers over me, then, before I can ask him again what we're doing, he buries his face between my thighs and starts eating me out.

And. *Oh. My. God.* It feels amazing. The restraints heighten the pleasure, and I cry out.

Fuck! What the hell?

"Caspian!"

He doesn't stop. He keeps going and going until the build of pressure rises through my body and explodes, leaving me writhing against the ropes like an animal in heat as I come.

A deep, low chuckle rumbles from his lips, and he goes back to continue eating me out. But this time, he's more intense, and my orgasm climbs higher and higher, faster.

He touches me as if he knows what my body wants and what it needs. So, he knows when I'm about to peak. He takes me there and then stops.

"Please, no, I need to come," I hear myself say.

"No, as punishment for last night, you don't get to come again, but I do."

He gets off the bed, leaving me in rapturous torture, and returns to my side to finish fisting his straining cock. Moments later, he sprays cum all over me. It lands on my face and my chest. It's warm and smells like sex and him.

When he finishes emptying himself on me, he dips a

finger in some of the cum that splashed on my chest and places it to my mouth.

"Lick my finger."

I do, tasting the salty, virile flavor of him.

"Now you smell like I own you; you taste my ownership of you, and I have marked you as mine, but there's still one more thing to do."

"What?" I mutter, still aching.

He loosens the ropes from my wrists then my feet. I watch him open the drawer and take out a little blue velvet box.

Shock races through me when he snaps open the box and I find myself staring at an engagement ring.

It's beautiful, and I can't look away from the diamond twinkling in the center that reminds me of the brightest star on a clear night.

My cheeks flush when he grabs my left hand and slips the ring on my finger.

"Let me tell you what we are, Malyshka. We're fated mates. The moon and the sun. Darkness and light. We're not supposed to be together, but when we come together, it's epic. That's why I can't cheat on you." He holds my gaze. "I'm so fucking obsessed with you that I see your face in every woman I've ever looked at. So no, I'm not fucking around, I don't plan to, and I didn't sleep with Becky. I haven't been around because I'm trying to catch the motherfuckers who tried to kill my girl."

He releases my hand, but I'm so dazed by what he said about me I can't talk.

Tucking himself back into his pants, he leaves the room, leaving me

there with the turmoil of emotions swirling around in my heart.

And his ring on my finger.

CHAPTER 24
CASPIAN

If I die tonight, I'll remember I gave her the ring.

Even I know the way I *proposed*—if I can call it that—was possibly the most unromantic of ways anybody could think of.

I stayed away all day to give Willow time to process what I did and said. I wanted her to look at her ring and think of what it's supposed to mean.

Because a lot of marriages in the Knights are arranged, and since we have different customs to everyone else, it's rare that engagement rings are given. Especially when the marriage is forced like ours.

My mother had an engagement ring. Willow's mother did not.

Nevertheless, Willow will know what it meant for me to give it to her.

Now I'm here, back at Boston Harbor, waiting for Raphael to arrive.

Thorne and I arrived at the old warehouses at the docks just before ten.

We're dressed in full black to blend in with the shadows of night and in one of the abandoned warehouses that used to be a shoe factory.

Thorne is stationed on the roof with a rifle while I'm concealing myself in the basement. From here I can see the building opposite where Raphael should be any minute now for that drug drop.

Bright lights illuminate the area, bringing my thoughts back to the mission at hand.

This should be him now.

Six motorcyclists pull up with guys dressed in black. All are armed with machine guns. I wasn't expecting so many. Two against six isn't ideal, but it is what it is. I just hope the element of surprise works in our favor.

The tallest guy stands before the group. I know that's Raphael even though he still has his helmet on. Once again, I recognize his build.

When he takes the helmet off and smiles at what must be his crew, I want to cut that smile off his face and stab him in his heart.

"Thorne, he's here. It's time," I say into my communicator.

We've got wireless virtually undetectable communicators we use for missions. They've come in perfect for tonight's heist.

"I'll tell you when I'm ready to take the shot."

"All right."

I'll move on his word, then I'll have to rely on him to cover me while I do the rest.

I wait patiently, but my blood is simmering, getting hotter the longer I watch the motherfucker.

Raphael jokes around with his friends until Thorne's bullets take down three of them. They all go down like puppets who've had their strings cut.

Those who remain standing look around frantically to see where the bullets are being fired from and start shooting back at the roof.

"Now!" Thorne's voice booms in my ear, and I snap into action, one hundred percent focused on the target before me.

That's what people like this guy become. Moving targets—*not human.*

I leap out of my hiding place, my two guns ready to kill, and run forward.

One guy shoots at me, but I manage to get out of the way. Thorne takes him down, leaving two of them. Now we're even.

Raphael looks at me and snarls before he and his friend start shooting.

I manage to kill the friend with a head shot. Now it's just Raphael and me.

I run behind a pillar for cover while he keeps shooting at me. When I snake around several other pillars, I surprise him, catching him off guard.

I shoot his arm, and he drops the gun. Panic rushes over his face, and he runs inside the dark building.

I chase after him, knowing I'll be on my own from here on out.

Dim overhead lights come on as we both run inside. I try to shoot his leg to slow him down, but he's too fast.

I follow him into the storage room with large crates, perfect to hide behind, and the asshole takes full advantage. I'm guessing he's familiar with this place because he seemed to know exactly where to go.

I can't see him anywhere, and I can't hear him either, but that doesn't mean he's gone, or he can't see me.

The bullet whizzing past my ear confirms exactly that. Fuck knows how it missed me.

"Motherfucker, come out and face me like a man!" I bellow.

"Think I'm afraid of you, Caspian Ivanov?" he calls back. "I just like fighting dirty when my opponent is a fucker who won't leave well enough alone."

"Fuck you. As if I would do that. Who are you working for?"

He laughs, and the echo reverberates off the walls. "I'm not telling you shit!"

"Then I'll make you tell me."

"I'd like to see you try. Zak didn't know when to leave things alone either."

At the mention of my brother's name, I lose focus—a big mistake I can't help.

"Did you kill my brother!" I howl.

When the asshole responds with a laugh, I follow the sound, but that's exactly what he wanted me to do.

He throws himself into me when I bound down the

pathway, and we both crash to the ground. As we roll, I lose my guns.

Blood spurts from my nose, and I see stars when he headbutts me. I just manage to catch my breath when he proceeds to land a series of punches in my face and chest.

It hurts like hell, but if he thinks that's enough to faze me, he's mistaken.

Summoning all my strength, I take the opening I see to get him off me by ramming my fist into the arm I shot. I can fight dirty, too, and I do.

Another hard punch connects with his face, and he flies back onto the ground.

Unfortunately, he doesn't stay down long enough for me to get the upper hand. He reaches for one of my guns, and I rush to get the other.

When he starts firing my own gun at me, I seek cover behind a crate, leaping out again when he straightens. I manage to shoot him right in his chest, and I hope like fuck it's not a fatal wound when he drops to the ground.

This is the part where I would normally end his sorry ass, but I need information.

He tries to shoot me again, but his hand is shaking so much he can't even hold the gun.

I kick it out of his hand and press my boot into the center of his chest, where he's bleeding out. He shouts in anguish, coughing up blood.

I laugh and smile, pointing my gun at him. "Look who's playing dirty now."

"Fuck you, punk."

"You're gonna die. I could make it fast or leave you to

die slowly. Maybe you'll live." The latter isn't going to happen, and he knows I'm just screwing with him. The only options are a fast or slow death, and both are as bad as each other. "Did you kill my brother?"

He smiles through the blood flowing from his mouth. "No. I didn't do it, but someone just like me killed his ass."

"Who did it? Who are you working for?"

The fucking smile widens. "You don't get to hear that part."

"Tell me, or I'll blow your head off right now." I cock the hammer on the gun. "Fucking tell me."

"No."

"You tried to kill Willow." I snarl, and he laughs again.

"Yes, that was me." Another coarse laugh leaves his bloody lips. "It won't matter if you kill me here. Your pretty little girlfriend is still gonna die. Someone else will take my place, and even if you get them, another will take his place."

My temper flares, but I'd be a liar if I said he didn't spark terror in me.

"Who are you working for?" I demand again, knowing it's fruitless. He's not going to say anything.

"The plan was set in motion long ago, and your Malyshka is going to end up as dead as her sister. Willow was always supposed to die. It was just a matter of when. Pretty girl. She looks like a good fuck. Such a pity I never got to fuck her. I would have fucked her senseless then sliced her throat. I thought death would look good on her when I threw her off the bridge. It's—"

I fire one bullet in his head, silencing him. He shuts down like someone switched him off. Blood splatters from the wound.

He's dead, but I keep shooting.

His words play around in my mind, unlocking wrath and madness at the same time.

The words sink in, and their gravity, but I can't move past them.

I saw Willow dead. She drowned and nearly left this life, because of him.

He mentioned Lillian and Zak. He knew of their deaths and said the plan was set in motion long ago.

How long ago?

I don't stop until I empty my magazine, and even then, I'm still pulling the trigger. All I hear is the clicking sound of the empty magazine.

"Caspian, he's dead." Thorne's voice cuts into my state of madness, but I can't tear my gaze away from the mess of gore, blood, and bone that used to be Raphael.

"Caspian." Thorne rests a hand on my shoulder.

I can't answer him. I'm too numb to speak.

WHEN I GET HOME, I clean off downstairs.

The light in the bedroom is on, so I'm assuming Willow is awake. The other night, I knew she was awake, too, or rather half asleep. I was downstairs but could hear her shuffling around in the bedroom in the early hours of the morning.

I avoided her because I knew she'd have questions.

I'm not going to stay away from her tonight, even though I probably should.

The left side of my face is a mess of cuts and black and blue I won't be able to hide. She'll know just from the sight of me that shit went down tonight.

Shit I should tell her about.

I make my way upstairs. When I open the bedroom door, the scent of roses and summer fills the hallway, hanging in the air.

My pulse quickens when I see her sitting on the bed with nothing but a towel wrapped around her body. Her damp hair cascades down her shoulders, falling into her lap.

She's sitting crossed-legged, reading *The Bell Jar*, a book I'm not overly fond of. She had that same tattered, dog-eared book at St. Jude's on my last visit.

Whenever I see it, I remember that bandage on her wrist from where she cut herself. The permanent scar is there now, another reminder of death.

Our eyes lock, and her skin pales when she sees the state I'm in.

"Oh my God," she gasps, crossing the room to get to me. "What happened to you?"

She stops a breath away, taking me in.

I look at her, too, and I think of everything I found out tonight.

She was always supposed to die.

How do I tell her that?

How do I tell her something else that will undoubtedly destroy her a little more? Only last night, she told me she didn't want to die.

I'm still not close to unraveling this web of deceit we've fallen into.

How do I give her hope?

I'm desperate to protect her from any and everything that will destroy her, but what chance do I have when there is no hope whatsoever?

As I stare into those eyes of hers, the angst I've held on to for so long over her secret fades from my heart. I allow myself to see who she truly is and what she means to me.

She's the opposite of everything I stand for and the emblem of good. Even after I've tainted her, she still carries the light of innocence that's too pure for someone with a soul as black as mine.

That's what makes her the fantasy—*my fantasy*—and all I need right now is her. I need to touch her, to feel her, to be buried deep inside her with her body wrapped around mine. I need to make her mine again.

My gaze drops to the ring on her finger, and my heart beats faster. I reach for her hand and kiss her knuckles, loving the silky feel of her skin against my lips.

"Caspian, you're hurt." She studies my face, worry clouding her eyes.

"I'm okay. You should see the other guy." I try to joke, but it's not working.

"What happened to you?"

"Not tonight, Printsessa." I shake my head, and she looks back at me with dismay.

"When are you going to talk to me about what's going on? I know it's all bad. Look at you."

She's about to continue, but I grab her and kiss the words away. When I pull out of the kiss, her cheeks flush and she gazes back at me, speechless.

"I promise we'll talk soon, but not tonight." I'm stalling again. I feel I need to. It's not the right time to tell her the truth yet, and there's so much to talk about.

Too much.

When I come clean, I need to tell her everything, including my plans for Zak, because it's all connected.

I'll also need her to trust me. I'll need her to trust that I'll never stop trying to protect her.

"When will we talk?"

I think for a moment and make the decision as it comes to my mind. "Let's get through the next few days, and we'll talk after the wedding." I'll take her somewhere we can get away from the strain of being at Raventhorn. "Can we do that? There's a lot I have to tell you."

"Okay. I'll wait."

I brush my hand over her cheek. "Tonight, I just want to escape with you. Escape to that fantasy where it's just us. You and me."

"Me?" she breathes. "You want me?"

"Only you. It was only ever you, Willow. Can't you look at me and see how crazy I've always been about you?"

The unhinged spell of hopelessness shifts when she

nods slowly. Nevertheless, it's clear her acceptance of what she sees in me forces visible fear into her eyes.

I don't want her to fear what she feels for me, so I touch her face and gently stroke her cheek.

"Don't be afraid of me. Don't be afraid to trust me."

She stares back at me for a long moment, contemplating my words. "Please, tell me you still believe me about Lillian. Please, Caspian. Tell me you still believe me. You did before."

Now it's my turn to confess. "I believe you. I never stopped. I told you we couldn't talk about Lillian anymore because we needed to be careful around my father and I didn't want to lose you."

A tear tracks down her cheek, but the light of hope returns to her eyes.

This time, she kisses me, giving me a kiss that feels like it breathes new life into my soul.

Her soft body sinks into the hardness of mine, and we mold together. I push her against the wall, inhaling the floral scent of her skin, her hair, her arousal.

My erection grows when she runs her dainty hand over my chest and grips my shirt. I tug the towel and expose her naked body, taking the time to appreciate every part of her.

She trembles under the weight of my stare, and I catch her face to kiss her once more. It doesn't take much for the kiss to intensify with greed.

A soft gasp hums from her lips followed by a needy moan that hardens my dick. I catch her nipples between my fingers then dip my head to suck as she arches into my mouth.

She takes a sip of air and smooths her hands into my head, encouraging me to devour her breasts. So, I do. I work my way from one breast to the other, giving her what she wants, then drop my hand lower to cup her sex. When I stroke her clit through her wet slit, she moans out loud and grabs my shoulders.

"Please don't stop," she begs, and the sexy, sultry sounds of her plea unlock every nerve in my body with vicious energy.

"I'm never going to." Fuck, I want every part of her. No one has ever held a candle to her, and in four days' time, she'll carry my name.

She will be Willow Ivanov, my wife.

I scoop her up and set her on the bed. She leans back on her elbows and gazes up at me when I start taking my clothes off.

"Ride my face, Malyshka. I want your tight little pussy on my face."

Her eyes widen the way they do when I talk dirty.

I continue stripping, then get on the bed and grab her leg, pulling her toward me so she can straddle my face.

As her perfect ass hovers over me, I grab it and kiss her luscious ass cheeks. I nibble on her skin, making her shudder, and I swear when she looks back at me, I see a little smile on her face.

I haven't seen her smile in weeks. Although it was brief, I commit it to memory and position her so I can start feasting on her pussy.

She rubs her pussy over my face, moving her hips, and fuck me, it's the sexiest thing I've ever seen or tasted.

I bury my face right into her folds, swirling my tongue inside and outside of her passage. I lap her clit until she comes on my face and her sweet juices flow into my mouth.

The taste makes blood rush to my groin, and I nearly explode when she grabs my dick. Then I feel her mouth on my length, taking me in.

We both give each other pleasure until my cock is about to detonate and she's had so many orgasms I've lost track.

I move out from under her and lay her down on her back so I can watch her breasts bounce when I fuck her.

Spreading her legs wide, I settle between her thighs and plunge deep inside her hot passage in one hard stroke.

"Caspian!" She screams my name and continues to do so over and over.

I TAKE HER ALL NIGHT, and we don't stop.

The next few days pass just like that, and I make up for the lost time we didn't spend together last week.

I keep her with me as much as possible, and the only breaks we take are the times she's with her godparents or her friends.

Before sunrise, on the morning of the wedding, I hold her in my arms as we lie together staring out the window.

"We get married in a few hours," she mutters against the silence with a tremor in her voice.

"You sound scared. Are you?"

"Yes. I know things are going to change between us again."

"You don't have to worry about that. They won't change."

"How do I know they won't?" She turns to face me.

I take her hand and place above my heart. "Trust this. You can feel my heart beating, can't you?"

"Yes."

"Every time you feel it, know that you can trust me."

As she stares back at me with awe, I pray to find a way to protect her.

Even if I die trying.

CHAPTER 25
WILLOW

I close my eyes, and I swear it's just for a moment, but it's not.

When I open my eyes again, thinking Caspian is still holding me, I realize I'm alone.

The bright morning sun greets me, along with the nervousness of what today will bring.

I sit up and pull the sheet to my breasts to cover me. I then look around the room, looking for him. He's not here, though.

Today is our wedding day.

A quick glance at the clock on the wall tells me Caspian would have left over an hour ago to get ready.

It's time I do the same.

I shower, put on a robe, and tidy the room. I then sit by the window bay and wait for the host of women who are supposed to come and help me get ready to look the part. They'll be here any minute now. It's nearly ten. Elaine will be part of the group.

When I saw her days ago, things were weird, but she tried to smooth things over by taking me to lunch.

I wanted so badly to talk to her again the way we did on Sunday, but we never got a chance.

Everyone's keeping things from me, and I don't know what today will bring, or if Caspian will be the version I had for the last few days.

He's different when he's with his father.

When a knock sounds at the door, I know it's time. They're here.

"It's open," I call out.

The door opens, and Elaine walks in looking absolutely beautiful.

The dress code for the wedding will make everyone look like they were pulled right from medieval times. The men will be in their Knights' tunics and the women in white gowns.

So, the dress Elaine is wearing looks similar to mine with the fitted bodice, long flaring sleeves, and full skirt. The only difference is that mine has an endless detachable train which she and Eilish will be carrying.

I would have liked to have worn something like normal brides do, but I knew that was never going to happen, which is fine because my dress is stunning.

Elaine waltzes over to me, and I expect the entourage to come in behind her, but it's just her.

"How are you feeling?" she asks.

"Nervous."

"You will be okay. Everyone is outside. I thought I'd check on you first before bringing them in."

"They can come in. I'm ready," I say, but there's a clear awkwardness between us that never existed before.

"Perfect." She brings her hands together then touches my cheek. "Be strong, Willow."

I give her a curt nod, and she leaves to get the women.

Two hours later, I'm at Raventhorn Hall again, but in the ceremonial hall.

I'm standing at the door dressed like a princess with my arm linked with Adrian's. Elaine and Eilish are behind me holding my train.

We're waiting for the violinist to start playing my wedding song.

Through my veil I gaze ahead to the altar, where Caspian stands with his father before him and Thorne on his left.

His father is going to perform the ceremony. I blocked that part out of my mind, but now it's about to happen. I have to face him—literally.

The trio of Ivanovs look like they're about to grab their swords and head off to battle.

I focus on the only man I need to as he stares back at me, and I wonder what my life will be like after this.

Caspian said things didn't have to change, but I can't see how that's possible when his father still owns me. Darkness settles in the pit of my stomach at the thought.

The Viking *Song to Odin* begins, and Adrian gives my arm a gentle squeeze as we start the wedding march.

I take in the people who are here, the majority of which I've never seen in my life, but they're here to witness the fall of the Raventhorns and the rise of the Ivanovs.

This union will be it.

I never thought my wedding day would be like this, but then I also thought my parents and Lillian would be here.

They aren't, and in this room full of people, I feel so alone and scared.

The urge to run hits me when my gaze lands on the self-righteous expression on Aleksander's face.

My steps even slow, and I want to beg Adrian to take me home. Take me anywhere but here—away from the monster.

Then Caspian steps forward, and when I lock eyes with him, the fear melts away. The trepidation fades the moment I take note of his eyes and see the difference in them.

It takes me a moment to realize what that difference is. It's the hatred. It's no longer there.

I search for it, but I can't find it.

When he extends his hand, I take it and hold on tight, as if I'm trying to hold on to this moment where he's looking at me with love.

Adrian releases me and lifts my veil, the last action a father would perform for his daughter before he gives her away.

He plants a kiss on my forehead and taps my head one last time.

"I now release you, my daughter," he says, looking from me to Caspian.

"Thank you, Father," I reply, and he looks exactly the way Elaine looked the other day when I called her Mom.

I move closer to Caspian while Elaine and Eilish take their seats together.

When Adrian joins them, Aleksander clears his throat and Caspian releases me, too.

We turn to face his father, and I try to think of anything besides that arrogant look on his face.

"Welcome, everyone, to the union between my son, Caspian Ivanov, and Willow Raventhorn," Aleksander begins. "Such a union has never before been witnessed in our lifetime. Today is a momentous occasion that will go down in our history."

I steady my nerves and swallow hard, trying to keep my focus so I don't faint.

"I will now begin the ceremony." Aleksander looks at Peter, who walks over with a gold tray that has a ceremonial blade sitting on top of it.

Aleksander takes the knife and holds it up.

"Give me your right hand and repeat these words after me," he instructs me.

I do as he says. This is where I take the oath, too, and will be bound by the same laws as Caspian.

"Luramentum est vita nostra et mors nostra," he states, which is Latin for *The oath is our life and our death*.

I say the words, my voice unwavering, sounding stronger than I feel inside.

He then places the blade to my hand and slices a faint line. It reminds me of when I slit my wrist. How strange that a man who hates that I live and breathe would draw blood from me on the same hand.

He glances at my scar briefly, and a smile dances in his eyes.

I need no other confirmation of his hatred toward me, and I know if I make it to my nineteenth birthday, I'll no longer have his protection.

What a bastard. I can't imagine how my parents could have been friends with a man like this.

He asks Caspian to present his hand, too, and Aleksander slices his palm.

"Please join hands."

Caspian and I face each other, and he takes my hand. Aleksander then places the traditional cord around our joined hands and ties the knot binding us together.

He proceeds to give the handfast ceremony in Russian, and we take our vows then exchange rings.

Caspian keeps his gaze trained on me the whole time his father speaks, and his eyes remain the same.

"I now pronounce you Lord and Lady Ivanov," Aleksander declares.

It's supposed to sound like a death sentence to me. Except it doesn't because when my husband smiles at me, I feel like I'm home.

I'm certain his father isn't expecting him to be smiling at me the way he is.

Neither does he expect him to cup my face as he kisses me and brushes his nose along mine.

When we pull apart and I look back at his father, the disapproval is apparent in his face.

I barely get to look at him, though, because Caspian takes the rope off our hands, hands it to Thorne, and ushers me back down the aisle.

We're supposed to be walking slowly while the music plays, but we aren't.

Our guests nod respectfully as we rush past, and I try to acknowledge them.

I catch sigh of Eilish, who smiles at me, and I return the same warm smile.

When we reach the end of the hall, we're supposed to go left. The guests will then follow us into the reception room, and we'll spend the rest of the day entertaining everyone. It was one of the parts of the day I dreaded.

But we turn right, and Caspian takes me through the open doors to leave the building.

My head whips around to face him the moment we walk over the threshold, and I stare at him in disbelief.

"What are we doing?" I mutter.

"Leaving."

My spirits lift. "Really?"

"Where do you think you're going?" Aleksander's voice booms behind us before Caspian can answer.

He stops and turns to face his father whilst still holding my hand.

"We're married, so we're leaving."

"You know we have all these activities planned for the day."

"No, Father, *you* do," Caspian answers firmly, shocking me because I've never heard him speak to his father that way. "You planned those activities, so go and enjoy them. I'm taking my wife away for a few days. I'm sure you recall the specs of our pact. We're married now, so don't interfere."

I can't believe what I'm hearing, nor the strength he shows against his father for me.

Aleksander moves closer and squares off with his son. "Enjoy those days while you have them, son. Make sure you're back on time for her other *appointment*."

He means St. Jude's.

Caspian dips his head and pastes a mocking smirk on his face. "Good day, Father."

Instead of pulling me along, Caspian scoops me up in his arms and carries me.

I run my fingers over his chest, feeling the steady beat of his heart through his tunic.

"You're taking me away for a few days?" I ask.

"Yes, Mrs. Ivanov." He smirks, trying out my new name.

"Where are we going, Mr. Ivanov?"

"That's a surprise, Printsessa. One I know you'll love."

CHAPTER 26
CASPIAN

As we turn onto the country road leading to Larchwood Lake, Willow's face brightens.

She looks exactly the way she used to when we came here as kids.

Our families used to come here for a joint vacation every summer. We'd spend two weeks together at the start of the summer break. I'd have the time of my life here. We both did.

The place belonged to my mother's family. She left it in her will to me because she knew I'd appreciate it the most.

"The Enchanted Forest," Willow beams.

The wind picks up her hair as she faces me with the biggest smile.

"Indeed. Was I right? Do you love it?"

"I do," she squeals.

It's the most excited I've seen her since we were kids.

When I park by the lake house, she gets out and rushes down to the edge of the lake.

Her dress flows in the wind. She took off the train so it's shorter, but it's still so long she has to gather up the skirt.

I took off my Knights' tunic before we got in the car, so I'm dressed more casual in a white button-up shirt and black pants.

I follow her down to the lake but stop paces away so I can observe her while she twirls in the wind.

Watching her like this reminds me of that day when I first thought she was the most beautiful girl I'd ever seen in my life.

Granted, I was eight years old when I thought that, but I couldn't have been wrong at the time if I still think so now.

That was the memory that kept me alive in Russia.

The years passed by, and we played in that meadow countless times, but I never forgot that particular day. I think it's because the seeds of what I feel for her now were sown at that moment.

As I watch her twirl in the wind, I'm glad I did this. My father is always trying to find ways around our oath to screw with me. This is mine. Today's entire setup was designed to showcase Willow as the evidence of his power. What better way than to show everyone that he's taken the last Raventhorn?

I might be married to her, but the laws that bind us give him all the power until the time when I take my legacy as Pakhan.

This trip was the only thing I could think of that would break down the remaining walls between Willow and me.

As I stare at her, I savor the respite I'm given from the darkness as I see colors for the first time in forever.

I see her radiant red hair sparkling in the sun under a clear blue sky. I see the lush green woods ahead of us, and yellow buttercups in the field. I see the crystal water flowing in the lake, sparkling as if someone splashed the brightest stars over the surface.

I see her, and she's mine.

She turns to look at me with that smile brightening her face, and in her eyes I see love.

It pulls me to her, and I touch her cheek.

"Thank you for this."

"I thought you'd like coming here. My mother used to come out here to write when she needed inspiration." The shine in her eyes saddens at the mention of my mother. "She left it to me because she knew how I felt about the place, and I brought you here because I knew it would make you as happy as it made her."

She dips her head, and when she looks back at me, her eyes brim with tears.

"I miss her, and I miss those days."

"Me too. She would have been happy today." My words clearly surprise her. "She would have been happy to see us get married. I think your parents would have been, too."

"You look at me differently. You did back at the hall, and you're doing it now."

"I guess I must look different because I love you." It's time I said it, and about time she knows.

A spark twinkles in her tear-filled eyes. The tears tip over her bottom lids, streaming down her cheeks before she brings her hands up to wipe them away.

"I love you, too. I... always have, and I'm so sorry I kept things from you that I shouldn't have."

I shake my head. "I don't blame you anymore, and I shouldn't have in the first place. I think I was looking for someone to blame because I lost my mother; she was everything to me. Both your parents loved you unconditionally and abundantly, but I never had that. You see what my father is like. My mother was my light, and when she died, I lost my way." That's the most I've said about my grief over my mother in years.

"That secret belonged to our parents. It was their mistake, not yours. You did what I would have done," I confess. "You think I'd do anything to please my father, but that's not the case. Of course, I've always wanted him to be proud of me, but there's a line I don't cross. My mother, on the other hand, was a different story. I would have done anything for her, no matter what that thing was. So, let's just let the ugliness from the past go and focus on us. Does that sound like a good idea, Printsessa?"

"Yes. Thank you. It means everything to me."

"You mean everything to me." I take her hand and kiss her scarred skin, loving her harder than I ever have.

Cupping her face, I gaze into her eyes and summon

bravery to shatter the ball of ignorance I've kept her in for the last few weeks.

"It's time to talk, Willow."

Time to break the fantasy.

CHAPTER 27
WILLOW

The old wooden floorboards creek as Caspian and I enter the sitting room.

It looks exactly the same as I remember.

The floral-patterned sofa is still sitting in the center by the fireplace, the little wooden table all the kids used to draw at is still by the glass doors, the happiness that comes with innocence and blissful freedom still clings to the air.

I take a moment to absorb the nostalgic memories that float into my mind.

If I listen carefully, I can still hear the echo of children running across the floorboards like a stampede of little elephants. And the aroma of cookies and cake and creativity.

Our mothers would wake up early, bake and tell us a story before we started the day. I'd linger behind after story time to hear more.

Either Irina would share something amazing she'd

written, or Mom would end up talking to me about one of her favorite writers.

I can't believe we're here and Mom and Irina are both dead.

My heart wilts at the thought and my brain still finds it difficult to comprehend that toxic truth.

Now I'm about to receive more truths. More dark truths that will scare the life out of me. I figured it had to be bad if Caspian wanted to wait until now to talk about it.

Eager as I was to know what was going on, I'm glad we waited.

In some ways my ignorance was a form of haven— my glass house.

We sit opposite each other. As I look at Caspian it feels weird seeing him as a man. We just got married and he told me he loved me.

He declared his love for me and in the same breath, forgiveness.

Words can't express what it meant to me to hear both. Hearing him speak those words unchained the guilt from my soul and took me back to how we used to be.

The last time we sat in this living room I was eleven and he was twelve. We were talking about hunting for grass snakes. Of the kids who were here, I was the only girl, and the only one willing to go off on one of his adventures.

I wasn't scared of snakes or creepy crawlies, but I

think I might have pushed aside any inkling of fear because I was obsessed with him.

Caspian leans forward, rests his elbows on his knees and the sun catches the lighter parts of his eyes, highlighting the shift in the mood.

"You ready?" He reaches for my hand and gives my knuckle a gentle squeeze when I nod.

"As I'll ever be."

"Okay. I guess I should start by telling you I took care of the guy who threw you off the bridge."

My eyes snap wide and the icy chill of fear freeze the blood in my veins. "You saw him?" My voice comes out a slow, hesitant rasp.

"Yes, he was following me at the Verge."

My God. "What do you mean by you took care of him?"

"I killed him, Willow."

My mouth falls open and I take a quick gulp of air.

Only moments ago I was processing the change in him from boy to man, but I forgot to factor in what he became. *A Knight. A killer. My protector.*

"Willow, my life is going to be like this. I had to kill him."

"I know." I do know and I shouldn't act so naïve.

"I was able to get out of him that there was some plan long ago." His voice takes on a guarded edge. "And you... were always supposed to die."

Terror slams into my soul like a Tsunami. The shock it leaves behind makes me struggle to take my next breath.

As the sting of the cold, hard truth works its way into me I shiver from deep within and cross my hands over my chest in an instinctive attempt to calm myself.

But the gesture is fruitless.

As fruitless as anything I could have done to protect myself.

Thinking of the guy makes me wonder if he was one of the men who chased Lillian and me through the woods.

I was supposed to die that night too.

"I was always supposed to die." I repeat the words slamming around in my mind and it sounds worst spoken aloud.

Caspian reaches for me again, gripping my hand tighter. "I'm doing my best so that doesn't happen."

That's more than I could expect or ask of anyone, but what happens when the best isn't enough?

Death. I die. Just like in my nightmares.

"Who wants to kill me Caspian? Why?" I fight the tears. I don't want to be the weeping Willow I've been all these years, but I feel like the lost little girl again.

"I tried to get more information from him, but he wouldn't tell me. What he did tell me, however, made it seem like Lillian and Zak died for the same reason."

"Lillian *and* Zak?" This is the first he's mentioned anything in relation to Zak. "You're saying their deaths are connected?"

"Yes. I've thought it for some time now. When my brother died, I never stopped looking for answers. I'm sure you would have suspected his death was an inside job."

"Yes, I did."

"Thorne and I have been investigating Zak's death under wraps. When we became Knights we were able to get into the system. We found out that the last person Zak spoke to before he died was either Peter or Dorian. The day before Lucian was shot, I went to see Dorian. At the same time you got that note days before so I was getting that checked out too. We thought the best way we could see what your father's sins were was to look through his files. Except we couldn't get in, so we got help."

"From who?" I have a feeling I know what he's going to say.

"Lucian. He was the only person Thorne knew who could hack a system like what your father set up."

"So that's how he got involved." Now I'm beginning to see how everything fits.

"Yes. I blame myself. I didn't know what was going on, or that I could be putting him in danger by asking for his help. I'm sorry."

I shake my head. "It's not your fault he got shot, Caspian."

He sighs with a pensive glint in his eyes and briefly presses his lips together.

"I worried you'd blame me. I confess—and I'm sure you know—I'm not fond of your relationship with Lucian, but I didn't want him to be part of this mixture of shit. However, he found out Zak was looking at your father's files days before he died, and I believe he found what Zak was looking at. I also believe that whatever Zak found is what killed him."

I'm so stunned I don't know what to say. I never expected this twist of events or connection.

"My God, I would never have thought Zak's death would be connected to any of this."

"Me neither. Finding that out was completely unexpected."

"What else do you know?"

He proceeds to tell me about Peter and the whole investigation.

He tells me everything, and when he's done I'm drained. So drained and hollow I feel like I might blow away in the slightest breeze.

Seeing the obvious effect the truth has had on me, Caspian pulls me into his lap. I rest my hands against the granite walls of his chest, and he slips a strong arm around my waist.

"I'm sorry it's all so bad. I won't stop trying to protect you, and I won't stop trying to find out what happened to Lillian either. I promise."

"Thank you so much." Deep gratitude sweeps through me along with the solace of knowing I can trust him with everything. "You will never know what that means to me. It was so hard to be alone when no one believed me, or if they did, I couldn't talk to them. I couldn't talk to anyone for fear of going back to St. Jude's."

"I know, baby." He strokes my cheek.

"It just means a lot that I have help. It would mean everything to her too. She always acted like my guardian angel. She told me she would take care of me, but I never got the chance to take care of her."

"She knew how much you loved her. She did Willow. She always did."

"Zak knew for you too."

"I hope so. I know him. If the tables were turned, he wouldn't stop looking until he found out what happened to me."

I agree. He's right and the same goes for Lillian too.

"Thank you for caring so much."

"Of course, I care." He brushes his nose over mine. "I brought you here because I wanted to take you away from the stress and danger. We got married today, Willow."

I smile when he gazes into my eyes, and I see the openness I've craved for so many years.

"We got married."

He gives me a sexy smirk that's brimming with all kinds of mischief.

"You're my wife now. Mine." He brushes his lips over mine lightly but with a hunger that sends arousal coiling straight to my groin. "You're my Willow. And I am yours."

Mine. He's mine. The thought tips the corners of my lips with a giddy girlie grin that feels out of place when I think of everything he just told me.

The last thing I should feel like is smiling. Who could

when they've just been told they were always supposed to die?

Yet, as our gazes collide, I allow this new life I could have with him as his wife to sink into my soul, and it makes me happy.

Caspian Ivanov is my husband.

I married the boy who unlocked my heart, swept me off my feet, and saved my broken being.

Despite the dark cloud of doom hanging over us, he is my light.

Being with him means I'll never be lost in the dark again.

"Let's go back to the fantasy, Willow. We leave Tuesday afternoon. Let's enjoy the time we have together and leave everything else outside. Let's just be married people. Can we do that?"

I touch his handsome face and nod. "Yes. We can do that." I slip into the fantasy and think of what I want him to do to me. "There's something I want you to do for me."

"What's that, Lady Ivanov?"

"Make love to me."

"I'll do more than that. How about we live out every single fantasy we've ever had of each other?"

"That sounds better."

CHAPTER 28
WILLOW

I t's Sunday night and we're still stuck in the fantasy.

I don't want to ever leave. There's something about this blissful sphere that opens my heart to believe maybe things will work out.

Maybe I could have hope.

Maybe we'll stop whoever is trying to kill me and we'll find out what happened to Lillian. I won't have to go back to St. Jude's. Lucian will wake up, and then maybe I could have some shot at a normal life.

I almost believe all those things can truly happen, but there's a shadow in the recess of my mind reminding me that this is a fantasy.

A smile, however, spreads across my mouth as Caspian licks over my lips. He quells my inner turmoil again with his spellbinding touch and I forget my problems, my worries, my life.

His fingers splay across my belly, and suddenly,

something cold runs down the deep valley between my breasts.

It's ice. He has me blindfolded again with my wrists bound by a rope hooked through the loop in the headboard above my head.

I just have enough room to move from left to right. My legs are free, and even though the rest of me is restricted, there's something freeing in what he's doing to me that I like.

He nibbles my skin whispering sweet nothings in Russian to me, telling me how he wants me again.

"I want you now," he mutters, moving up to my ear.

This is the second time today that he's tied me up. I started the day in sweet bondage.

He moves down to my pussy and flicks his tongue over my clit, sending a whirlwind of pleasure spiraling through me. The dazzling effect heats my body like I'm standing right next to the sun.

"Are you ready for me, Malyshka?"

"Yes." I move to touch him instinctively, but my restraints swiftly remind me I can't.

The deep rumble of his chuckle turns my head to the left, and he caresses my cheek with his calloused palms.

"I want to touch." My voice sounds like a sultry hum.

"You'll have plenty of time to touch me. Right now, I want you to give yourself to me again." He strokes the insides of my thighs. "And trust me."

A hint of longing that lingers in his words.

"I do."

He kisses me gently then there's a moment of nothingness before his hands grip my hips and his length spears into me.

I gasp as wildfire blasts over my skin from head to toe. It intensifies when he starts moving inside me and the pleasure is unreal.

I feel everything all at once and lose control, but his grip on me keeps me anchored there so I can experience all he wants me to feel.

"You're perfect, so fucking perfect," he groans.

I throw my head back, coming straightaway as I fall from the rise of ecstasy pulsating through me.

The other night when he first tied me up, I remembered that girl at the club who was tied up, too and the look of pleasure on her face.

I'm doing it again now because I know the depth of pleasure she experienced. It's true pleasure, raw and undulated.

As soon as he gives me my first dose, I crave more and Caspian pounds harder into my body, giving it to me.

Time passes the way it has all night, like a languid stream, and he moves faster and faster, fucking me harder, filling every nerve in my body with pleasure.

Soon it becomes cold, hardcore fucking, and then we both come so hard I feel like I'm going to spiral off out of existence.

He collapses on top of me, pulling me closer toward him as we calm, and we stay like that for several long minutes.

My skin is still buzzing when he loosens the ropes from my wrists and takes off the blindfold.

"More?" He gives me a seductive grins.

"I want more."

"Then let's go skinny dipping in the lake."

Before I can answer he scoops me up and carries me away.

We spend every second we have together addicted to each other.

Then Tuesday morning comes like the grim reaper ready to claim our souls.

The heaviness of having to go home hits me. It hits Caspian too, but I can see he's trying to keep the fantasy going for me.

He takes me out on the lake, and I rest on his chest while he smokes.

We stay on the water in silence for what feels like an eternity, but we've only been out for about two hours. We still have some time left before we leave.

Then I have three days before I leave for St. Jude's.

I'll be there for three weeks. What will I do then?

What the hell will I do?

I've wanted my life to be normal, or as normal as can be for so long and now it might now happen.

Caspian squeezes my hand. "Penny for your thoughts, Malyshka."

I shuffle to face him and run my fingers over the smooth ridge of muscle under his left pec.

"I'm just worried. Worried about everything. Worried even more about St. Jude's. I guess I would be, though."

"I'm going to see you every day."

"Will you?" I glance up at him and take in the conviction filling his eyes.

"Of course. I'll make sure you're okay. I think my presence there will help you stay focused."

It will definitely help. With him around I won't feel so alone. "Thanks. I really appreciate that." I caress his skin. "So much for that normal life I wanted." I was trying for light humor, but it doesn't quite come.

"What is normal for you, Willow? Normal can be anything."

"I guess so. I suppose sometimes I think back to when we were kids. Our parents kept things so controlled I would never have guessed we were a mafia family, much less in a secret society."

I never knew the full gravity of who or what we were until after my parents died. It was when I went to live with Adrian and Elaine and certain things were being sorted out that I understood.

"Would you prefer it that way? Not knowing?" His voice is cautious, like he's trying to figure out something more meaningful than the question indicates.

I sigh. "I would have at least liked the standard, boring version of normal people imagine up with the house, the white picket fence, and the dog."

"We can have those things, Willow." He laughs, then the humor in his voice fades and is swallowed by seriousness. As if something sucked the spark from him. "We can have those things and I will try to make everything as normal for you as I can. But... I'm not normal."

He pauses and I wonder if he's going to elaborate. I almost think he won't then he takes a quick breath and continues.

"Aside from the fact that I will be Pakhan one day and lead the Knights, nothing about me will ever be normal again."

I straighten too, knowing he's referring to what happened to him in Russia. I search his eyes and try to see past the guarded walls he has locking me out, stopping me from seeing what he's hiding.

"You have that question in your eyes again, Malyshka." He presses his forehead briefly to mine then pulls away.

"If I ask it, will you give me the answer?"

"I'm not sure I should. Then you'll definitely know just how fucked up I am."

"I'm not normal either, in case you didn't notice." I'm far from normal. I'm almost certain of the two of us, I'd win hands down on the fucked-up scale. But then, that's just based on what I know. I don't know what horrors he might have gone through in Russia.

"The anxiety?" he offers with understanding, cutting into my thoughts.

I nod. "You did notice."

"Counting and going in water when it's bad? Yeah, I

noticed. I don't know much about anxiety, but I figured it had to be that. It's bad, isn't it?"

"It can be. I don't think I'll ever be rid of it. It started in St. Jude's when it truly hit me that Lillian was dead. But I guess that was my mind's way of coping. What do you do?"

He stares back at me for a few pregnant beats and then his eyes flit over to the vast space ahead of the lake and trees.

"I draw, but it comes out like what you saw back at the apartment."

"Because of Russia?"

"Yes."

"What happened to you there Caspian? What happened to the boy who used to paint in such vivid colors?"

"That boy died in the bottom of a well." A faraway look comes into in his eyes. "He had the colors beaten and tortured out of him. That was just what they did to me. What they did to my family was something else that blackened my soul. They forced me to watch as they killed them one by one. My uncle, my aunt, my cousin. They were killed because of some deal gone wrong and I was the toy until the men got bored."

My heart squeezes into a tight fist, forcing my blood pressure to rise. "I'm so sorry."

"I know." He taps my hand and even though he gives me a little smile, it's a dead one. Not a smile to even humor me. It's lifeless. Soulless, like death. "My parents sent me to therapists when they got me back, but I couldn't talk about what I saw, so I'd draw it. Everything that comes to my mind is darkness and that face of the devil who took me."

"Did your father ever find out what happened?"

"It was an inside job, but one we won't be able to resolve because everyone we knew who could have been involved died the same day I got taken. I was told Thorne was the only person left on the property. The whole thing changed me. But maybe..." He takes a lock of my hair and allows the ends to coil around his thumb. "Maybe one day I'll get to the stage where the darkness leaves me, and I can be normal for you."

"How about we try to be normal for each other?"

"That works. Come here, don't leave the fantasy yet."

I wish we didn't have to at all.

At least I got to be with him the way I always was in my fantasies, and we were almost normal.

Almost.

CHAPTER 29
CASPIAN

The beast inside my soul roars at the same time I gun the engine to life, and we drive away from the lake house.

The deafening sound ricochets off the walls of my heart, pleading, begging, warning me to take my girl and drive the other way.

All I would need to do is flip the car into a U and drive away from the convoy of guards like I have napalm on my ass.

But I know I can't do that.

I feel like I'm taking Willow back into danger because I am. I've thought of every way possible to avoid returning to Raventhorn, but such a plan would need more than my defiance and wit.

It would also need me to be free of the fucking fear that holds me hostage.

I could almost laugh at myself. Since when did I allow fear to rule me?

I've always been the rebel. I was born to give the world a giant fuck you and I've always done what I wanted to do. This is one of those times where I know I should.

However, once again I've had to take the higher ground and *think* of the consequences if I don't play by the rules—my father's fucking rules.

I have seen no possibility where my actions to defy him don't screw me over in some way, and in turn affect Willow.

Willow looks back at the lake house with longing, tired, please-don't-take-me-away-from-here, eyes.

I loathe seeing her look that way, knowing the best thing I can do to help her is to keep going, keep trying. Keep trying to fix the situation until I see a way, a path, an answer.

The silence we drive back in is stifling. It's not the angst-filled silence that engulfed us weeks ago on the way back from New York, but the kind shared by two people who know nothing good will come of whatever they do next.

The entire journey sees me trying to process everything and I couldn't get Willow's wish for normalcy out of my head. My brain was a broken record stuck on a loop and hours later something I wish I never figured out sunk into my head.

She mentioned our parents when we were on the lake, but it dawned on me why her father would never have chosen me to marry her.

The same reason made him choose Dorian to marry

Lillian and not Zak, who would have made more sense because our parents were so close. The same reason might have also prompted him to leave Dynamic Corp to his daughters.

The choice was made because of *what* my brother and I were born to be. *Leaders.*

Whether Zak had become the Pakhan or me, the laws of the Knights would have still placed us both in leadership. And Timofey Raventhorn did not want that for his daughters.

More and more I see that he wanted them to have a normal life and maybe even run the company together outside the influence of the Knights or anyone from the Bratva.

I'm sure he would frown upon my helplessness in this situation of shit to protect his daughter from my father's clutches. But that part isn't entirely on me.

Timofey's sins pushed us here. He was the one who stabbed my father through the heart with betrayal.

At the same time, Timofey and I have things in common because I *will* betray my father at some point in the near future and break my vows all over again for the girl.

I will never be normal, and I know now I wouldn't have been anyone's choice but I'm the guy who will try. I'm the guy who wants to give Willow a good life and protect her with mine.

When we get back to Raventhorn, I hold Willow's hand as we make our way to *our* apartment. The place has felt like ours since she moved in with me but being married has a different feel.

I break the silence when I open the door and stop her as she's about to walk in by scooping her up into my arms to carry her over the threshold.

She laughs and smooths her hand up my beard, then kisses me.

"I had to. We only get to do this once. Although I might do it again in a few years when we move into our real home." I nuzzle my face into her hair and we kiss again.

"You're sweet."

"Baby, you know I'm more like poison."

"No, you're sweet to me."

"Whatever you say, Malyshka. Do you want to go out for dinner later?"

"Are you asking me out on that date we're supposed to go on?"

"Yeah." I chuckle and try to push the darkness out of my mind. Dinner might be a good idea. It gets us off campus. *Again*. "Do you want to go to dinner with me?"

"Yes."

I set her down once we get past the living room. I'm about to make some wisecrack about getting her naked when we get back, but I spot something on the floor at the end of the hall by the door.

That door leads to the rest of the frat house and is the entrance I'd normally use when I see Thorne.

"What's wrong?" Willow follows my gaze.

"Gimme a sec."

I make my way down the hall and as I realize what I'm looking at is a white envelope my steps dawdle.

My nerves spike with fury when I reach and see the fucking envelope has Willow's name on it.

Jesus. What the hell is this now?

I pick it up, and of course the moment Willow sees, she walks up to me.

I meet her terrified eyes and pale face.

"It's... for me, isn't it?" she stutters.

My lips part, and I stare back at her wondering when this was left here.

The guards came with us to Larchwood Lake, so they wouldn't have been around. When we're home, I always have a guard on the outside of that door watching the place.

"I'm going to open it," I tell her.

She nods and brings her hands together.

Carefully, I open the envelope and look inside. There's a note but also a silver necklace with a pendant attached to it that looks familiar.

When I pull the necklace out and hold it up, Willow looks like she's going to pass out.

She begins shaking violently and tears pour out of her eyes.

"That's Lillian's necklace," she cries, lifting the pendant attached to her own necklace. That's why this looks familiar. Willow has one just like it. The only differences are the runes engraved on the pendant.

"Lillian was wearing it when she died," she adds.

CHAPTER 30
WILLOW

Terror squeezes the air from my lungs and every muscle in my body goes rigid.

I'm struck speechless because seeing the necklace could only mean one thing.

One fucking thing.

The person who's been leaving the notes was with Lillian when she died.

"Willow, are you sure this is Lillian's?" Caspian asks.

I can't even look at him; my eyes are glued to the necklace in his hands, and I remember when Lillian gave me mine and she put on hers.

We promised each other we wouldn't take them off.

Someone took hers off.

"Yes, I'm sure. She was wearing it when she pushed me over the side of the cliff." It was one of the last things I saw before I went over. I cry harder as my emotions spiral out of control. "Caspian, it's hers. It's Lillian's. She never took it off."

"Baby." He reaches out to brush my cheek.

"Is... there a note?"

He nods slowly and pulls out the dreaded note. He reads it first then hands it to me.

With trembling hands, I take it and read the simple words:

You're still here. Stay, and you'll end up like your sister.

MY HEART CONTRACTS AND FREEZES. But when it starts beating again, it's a pattery mess.

Suddenly, my terror transforms into wrath and the veins in my head feel like they're going to pop.

I ball my hand and slam a fist into the wall. It hurts, but right now, I want to feel something more than the grief over losing Lillian.

"This person was there when she died!" I explode. "They were there, and they're here warning me away?"

I can't make sense of anything. This person sending me notes is definitely not good if they had possession of this necklace.

Yet they're trying to help me?

And they think this is the best way?

Something snaps in my mind, and I rush back downstairs.

Caspian follows me. "Willow, where are you going?"

I have no idea. I don't know if it's air I need or something else, but I'm heading outside.

When I get out there, the guards all look at me and straighten, turning toward Caspian for direction.

It's late afternoon, so people are still out and about. A group of students walk by the house, and they all look at me when I stare them down.

Is the person who left me the note one of them? Is it one of the people on the fucking lawn, or over on the quad playing football?

Is it a teacher, a parent, a guard, the cook, the cleaner, the engineer?

Who is it?

Who left my sister's necklace here?

Who the fuck is it?

"Who are you?" I scream. "Who the hell are you?"

Those who weren't looking at me before look now. I have everyone's attention. *Good.*

I'm sick of suffering in silence and being afraid. The person who's sending me these notes is here somewhere, probably looking at me, or hiding behind their smoke-screen, watching.

"If you think this is the way to help me, you are wrong!" I continue, and I'm glad Caspian doesn't stop me. "You know I can't leave! So, stop telling me to. If you want to help me, then help me. This is not the way. If you don't, I'll die. Just like her."

That's when I break and crumble into nothingness. Then my legs give as the tears flow and Caspian catches me.

∾

By nightfall, I sink into a catatonic state.

I know my outburst earlier didn't do my social life any favors. The word has probably traveled back to my new father-in-law that I've lost my mind, but I'm past caring.

I'm sitting by the fireplace in the armchair with a blanket wrapped around me and a book I can't calm myself down enough to read. It's *Pride and Prejudice,* the book I could normally get comfortable with, but I'm not in the mood.

I was already feeling low; seeing the necklace just made everything worse.

I always wondered what happened to Lillian after she was shot. Now I can't stop thinking about it and what's happening now.

Clearly something is about to happen, or I wouldn't have gotten another note.

I feel like an animal waiting to be slaughtered.

Caspian walks into the living room carrying a steaming mug of hot chocolate.

He sets it down on the side table next to me and takes my hands into his. "How are you feeling?"

"I don't know." My voice sounds hoarse.

"We're looking at the cameras to see if we can identify this person. I'm not sure that will work, though, because they know what to do to stay hidden."

"Yeah, I figured."

"What can I do to make you feel better? We can still get something to eat."

I shake my head and blink back the next wave of tears that threatens to fall. "I can't go out. I feel like shit."

"Just let me know what to do."

"Hold me," I mutter. "I just want you to hold me."

"I can do that."

He sits beside me and takes me into his arms. There we stay for the whole night.

Morning comes and I wake before Caspian. His arm is secured around me. It's nice to be safely cocooned against his chest, a privilege I won't have when I'm at St. Jude's.

A knock sounds on the door; it wakes him up.

He straightens but still keeps a grip on me. "You okay?"

"I'm okay."

"I'm going to get that."

I watch him. He opens the door then slips outside. Moments later, I hear raised voices, so I follow him into the hallway.

Sergei, one of the other guards, is standing next to Caspian, and there's a guy I recognize from campus security holding another white envelope. This one, however, is sealed like a delivery package.

My chest automatically tightens when I see it.

"What's going on?" I ask.

"This was left at campus security with explicit instructions to bring it here to Willow," the campus security guy answers.

"And you don't know who it's from?" Caspian demands.

"Like I said, no. I found it in the mailbox when I arrived this morning. No one from the night shift knows anything either. I just thought I'd bring it here to you. We've already scanned it to make sure there's nothing explosive or likewise inside."

"Make sure you check every camera," Caspian demands.

"We're in the process of doing so. I'll report back if we find anything."

He holds out the envelope to me, so I step forward and take it.

"Come, let's go back inside and open it." Caspian ushers me back into the living room.

He locks the door, and we move to the sofa.

The envelope feels dirty in my hands, like I have Lillian's blood on me.

"Willow, open it," Caspian says.

"I'm scared. What could it be this time?"

He sits next to me and steadies my hands. "I'm right here. Let's open it."

I nod and rip the seal open.

Swallowing hard, I reach in and pull out the note. It's longer this time and looks more like a letter.

I draw in a deep breath, and we start reading together. It says:

Dear Willow,
I heard you.
I heard your words, but I can't tell you who I am. Yet.

But I will help you.

The first thing I'm going to tell you is this: If you seek answers for your sister's

death and want to know what happened in the past, you will need to find a way to go back to Bluff Island.

There's a cottage on the edge of the lake near where you stayed. It's called The Bluebell. That's where you need to go.

I'll leave a message for you at the cottage, so you'll know what to do next. I don't think I have to tell you to keep the number of people who know your plans secret. I have gone to great lengths to do the same.

There are things at that cottage that will explain much about the past, but it

will also put you in more danger as dark secrets are revealed.

You must not come back to Raventhorn until it is safe.

This is my final warning and the last time you'll hear from me in this manner.

Everything you find next will break your heart beyond repair, but I suppose, in the end, we always desire the things that will destroy us,

A POSSIBLE FRIEND.

CASPIAN and I look at each other. He searches my eyes, and I allow myself to do the same to him.

Go back to Bluff Island?

How am I going to do that?

Caspian stands and grips the back of his neck with one hand. He stares out the window in silent contemplation.

"I don't know what to do." I look back at the letter and read over that last paragraph.

Apart from the horrible warning that my heart will be broken beyond repair, there's something about it that stands out. It's a feeling of familiarity that stirs my soul.

Maybe I'm thinking about it because I have desired the things that would destroy me. The man before me is evidence of that, and so is what I want to do.

It wouldn't matter if going back to Bluff Island would kill me; I'd still want to go to find out the truth.

Caspian turns around and presses his lips together, then comes back and crouches before me, where he leans close to the shell of my ear.

"We'll leave Friday," he whispers. I turn to face him, wide-eyed.

"How are we going to do that? I have to go to St. Jude's."

"No." He shakes his head. "We're going to Bluff Island. I'll take you there and we'll find whatever this person wants us to see. Then we'll leave. We'll leave the Knights."

CHAPTER 31
CASPIAN

Thorne releases a heavy sigh, sets his hands on the table, and nods.

I've just told him about the most dangerous plan I've ever come up with.

The plan is this: Willow and I will act like we're going to St. Jude's on Friday. We'll head to the diner we went to the other week under the pretense that we're getting breakfast, then we'll change cars.

I've already sorted out a car. One of my underground contacts is going to take it there and have it ready for us in the parking lot where there's no surveillance.

It's imperative that car isn't tracked, or it's game over.

Willow and I will escape the guards who will be accompanying us and then head to Bluff Island.

It sounds simple enough, but it won't be. We'll probably have half an hour tops before the guards realize we're gone. Then we'll have problems.

At least when I told Thorne what we were doing, he didn't ask me if I was crazy. I would have told him what I was doing anyway, but I need his help again.

This time, my request for assistance surpasses every other time because unlike before, I'll be flying blind.

It will just be Willow and me.

"What do you need me to do?" Thorne gives me a look of understanding.

"I need you to keep tabs on everything here and let me know. I'll find a way to check in with you."

"Please tell me you have a number I can call."

"I'll get a burner, and we'll use that until I can't."

"What happens if you end up in danger and you need help? What happens then?" Worry creases his brows.

"I'm praying that doesn't happen, Thorne."

"Let me rig up a tracker you can activate if you need help. All you need to do is switch it on when you decide you want to be found. It's less risky and ensures you have some form of backup if you need it."

I nod, agreeing. "Thanks, that will work."

The last thing I want to do is jeopardize everything with this risky plan.

My father doesn't want me dead, but there are other things he could do to end me. Like sending me to the Hallows—the Knights' prison.

Like Alcatraz, it's highly secure and situated on an island. Unlike Alcatraz, the location is secret and only the Pakhan and his elite know where it is.

The laws there are above everything else because the

fucking island is classed as its own country. So, the type of inhumane torture a man would suffer would likely kill him. He would prefer to beg for death rather than endure their brutality.

All my father would have to do is send me there and tell them to punish me but not kill me, and that would be death. I could imagine he would then make good on his threat to destroy Willow.

"Keep a keen eye on my father, Thorne. He's planning something, and I know my departure will throw him off his game."

"He's planning something big, for sure." Thorne sighs. "He's meeting with the board at Dynamic Corp again tomorrow. They're meeting to vote and discuss the new leadership structure of the company. He's also requested Willow's medical records from St. Jude's. I think his takeover of the company is happening, Caspian."

I recall that strange phone call I overheard between my father and that guy. I told Thorne about it, and he'll be listening out for anything that might happen while I'm away.

I want to know what my father is going to finalize. This meeting with the board could be part of what he needs to discuss with that guy.

"I'll bet whoever he was speaking to on that call will know his plans."

"I got it covered. If anything happens, I'll let you know." He tilts his head to the side and regards me with curiosity. "Where are you going after Bluff Island, Caspian?"

That's a good question and one I've mulled over since this new crazy hit us this morning. It's difficult to plan anything specific because we don't know what we'll find at Bluff Island.

When I read that letter, my first thoughts were that we'd find some kind of evidence. If that's the case, it might help us solve some of our problems.

That letter highlighted the gravity of danger Willow is in, and I realized that as much as I want her to find her truths, I have to get her away from here.

"I think L.A. would be the best place for us. It's across the country and easier to stay off the grid."

"Just keep me in the loop."

"You know my father is going to come to you first. He'll know I told you something."

"I know, but there are ways to get around your father."

"Thanks for your help and for having my back."

"Always, Cousin. I'm still true to the pact we made long ago." He sighs.

"I keep telling you, you are not obligated to me or that pact. We were eight."

"I know, but at the same time I hold that pact as binding as the oaths we took when we became Knights. You endured horrors I never had to and were with my family in their final hours. I will always have your back."

We bump fists and gratitude fills me for his loyalty.

My phone starts ringing. When I reach for it, I see it's

an unknown number calling. I don't like those types of calls.

"Hello," I say into the phone.

"Hi, this is Jennifer from the hospital. You asked me to let you know when Lucian Sokolov wakes up. He's awake."

CHAPTER 32
CASPIAN

E ilish is already here.

She's sitting by Lucian's bedside when Willow and I walk into the room.

I'm not surprised to see her, nor her tear-stained cheeks when she turns to acknowledge us.

We had to wait until this morning to see Lucian because the doctors were running tests yesterday, but Eilish looks like she slept here last night.

Even though I was an asshole when I was last here, it's a welcome relief to see Lucian sitting up in his bed, propped up against a stack of pillows.

He still has IV tubes attached to his wrists and wires going to the monitors, but he almost looks like his normal self. Especially when he smiles at Willow, who rushes toward him with tears of relief. She cried yesterday, too, when I told her he was awake.

I watch them together, and for the first time ever, I

see them as the friends they are and not what I was jealous of.

But I still think he's a better man than me.

"Look at us here together," Lucian states in a raspy voice, focusing on me once Willow has finished fussing over him.

If this were another time, we would have been the friends we all were years ago.

"Yeah. How you doing, Sokolov?" I ask.

"I'll live. I suppose I *have* lived."

"You did."

He turns to Eilish and takes her hand. "Babe, why don't you go and get something to eat. We'll talk some more later."

"Sure," Eilish agrees.

I take it they must have talked already. Eilish glances at me and dips her head before she walks away, something she wouldn't have done before. I do the same and move closer to Lucian and Willow.

"I have a lot to tell you guys," Lucian states when Eilish leaves the room.

"Are you okay to talk?" I can't deny that I'm eager as hell to hear what he has to say, but I'm mindful he's been fighting for his life for close to a month.

"Yes. I need to. While I was in that coma, all I wanted to do was wake up so I could tell you guys what I found out, and what happened to me." His brows knit. "I didn't want many people knowing I was awake. My parents know, but I've asked them to keep it quiet. Of course, they'll only be able to do so within reason. I needed this time to speak to you. You're the first and the only people to hear what I'm about to tell you. What I found out is completely unreal and part of some secret plot that began long ago."

Long ago. That's what Raphael said.

"What happened, Lucian? Who shot you?" I ask.

"Oleg."

Willow and I exchange stunned glances.

"*Oleg?*" I grate out in disbelief because he was the person I least expected.

"Yes, but he wasn't alone. His son Ilya was with him."

Willow goes pale and brings her hands up to her cheeks. "Oh my God, I saw them at the library just before I went up to your apartment."

"Well, they were probably coming straight from mine." Lucian drags in a breath, and he looks at Willow. "How much do you know, Red?"

"Caspian told me he asked you to look into my father's files, and you found a record that Zak was the last to access them," she replies, glancing nervously back at me.

"Yes. Good, you're up to speed." He nods. "That day when we got back from the city, I went home to continue going through the files. I'd stumbled onto something earlier in the morning and wanted to check it out because I had a hunch. It turned out my hunch was right, and I found the files Zak was looking through. I'm positive that what I saw was the reason for his death."

I never knew just how badly I wanted answers for my brother's murder until now.

"What did you find?" I demand.

"The first thing Zak accessed was an email from Timofey to Adrian letting him know he was collecting evidence against two of the judges, but he never told him which two. Timofey sent it to Adrian in the early hours of the morning the same day he died. He said the evidence would be hidden away in an encrypted file which he was going to give him later in the week. I found that file. It contained evidence against Oleg *and* Peter."

Fuck. I was right about Peter. I knew it.

"What kind of evidence was it?" Willow asks weakly.

"Extremely incriminating evidence. The two of them were planning to kill the Raventhorn family."

Willow sucks in a breath. "What? My family?"

"Yes, Red, all of you."

HIS WORDS DELIVER a punch to my gut and awaken my old suspicions.

I always thought the whole incident surrounding Timofey's death sounded off. It's starting to sound like I might have been right about that too.

"My God," Willow breathes. "So, you think they could have had something to do with my parents' deaths? And it wasn't an accident?"

"I do. They'd also stolen forty million from the bank and twenty from Dynamic Corp. They had various contracts with drug cartels in Mexico and were also selling Timofey's biomechanical designs on the black market. Timofey was collecting the evidence because he planned to execute them for their treachery. I think they knew he was investigating them, but they didn't know what he collected or where to find it. Every single piece of evidence provided sufficient grounds to not just kick them out of the Knights but also execute them. I'm sure they would have tried to find the files, but they couldn't locate them."

"How the hell did you find it?" I ask. "Peter is a genius, and Adrian works for Dynamic Corp. Why wouldn't any of them have seen it?" Or anyone else? The company is teeming with geniuses.

He smiles proudly. "Timofey created something called a Phantom file. It's like the old ghost files that attach to another the underground used to use but are a little more intricate. You need to either have a password to open the encryption, or, if you're like me and *Zak,* you know what you're looking for and can hack it. My assumption is that they didn't find anything because they didn't know what to look for."

"How did you learn about Phantom files?" I've never heard of them.

"The same way Zak did. We both did our summer internship with Eric Markov at Markov Tech. Phantom files were something Timofey and Eric were working on. The designs are with Eric."

Eric Markov is from the Voirik Brotherhood, who are in our alliance. Eric designs weapons. My father has arrangements with him for the summer internship in San Francisco for those who hope to study computer sciences at Raventhorn. Of course, anything like that is geared toward our future training and career choices in the Bratva.

"So, Peter might be hot shit in the tech world, but those types of skills are beyond him." He smirks. "At first, I was looking through the usual files as well, then it occurred to me to check for something Timofey would use to hide something top secret. I'm sure he preempted that his system could get hacked. With that said, I believe the only person to ever open the files with a password was Lillian."

"*Lillian*?" Willow goes rigid and looks at me.

"There was a record of the files being accessed at a library in Bluff Island. The password was used then. I figured it had to be her, and she must have gotten the password somehow. I couldn't imagine it being Adrian or Elaine and neither of them doing anything about the evidence. That password seemed to be a master one to open his entire system. I think Timofey made it for Adrian to be able to access the files easily. It would have unlocked the Phantom file as well, so it would have been visible to him straightaway. The file was labeled *Evidence,* so it would have been very easy for Lillian to spot it."

Willow brings her hands together. "There was a sighting of Lillian inside a library."

"Sorry, Red." Lucian takes her hand and taps them sympathetically.

"This was why she said we were in danger."

"I think she and Zak both saw that email to Adrian, and that prompted them to look deeper."

"Something would have happened before that, though," I state.

"I agree. But I don't know what that was. My guess is both she and Zak saw or heard either Peter or Oleg do something. It's possible they knew she accessed those files in Bluff Island."

We might never know what that something is, but I wonder how and when it was they knew Lillian accessed the files. There's something amiss there, but perhaps they knew she was digging around and were keeping tabs on her.

"It also seems like something has recently changed between Peter and Oleg. I don't think they're the allies they once were," Lucian adds. "I think Oleg might have a different agenda than Peter because Oleg killed Dorian."

Dorian was going to be my next question. "What happened to him, Lucian?"

"When I found the files, Oleg and Ilya stepped out of my kitchen pointing their guns at me. I guess I was so immersed in what I was looking at that I never heard them come in." He sighs. "Oleg said there was no way he was going to allow me to ruin his plans because he'd been burned before. When he demanded to know what I found, I quickly closed the file. Ilya came after me, and we smashed into my closet. That's when we found Dorian. Oleg shot him before he could even say anything."

"People have been watching all of us since the start of the semester. But it seems their eyes were turned to you after I asked for your help. Dorian knew I was looking into Zak's death, and if they were all aware of these files, it makes sense that they knew I was going to see you because of your skills."

"Yes, that does make sense. I think Dorian must have been snooping around while I was out because of the incriminating evidence against Peter. Dorian also heard everything that was said, but my guess is Oleg didn't want him telling his father he was in my apartment because of his agenda. That was clear from what he said about being burned."

This explains why everything is so confusing and doesn't quite connect.

There are two different agendas that might have started out the same but aren't anymore. So, what was the initial plan, and why did it change?

Why did Oleg get burned?

Peter wanted Willow to marry Dorian. He would have taken the empire that way. But Oleg wants Willow dead so her empire can be split, and he gets a portion. Something would have caused Oleg to suddenly go off on his own quest. That's recent and whatever burned him.

"Lucian, the files got wiped," I tell him. "Everything is gone."

He shakes his head. "No, to my knowledge, you can't wipe those files. What whoever did was wipe everything else including the file the Phantom was attached to, but the Phantom file is still lurking there. No one would be able to see it, though, not even me. The only thing that can open it now is the password. There might be another way to unlock it, but it could take a while. So, for now, we just have my word."

"Your word is enough to know what direction to move in."

"I guess so. What about the notes and the person following Willow? This has to be linked to them."

My guess is either Oleg or Ilya is the other guy who attacked Willow in her apartment.

Lucian doesn't know how serious that attack was or about the whole St. Jude's fiasco. Since he already looks like he's exerted himself more than he should just by talking to us, it's probably best we don't go into anything more that could stress him out.

"I'm still investigating," I decide to say and Willow casts me a grateful look.

"Did something else happen while I was down?" Lucian looks at her.

"Yes, but how about we talk about that another time? I'm okay."

"You sure?"

"Yes, I promise."

"Okay. I haven't told Eilish anything much because I didn't know how much she knew, and I don't want her in danger. She and my parents think I've lost my memory. While I think the best person to tell what's happening is the Pakhan, I think maybe we should speak to Adrian, as Timofey was preparing those files for him, and trusted him." He glances at Willow. "Maybe he might be able to figure out a password. Things are always rocky between my stepdad and me, but I know if I told him it was Oleg who shot me, he'd kill him. I need that evidence against Peter and Oleg, so they get what they deserve with no repercussions for anyone else."

"We'll tell Adrian, then," I agree.

"Can I do that part?" Willow offers. "Adrian is on campus on Thursdays for meetings."

When she looks at me again, I know she wants the chance to say goodbye properly to her godfather before we go to Bluff Island and probably leave for good.

"Yes, you can." I brush over her cheek.

"I'll keep my silence until it's safe to talk." Lucian glances at my wedding ring and then at Willow's. "I heard you two got married."

"We did," I answer for us both, interested to hear what he has to say.

"Take care of my friend, Caspian. She's the best thing to ever happen to you."

"I know."

Willow and I sit opposite each other in the kitchen.

We just got back from the hospital, and she's getting ready to see Adrian.

She sips on a cup of water and looks at me when I stand.

"Thanks for not telling Lucian about what happened to me," she mutters. "I could see it was taking a lot out of him to tell us what he knew."

"I saw that, too."

"Caspian, what if Lucian was right about our parents? Suppose Peter and Oleg had something to do with their deaths? I always felt in my heart that my mother wouldn't kill herself." She presses her lips together.

"I know, but we don't have answers right now, and short of capturing Peter and Oleg, I'm not sure how we're going to find them. I wish those fucking files hadn't been wiped."

"Me too." She brings a weary hand to her head and her breath catches.

"You okay?"

"No. I'm not ready for anything. Everything feels so weird to me now, and then there's tomorrow. I'm not sure what worries me more, what we'll find at Bluff Island or being stopped from going there."

I release a heavy sigh. "Try not to worry. Let's take everything as it comes to us. That's all we can do."

She nods and stands, too. "Then I'm ready. Thank you for everything, Caspian. I know what you're doing for me is huge and a massive sacrifice."

I lean forward and kiss her. "As Lucian said, you're the best thing to happen to me. Let's go, Printsessa."

I take her hand and lead her away, but I have a million thoughts on my mind, and I still don't know who killed Zak.

CHAPTER 33
WILLOW

"Willow." Adrian smiles when he sees me sitting in the waiting room by his office.

I stand up and rush over to him as he spreads his arms wide to give me a hug.

This is the first time I've come here. These are the offices outside Raventhorn Hall that the judges use.

"It's so good to see you." He plants a kiss on my forehead.

"You too."

"How's married life?"

"It's really good."

A proud fatherly smile spreads across his face on hearing my answer. "I'm glad to hear. I was hoping you'd take me up on the offer to meet, but I didn't want to interfere if you and Caspian had plans."

"I needed to speak with you about something important."

Instantly, he looks worried. "Is this about St. Jude's?"

"No, it's something else. Can we go in your office?"

"Of course."

He slips an arm around me and ushers me into his office, which is twice the size of the one he has at Dynamic Corp.

"What's going on?" he asks, motioning for me to sit.

I do, and he joins me on the chaise.

There's so much to tell him and so much to process that I feel like I'm being ripped apart. Every time I think of Oleg and Ilya, I of course think of Nina. I wonder if she's aware of what her father and brother are like.

She seems normal, and I took her for a friend, but what if she wasn't? What if she was watching me, too?

I push the thoughts out of my mind so I can focus on what I have to tell Adrian.

"Lucian's awake," I begin, and his mouth falls open.

"When did that happen?"

"Yesterday, but he's keeping it quiet because he found out a few things about certain people that I need to tell you."

"Tell me what's going on, Willow. Does he know who shot him?"

"Yes. It was Oleg." Adrian looks as astonished as I was when I first heard. As I proceed to relay everything Lucian told Caspian and me, Adrian looks even worse. "We thought you were the best person to tell. I agreed because my father trusted you."

"Thank you for telling me. I'm sickened by the actions of people your father and I called friends. When I received that email from Timofey, I didn't know what to think. I wasn't a judge then, and I didn't have a clue where to start looking for what he was talking about. I kept hoping something would turn up, but it never did. I've been wary of everybody ever since, especially Caspian's father. I guess I never thought the traitors would be Peter or Oleg."

"I'm sorry."

"You can't be sorry for that."

"I am because they were your friends. Look how I almost married Dorian."

"Don't go down that road. It's the last thing you should be thinking of before tomorrow. I have spoken to your old doctors, and Elaine and I are going to arrange to see you on Saturday. I thought that might give you some comfort."

I nod, feeling like such a hypocrite. I wish I could tell him I won't be going to St. Jude's, but I can't. All being well, whatever I find there might give me answers and when I see him again—if I ever do—I can come clean.

"Thank you so much, Adrian. Thank you for always being there and being a father to me."

"You are so welcome, my daughter." He taps my head. "Leave this with me. Now that I know about the Phantom file, I will contact Eric Markov and see how best to unlock it. At the same time, I will speak to Aleksander, and we'll direct the investigation toward Peter and Oleg. Don't worry about this anymore."

"Thank you." There is something I feel I should mention so I will. "Adrian, I've thought before that the only person who could want me dead is a judge. This makes sense now."

"Yes, it does, and believe me, we all thought the same thing. Everyone suspected the other. Now that we know who it is, I will make sure they pay."

A flash of something dark I've never seen before blazes in his eyes. It sends a shiver through me.

"I will, Willow. Rest assured." He touches my cheek and nods.

"Thank you."

MORNING COMES, and I'm a nervous wreck.

I feel awful that I won't see Lucian or Eilish before I leave. I asked Eilish to tell Lucian about St. Jude's, and then I prayed to whomever would listen that I might see my friends again someday soon.

At least I got to see Lucian wake up, and when he was holding Eilish's hand, they looked happy together.

If things don't work out for me and I never see them again, I hope they get together, get married, and have kids.

Whatever they do, I wish them happiness.

Before I know it, it's time to leave, and I don't know what the day will bring.

I've packed my things, but the real bag I'll be taking is a small tote that contains cash, clothes, underwear, and some accessories.

Caspian has some other stuff packed that went into our getaway car last night.

As we drive off the campus grounds, I look at the statues of the Knights and wonder if this will be the last time I see them.

I focus on the statue of Raventhorn until we drive through the gates, and I can't see him anymore.

Caspian reaches over to take my hand and gives it a gentle squeeze.

"Try not to worry."

"I'll try my best."

"Be strong, Printsessa."

At this moment, strength is a thing that feels difficult for me to muster, but all I can do is try.

When we arrive at the diner, the plan truly begins.

We're going to go through the motions of ordering food, then I'll go to the ladies' room. Caspian will follow five minutes later, and we'll slip out the back.

When our food is served, I'm so nervous I can't eat it. I have to force it down my throat.

When I do manage to finish, Caspian gives me the signal, heralding the time to break free.

I pick up my bag and make my way into the ladies' room, averting the stares I get from the two guards who watch me.

When I reach the bathroom door, I continue walking down to the exit and wait for five minutes. Sure enough, Caspian joins me when he's supposed to and takes my hand as if he knows how frightened I am.

He doesn't even look back when we jump into the

black SUV and pull out onto the road. He just drives, and we escape to Bluff Island.

~

It's after five when we arrive; the sun is hanging low in the sky.

The area we drive into is as beautiful as I remember, but because of the bad memories I have of this place, I don't feel the beauty. Only pain writhes through me, fueling my anxious state.

I'm also exhausted from the long drive and the tension created from worrying someone will find us.

"We're not far," Caspian says.

I glance at him. He's been focused, extremely focused, and we've barely spoken. I am aware of the lengths he's going to, to help me, what he's giving up, and that he chose me.

I'll never forget that he picked me, and I was the only thing that mattered when he had to make a split-second decision.

"This is the place, but it looks like there's someone here," he states as we turn down the next road, which is narrow and more like a dirt road with the woods pushing in on either side.

There's a black Miata ahead, parked under an oak tree. The moment I see the car, a pricking sensation crawls down my spine.

"Who could this be, Caspian? I'm scared."

He reaches for his gun and a knife pack. I'm not used

to seeing him with weapons. I'm glad he's equipped to keep us safe, but I hope we won't face that kind of trouble.

"Stay close to me. Perhaps this is our note person. They said they'd leave something for us, and we'd know what to do next."

"I didn't think they'd be here, too, though."

"No." He searches the area and frowns. "We have to park here and go the rest of the way by foot."

I'm not liking this at all.

When we park in front of the Miata, we jump out of our car, and Caspian checks out the area before we follow the path that leads to The Bluebell.

Moments later, a cottage comes into view. It looks like something from a country home magazine. The grounds seem well kept and so does the exterior of the house. It's made of wood, like the cabin I stayed in when I was last here. That campsite isn't too far.

Caspian keeps an arm around me as we move forward to the cottage door.

He tries the handle, and the door clicks open.

We exchange glances and he readies his gun, moving in front of me.

When we step inside, I hear music—classical music. It's Debussy.

The melody is faint and seems to be coming from the back of the house.

We move closer, and I can see the back of someone sitting in an armchair.

It's a woman with dark curly hair.

The moment I see the curls, I know in my heart who it is and who's been leaving me the notes.

Suddenly, the familiarity of that last paragraph of the note I got the other day makes sense.

It said I would desire the thing that would destroy me. It was a play on a Sylvia Plath quote. The original quote is:

I desire the things which will destroy me in the end.

My stomach churns as the realization hits me, along with the sting of betrayal.

The only person I spoke at length with about Sylvia Plath was Nina.

That's her sitting in the chair, but she's not moving.

Caspian and I walk in front of her, and I realize why she's not moving.

Her lifeless body is resting in the chair, with her hands folded in her lap.

Next to her on the table is a letter with my name on it.

Her eyes are staring straight ahead as if she's watching something fascinating.

Except she's not because she's dead.

CHAPTER 34
WILLOW

It's Nina who left me all those notes, but how did she do it?

She would have had to have eyes on me almost everywhere. I spent a lot of time at the library, but there were places I went that I can't imagine how she would have slipped me a note without me seeing her.

Perhaps she had others working with her.

"Nina," I say, even though I know she can't answer me.

I reach out to touch her face, but Caspian stops me.

"Willow, don't touch her. Just take the note. We don't know how she died. It could be poison."

Poison—like what I was given.

But I'm certain she gave it to herself. She killed herself.

Nobody else did this. And this setting is exactly the type of macabre poetic death a writer would orchestrate.

As I stare at Nina's dead face, her blue lips, sheet-white skin, and lifeless eyes, my head spins and my lungs burn with the breath I'm clinging to.

I feel like I should be surprised, but part of me isn't.

Caspian rests a hand on my shoulder. I tear my gaze away from Nina's face.

"Baby, we should read the note and get out of here." His voice is hushed.

I swallow hard and reach for the envelope, forcing myself to focus.

I open it and find a letter inside that is two pages long.

Caspian moves closer so we can read it together.

DEAR WILLOW,

Now you know who I am.

By the time you read this, I should be dead.

The first thing I want to say to you is that I'm sorry. Not just for my part in this, but for everything. I feel like I should tell you our time together wasn't fake, but I will confess that I was told to befriend you.

I'm embarrassed to say, the fact that we shared similar interests made it easier.

Sending you Lillian's necklace the other day was meant to scare you into finding a way to leave Raventhorn. Of course, I knew it would freak you out, but I did it in a desperate attempt to keep the one promise I made to Lillian before she died.

I'm sure by now you must have figured out that she didn't die on that cliff, but it wasn't long after. She was alive for a few days, and I took care of her, or rather I was tasked with watching her.

I wanted to help her, but I couldn't.

She kept saying, "Don't let my sister die." Those were her last words, and I promised her I wouldn't. So, I watched and waited for the time when I knew you'd be in danger.

My father, brother, Peter, and Dorian are only some of the devils in this plot. I won't excuse my guilt, so I class myself as a devil, too, but there are others. There are more people you need to be aware of. I don't, however, know their identities.

Peter is the leader of the pack, and everyone involved allied to take everything from your father. That was the plan. Take everything including his heirs and share the Raventhorn fortune amongst them.

They thought your father became a dictator and no longer shared wealth and opportunity. They believed he started to undercut them and take all the resources for himself to invest in Dynamic Corp. They believed he would never allow them to progress, and they would never have the wealth they desired.

They started stealing from the bank. That was where my father came in because he was responsible for taking care of all finances. Because Peter worked across businesses, it was easy for him to keep tabs on things. He was the first to be alerted when he realized your father was onto them and had started collecting evidence to execute them. No one was able to find the evidence, but they knew it would mean their death if Timofey unleashed it.

Your father chose to communicate with Adrian because he was a neutral party and Peter was keeping tabs on Alek-

sander. The day came when they decided it was time to kill your father.

So, if you thought your parents' deaths were suspicious as fuck, they were. What happened that day was planned. I wasn't there, but it was planned. Your parents were baited to the lake house to die. I don't know why Caspian's mother was there, but that was an accident, and she became collateral damage.

I HAVE to stop reading because my entire body is shaking so hard I can't think straight. My trembling hands drop to my sides, and my body goes limp as if all my bones have dissolved. The only sign that my body is still working is the punishing cacophony of painful emotions clashing through my mind.

Jesus. I can't believe any of this. I just can't, and the worst thing is knowing all this time, my instincts were right. Nothing happened the way people made it look, and Mom didn't kill herself.

What happened, then?

What the fuck happened?

"Willow, baby, let's keep reading." Caspian takes the letter and holds it out so we can keep going.

USING the old laws of the Knights, they positioned themselves so they could take the empire. So, one of the first people they had to get rid of was Aleksander. He was the only person in their circle of friends who posed a threat because he didn't want anything from Timofey. However, his partnership with the company and executorship over your estate blocked them from doing what they sought to do. The day your parents died, everything was set in motion, including removing him from control.

The next plan of action was to kill you and Lillian, but they wanted everything to look legit. They also needed to wait until one of you was of age to claim your inheritance.

Because Lillian was promised to marry Dorian, she was supposed to die first, then you next. They were going to make your deaths look like the same kind of accident as your parents'.

However, Lillian used her suspicions about your parents' deaths to dig around. She told me she overheard Peter talking to Oleg about the plan to kill

you both and knew they were still looking for the evidence among your father's things. She found his passwords and was able to dig up that evidence, but they discovered her. I don't know how, but they did.

She was kept alive because they needed to know where the evidence was, but she never told them because she feared they'd kill you.

They allowed her to die and planned for you to marry Dorian instead. As long as they had one Raventhorn sister, they could still carry out the plan.

They were almost discovered again when my father slipped up in a bad way and Zak Ivanov overheard a conversation he shouldn't have.

Because Dorian was the best person to get close to Zak, Peter arranged for him to kill him. They all covered it up.

However, because of my father's mistake, they cut him out of the plan and threatened to dismiss him as a judge if he retaliated.

That brings us here.

Instead of getting nothing from the fortune, my father planned to kill you before you received your inheritance. That way, he'd still get a portion and the others would be bound by the same laws as him.

He knew the best time to get to you was when you started college, so he planned for that point.

The last thing I have left to tell you is where to find Lillian.

I figured if you're like me, you'll want to see her to get closure, so I left a shovel in the back on the spot I buried her.

I'm so sorry, Willow.

But please don't forgive me in any way. I couldn't forgive myself. I stayed alive so I could help you, and now I must depart.

Leave as soon as you can. I think my father was keeping tabs on me, so I don't know if I was tracked here. It won't be safe for you to stay.

Goodbye.

From Nina.

A possible friend.

MY BRAIN IS NUMB, my body stone. When I lift tear-filled eyes to look at Caspian, we stare at each other for what feels like eons.

I want to scream, I want to run, I want to rip the fabric of reality apart and burn everything to the ground.

He looks the same. Of course, he would; he just found out how his brother died.

And I'm yet to get closure because Nina is right. I want it. I want to see my sister.

I want to see what happened to her.

When I move away from Caspian, he catches my arm.

"Don't. Don't, Willow." He shakes his head vigorously. "You know what you'll find if you dig up that grave. I think you knew all along we could find something like this if we came here, and that's why we're here."

"I have to see," I mutter. "I have to. So many people wanted me to believe she ran away, but I held on to the truth. Now I want to see the sacrifice she made for me."

"It's going to break you."

"I'm already broken." My breath catches. "I have to see her, Caspian. Please let me see my sister one last time."

The moment he releases me, I rush to the back of the house fueled by untamed adrenaline and raw desolation.

When I scan outside and see the red shovel resting on the patch of slightly raised earth by the edge of the lake, I'm overcome by anguish.

The dark dread of what I'm about to find drops to the pit of my stomach like a steel weight, but I push past it and keep going.

I reach the shovel and am about to pick it up when Caspian rushes up to me and takes it.

I expect him to protest again, but he doesn't. Instead, he starts digging.

I watch him unearth the dirt; each speck as filthy as the secrets we've exhumed.

He digs deeper and deeper until I spot a flash of color that stands out stark against the rustic earth. It's a patch of blue cloth—denim, like the jeans Lillian was wearing that dreadful night.

As more earth is removed, more of what remains of my sister comes to light. The bones of her arms, her feet... and then her skull, which still has her hair attached to it.

Caspian stops there, and as he throws down the shovel, I drop to my knees and scream.

The pain that overwhelms me stabs my body like a million knives. The agony pierces my entire being.

It sears into me with such intensity I feel like I'll never experience anything but this darkness again.

Deep sobs rack my insides as I stare at my sister's remains, but then warm arms encircle me with love.

When I gaze into those green eyes of the boy I love who became my husband, something anchors me, stopping the grief from swallowing me whole.

"She loved you," he mutters. "Just remember she loved you, that you are here today because of that love."

I try to catch my breath, but I can't.

My lips part to say something. No words come, though, when I see men moving around in the house carrying guns.

"Caspian, we have to get out of here!"

He follows my gaze and grabs my hand, yanking me

to stand so we can run. We just miss the first bullet as it whizzes our way.

As bullets fly, Caspian tries to cover me and fires back.

I don't look behind me; I just try to run as fast as I can.

The moment we head into the woods, it feels like déjà vu. I'm running for my life again, through the woodlands at Bluff Island. The difference is that this time, I'm with Caspian and it's not in the pitch-black darkness of night.

We race through the trees, and I hear the heavy footfalls of the men coming for us—coming to kill us.

The trees clear, and I move toward the opening, to what I see is the road.

A car speeds down it toward us, going way too fast. Imminent danger is all I can think of, and this must be more men.

I catch sight of the panicked look on Caspian's face, and my breath freezes in my lungs.

As the car draws near, he shoves me behind him and readies his gun to shoot.

We are both astounded, however, when we look at the driver and see it's Elaine.

"Get in!" she shouts. "Come on! Get in!"

CHAPTER 35
WILLOW

When we jump into the back seat of the car, Elaine takes off.

She glances back at me through the rearview mirror, her face filled with worry.

As I stare at her, I recall the words she said weeks ago about putting me in her car and driving away.

At that time, I thought it would mean freedom, that she would take care of me the way she always had. However, right now, I don't feel that way, even though she just saved us.

I don't think this is a chance meeting or that she's the real cavalry coming to the rescue. Because what is she doing here?

How did she know to come, or that we would be here?

And if she knew about this location, would she have known about Lillian, too?

A quick glance at Caspian tells me he has the same thoughts.

"What are you doing here, Elaine?" My voice is still haggard from my anguished sobs.

She glances back at us. "We'll talk when we get to safety. I'll tell you everything then. Let's just get out of here."

She accelerates and speeds down the road.

We drive in silence, but Caspian keeps one hand on his gun and the other on me.

Hours later, the sun has set and we pull up at an old farmhouse that looks like it's seen better days. The place is dark and deserted and surrounded by a lot of land with shadowy woods in the distance. I have no idea where we are, but since we drove east of Bluff Island, I'm assuming we're near the border of Vermont.

Elaine jumps out of the car, and we do the same. She looks around to check the place out and then releases a sigh.

"Let's get inside," she says. "Hopefully, we should be okay here for a while."

She leads the way, taking us through the rickety door and then into the house, which smells like dirt.

Elaine switches on a dim light then nervously looks from me to Caspian.

It's time to talk.

"Are you going to tell us your part in the plot, or should I try to fill in the blanks?" Caspian demands, tapping his gun against the side of his leg. "I'll let you in on a little secret. I always suspected there was something up with you, but I never thought it could be this."

Well, he has one over on me because she had me fooled. I'm guessing if she's in this mix of shit, then Adrian must be involved, too.

And what did I do yesterday? Tell Adrian what Lucian revealed.

"I wish I could say you're wrong, but you aren't," Elaine stutters, hardly able to look at me.

"What happened to my mother, Elaine?" he snarls. I'm glad he can speak because I can't. "We know she wasn't supposed to be at the lake house the day Timofey and Isabella Raventhorn died. Or should I say *were killed*? They were killed, weren't they?"

When Elaine nods her head, a hot tear rolls down my cheek.

"Your mother was there because of me," Elaine confesses in a raspy tone. "I called her when I couldn't reach your father."

"You tried to call my father?" Caspian narrows his eyes.

"Yes, I was aware of the plan to kill Timofey and Isabella. When the day came to do it, I couldn't sit back and allow it to happen. I knew Aleksander would be the only person who could help. I was at home when I called your mother at the magazine. I ended up telling her what was going on. The moment she knew Timofey was in danger, she went to the lake house to warn him and fell into the same trap he and Isabella did. I went there to try and stop her, but I was too late. I think she might have tried to call your father too but couldn't reach him either."

On hearing that, Caspian's back goes ramrod straight.

"And what about Adrian?" I cut in because I'm dying to know. "Could he kill my parents? Did he know about the *plan*?"

Elaine turns her focus to me. "It was his idea, Willow. He arranged the whole thing."

Shock slams into me, and I stare back at her feeling utterly flabbergasted.

"His idea?" I mumble.

"He was the middleman, but he was just as bad as Peter. Adrian wanted power. He was never going to be anything but what he was because he had no link through the bloodline. So, when the others realized that Timofey trusted him, they approached him to help in their scheme, and he quickly jumped on board."

"You're my godparents. My parents trusted you. You speak so highly of my mother. How could you be involved in this?"

"Everything you're thinking right now is right. I shouldn't be involved in this, but I am." She wipes away tears. "Adrian changed from the guy I married after we lost our baby. He became manipulative, mean, and selfish. I don't think in all the time you lived with us that you ever saw his true face. That day at the lake house, he kidnapped your mother and lured your father there. He held a gun to her head and forced your father to change his will, vote him and Oleg in as judges on the Knights' council, and remove Aleksander from the company and his estate management."

I'm so stunned I can't breathe past the constriction in my chest.

"And what did you do?" I glare at her.

"I made things worse. When I tried to intervene, your mother was shot. He shot her to shut me up." She sobs while I gaze back, tongue-tied. "A fight broke out, and Timofey tried to save Irina. They got in the car and managed to get away, but Adrian went after them and ran them off the road."

"My God." My voice breaks. "*Him*? It was Adrian?"

"Yes. It was him. All this time, we pretended to be the supportive godparents, but we were a lie."

"Yes, you were. Why did you stay with Adrian?"

"He threatened to kill me if I left him or didn't do as I was told. Then I stayed with him to protect you. Lillian had her suspicions about him, but they weren't strong enough to evade his manipulative side. She knew something was off about the way your parents died. When she started snooping around, he was aware of it. When we went to Bluff Island and she found that evidence, she called Adrian and told him. He knew the danger in having that evidence, so he contacted Peter and Dorian. They flew over and found her in the village. The moment she noticed them, she knew she was in trouble, and I'm guessing that's when she got you."

"So, it was Peter and Dorian who were chasing Lillian and me through the woods?" I snap, having the sickening recollection when I was around Dorian that there was something familiar about him.

I never saw the men in the woods properly, but I'd looked back at one point and saw the outline of one. That must have been Dorian. The fucking asshole would have been sixteen at the time, not even a man yet.

"It was Adrian and Dorian," Elaine corrects, adding another layer to my shock.

"What!"

"Adrian and Dorian chased you through the woods. I was just behind them. In his rage, Adrian shot Lillian."

My hands fly up to my mouth as I weep, disbelief clawing at my insides.

I can't believe it was Adrian who shot Lillian. The knowledge makes me feel so sick my head spins and my legs wobble. Caspian secures an arm around me when my legs give, and I clutch on to him as the tears flow from me like a river breaking through a dam.

"When he realized she'd pushed you over the cliff, he thought she told you what she found," she grates out. "Then he and Dorian took Lillian to The Bluebell to torture her into giving up the information, but she wouldn't do it. When the police found you and you didn't know anything about your father's evidence, he left Lillian at the house to die. It was his idea to send you to St. Jude's. That way, we'd be able to cover up what happened to Lillian and get legal guardianship over you. Peter blamed him when he thought Lillian was going to blow the operation. St. Jude's was Adrian's way of fixing it. The original plan was for Peter to get the empire, then he'd give Adrian and Oleg a percentage. When Oleg was cut out of the plan, Peter was going to split everything with Adrian. Then, when Dorian died and Aleksander took over your legal guardianship, everything went to hell."

"You knew the truth the whole time and you let me go to St. Jude's," I stutter. "You sat there and watched me suffer. They gave me so many different medications to fuck with me, I nearly killed myself. You knew the truth, and you lied continuously to save yourself."

"I'm sorry, Willow. I didn't know what else to do."

Now it all makes sense. And that argument I over-heard the other week was about Peter. He was the man they were talking about who wouldn't be happy.

"Something else must have happened recently," Caspian points out. "Dorian died weeks ago, and my father has held that legal guardianship for the same amount of time. You knew where to find us earlier. Something else has changed. Hasn't it?"

"Yes. When Willow told Adrian about Oleg, he knew straightaway it had to be him who tried to kill her. He knew Oleg must have had a separate plan to secure a part of her inheritance. He worried he would succeed and expose him and Peter for their crimes of the past." She pauses for a beat to glance at me. "When Willow was attacked, the first people Aleksander suspected were the judges because they were the only people who stood to gain from her death. He also suspected it was one of them who killed Zak, so it didn't take much to spark his suspicion. Aleksander started investigating everyone, so

Peter and Adrian decided to play things safe, be compliant, and fall back on the money they were siphoning from Dynamic Corp. They have a combined debt of close to a billion, so they knew if Aleksander suspected them of trying to undercut him, they'd lose everything. But that plan also backfired."

"In what ways," I spit.

"Yesterday, the board at Dynamic Corp voted Adrian out and Aleksander in as the new C.E.O. with a view to owning it based on your guardianship. That wiped out the backup plan to use the company profits to fund their deals and pay off the debts." Elaine's lips press into a thin line. "Because Adrian lost his power in Dynamic Corp, he decided to kill Oleg and take over his plan to kill you, so he'd get the money to pay the debts. I knew to come here because he and Peter tracked Nina down. They knew she was up to something just for being here, so they were watching the house. They saw when you arrived and decided to strike. I did, too."

"So, it was Adrian's men who came to kill us just now?"

Elaine nods slowly.

"Once again, I'm reminded that I'm a thing."

"No, you aren't, my darling."

"Stop it. Don't you dare try to talk to me like we were before."

"But Willow—"

She reaches out to touch me, but I slap her face and she recoils.

"Don't touch me ever." I shake my head at her. "You

stand there and tell me you tried to help, but you didn't. I spent two years in a mental hospital. You knew the truth, and you let me stay there. You allowed people to think I was insane."

I hold up my wrist to show her my scar. Tears roll down her cheeks.

"Remember the day this happened? I do." I raise my voice. "The other day, I begged you to help me because I didn't want to go back to St. Jude's, and you basically told me to do as I'm told. You're a poor excuse for a human being."

"I'm sorry—"

"Save your fucking breath. It's not me you should apologize to; it's my mother. The woman you called your best friend."

I walk away from her and go outside in the dark where I can cry.

That dreaded doom settles over me, and I'm not sure if I'm going to survive this. My soul is too broken.

CHAPTER 36
CASPIAN

I follow Willow as she rushes through the door and coax her back inside.

Emotions are running high, but we need to be extremely careful.

I assume this place is somewhere Adrian will look for Elaine.

"There are beds upstairs," Elaine says. "She should rest."

I give her a hard stare, displaying my disgust. People like her are enablers.

They know when to do the right thing and stop themselves from doing it, not always out of fear.

I observed her as she spoke. Her terror over defying Adrian was clear, but I imagine there were instances when she could have done better than she did.

Helping us today is perhaps the only time she's truly done what's right. I can only imagine how terrified she must be now.

With my gaze trained on her, I take Willow up the stairs.

We enter a room with a queen-sized bed that looks freshly made but like it was done many years ago.

It makes me wonder what this place is.

What is its use?

I asked myself the same thing about The Bluebell as we read the letter Nina wrote.

I check the bed is free of dust before letting Willow lie on it, then I sit next to her and hold her while she cries herself to sleep.

It's not until then that I allow the truth to sink in about my mother and Zak.

I release her when she falls asleep then check the tracker. In our attempts to get away from the gunmen, I lost the phone, but thank fuck I had the tracker. I activated it on the way here, so I'm hoping help arrives soon. A message is supposed to come through when help is on the way. There's nothing yet.

Things have gotten to that stage again where it would be counterproductive for me to do things on my own.

I need help to protect Willow, and I have more than enough evidence to show my father what's going on.

He has three rogue judges on his hands. I can't imagine anything worse for the Knights.

Then there's me.

I became the Viper when I wanted revenge for my brother's death. Now that I have answers, I feel like I'm something else, and not in a good way.

I always thought I'd feel more liberated when this day came, but how can I when it wasn't just the one truth I discovered?

There was one for Zak and one for Mom.

My mother must have loved Timofey a lot to go rushing off to warn him of the danger.

I guess I still wish there were something someone could have done to stop her. I can't think of why she didn't take backup or try to contact my father.

If my father had gone, chances are he would have walked into a trap, too, but he wouldn't have allowed them to kill him.

An hour later, noises drift up from downstairs. It's Elaine, but I don't know what she's doing.

I make my way downstairs to find her in the kitchen with a host of weapons laid out on the breakfast table. There are six different types of guns, a few grenades, and other explosives.

She lifts her head and looks at me when I walk in.

"Where did you get all this?" I motion to the weapons.

"This is a safe house my family used, so it's packed with all sorts of ammo and food supplies." She sighs and runs a weary hand through her hair. "We have a couple of houses like this one. This is the furthest."

"But one Adrian will look for you?"

"Yes."

"How many men does he have?"

"Too many."

"I've activated my tracker, so help should come from Raventhorn soon."

"Good, we will need it. I had to leave my phone behind, or Adrian would be able to track me. Until help arrives, I'm hoping this will hold them off if we get trouble. I only stopped because the car was going to run out of gas. I didn't want us to get stuck on the road in the middle of nowhere in the dark. At least here we have ammo. There is a gas station about five miles away that opens at five thirty in the morning."

"How much gas do we have?"

"Enough for another ten miles."

"And there's no other gas station around that's open?"

"No."

"We're going to have to get to the gas station before they open so we can get ahead." *If we're still around.*

She nods. "I know."

"Thank you for doing this." I think thanks needs to be said because if not for her, I don't think we'd be here.

When someone wants something from you, that something protects you. Now that Adrian and Peter want Willow dead, there's nothing to hang on to.

"I'm sorry for everything." She sets her hands down on the table.

"You knew about the affair before Willow did, didn't you?" The question is irrelevant, but it's something I wondered about earlier as she explained herself.

"I did. Timofey and your mother met at Raventhorn, but

she was promised to your father. They stopped seeing each other after they got married but very quickly resumed a secret affair. They were together for as long as I knew them."

"God." I blow out a haggard breath, feeling even worse for blaming Willow for keeping their secret. "I can't believe it went on for so long."

"It never stopped until the day they died. That's why your mother went to try and rescue Timofey. She was in love with him. I wouldn't say Willow's mother wasn't aware of it, but I know your father wasn't until just before they died, and he took it hard. It pushed him over the edge."

"It did."

She stares at me, but then her gaze switches over my shoulder and the blood siphons from her face.

"They're here, Caspian." Her hands fly up to her cheeks. "Oh God, Adrian found us."

I snap around to see a truck and three motorcyclists racing down the path in the distance.

Fuck. There are too many of them.

A bad idea forms in my mind, but it's one I knew I might have to execute at some point.

Turning back to Elaine's ghostly face, I grit my teeth. "Get Willow and go. I will hold them off."

"No, you can't do that."

"Do it, Elaine. The two of you need to get to safety. I can handle myself. Get Willow and go."

She quickly grabs a gun and moves. I take the shotgun, a Glock, and a few grenades, then move, too.

I know I can't kill all of them, but I will kill some of them.

That should hopefully be enough to allow Willow and Elaine to get away.

I just don't know what will happen to me after.

CHAPTER 37
WILLOW

Elaine and I run outside.

My eyes are so swollen from crying earlier I can barely see, but when I notice Caspian walking across the path with his shotgun raised, I stop and freeze.

He's not getting in the car with us. I can't leave without him.

"Caspian!" I shout.

He turns to face me, and as the moon shines down on his face, I remember how Lillian looked just before she pushed me off the cliff.

For that moment, time froze as I tried to process what she was going to do next, and I didn't know until she did it.

As I gaze at my husband now, the same thing happens, but this time I know.

I know he's not coming with us.

"Willow, get in the car!" Elaine grabs me. I fight her.

"No, let go of me." I try to fight her off, but she doesn't let me go. "Caspian, come with us!"

"Go now!" Caspian shouts. "Go!"

The sound of bullets firing snaps me, and he rushes into the night, toward the oncoming vehicles, and starts shooting.

Elaine pulls me into the car, and we drive away. All I hear as we speed down the dirt path is gunfire.

There's so much of it, too much. It's the sound of war. I can't imagine Caspian surviving.

Elaine revs the engine, and when I glance across at her, she looks back at me with the deepest sadness in her eyes.

"He told me to take you. I'm going to try and get you somewhere safe, then we'll call the Knights."

I can't speak. I can barely breathe.

"Willow. I promise I will do everything in my power to fix this."

"It's too late, Elaine," I rasp. "Can't you see it's too late? Look at us."

"That doesn't stop me from promising to do what I can. I know you hate me right now and I can't blame you, but please know that I love you always and I will always think of you as my daughter."

I'm about to answer when a car pulls out in front of us from the adjacent road. Another car appears, and the speed they're coming at already suggests they mean to cause trouble.

Elaine tries to get past them, but they block her, and she ends up driving off the road and into the trees.

We crash into a thicket of oak trees, and I slam my head against the door.

Before we can even think to get out of the car, men are jumping out and rushing toward us. My door is yanked open, and I find myself staring into my godfather's face. To think I called this man Father on my wedding day and always thought of him as a pillar of strength disgusts me now.

"Hello, my daughter," Adrian says as if he knows what I'm thinking.

"Leave her alone!" Elaine cries.

Adrian raises his gun and points it at her. "Elaine, when I knew you betrayed me, I thought it should be me who gets to kill you. As much as I love you, you have to die."

"You bastard—"

He silences her with a bullet to her chest and grabs me by my throat.

I scream and thrash against his grip, kicking and punching to no avail.

"As for you, my darling goddaughter, I have something special in mind for your death. I figured it should be me who kills you, too."

He stabs me in my neck with something sharp, and I black out just like I did on the bridge.

CHAPTER 38
CASPIAN

I speed down the road on the motorcycle I took from one of the guys, and my frantic gaze finds Elaine's car smashed against the trees on the side of the road.

That grenade took out the whole convoy of men who came, and I was able to get away.

I was hoping to catch up with Willow and Elaine. I didn't expect to see this.

I rev the engine harder, driving faster to the crash site.

My fucking heart is in my throat by the time I jump off the bike.

I fully expect to see my wife dead in the car, but what I find is Elaine's bloody body.

She moves when I approach, but I can see from where she's shot that she's not going to make it. The wound is too close to her heart.

I climb into the car. When I pick her up, her eyes flutter open and she tries to focus on me.

"Adrian took her. The caves," she stutters, blood running down the side of her mouth. "Try... the caves at Smokey's Den...by... the river. Adrian and Peter use it for business. I'm so sorry, Caspian, so very sorry."

"It's okay, Elaine. You tried to help."

"Willow was like my daughter, and I did truly love ... her. Please tell her I said that and I'm sorry."

"I will."

She closes her eyes, and then she's gone.

Damn it, I'm flying blind now. All I can do is feel my way forward in this unknown place of darkness and doom.

I check the tracker in my pocket. Hope sparks in me when I see a message from Thorne.

It says: *we're on the way.*

I'm glad I have backup coming, but I'm not sure they'll get to me in time.

Staring down the dusky road, I pray I can find Willow before Adrian kills her.

CHAPTER 39
WILLOW

When I come to, I open my eyes to a strange dim amber light.

I move my head from side to side but find I'm restricted.

It takes a moment to realize I'm tied up, and although I'm propped upright, I'm inside something.

What is it?

"Looks like she's awake. Let me shed a little more light." Adrian's voice fills the space, echoing around me.

The light brightens, illuminating the area before me, allowing me to see Oleg and Ilya's severed heads on a stone slab.

I scream, and Adrian responds with a crude laugh.

"This is what we do in the Bratva when someone double-crosses us," he says, coming into my view now.

As I look around me at the raised sides of the enclosure surrounding me, I realize with horror that I'm in a coffin.

The knowledge tightens my chest and I start panting.

"Why are you doing this? I trusted you. I loved you like a father."

The smile drops from his face. "And I tried to love you like a daughter, too, but it wasn't real. I can't have kids. They'd die. Did Elaine ever tell you that? There were times when I'd look at you and you'd feel like mine, and I thought I had to try and find a way to save you. At one point, I thought maybe you didn't have to die. But in the end, especially with this recent spell of shit that lost me everything I worked for at that fucking company, I had to remind myself that you were always the lamb. You were always supposed to die."

"How can you say that?"

"Because it's true. I have to give Oleg credit for what he did. The poor fool tried to fuck us over. I take it you know the truth."

"I do, and you are despicable." I choke back tears. "You killed my family."

"I know. They were what you call collateral damage. The same as you."

"How could you do this to us?"

"Because I only became somebody when your father died. I was the guy you get to do everything but who never got enough credit. I was the asshole. Oleg, Peter, and I were supposed to split your inheritance. But when Oleg fucked up beyond repair, I felt it was reason to cut him out of the agreement. With him out of the way, Peter and I would have gone halves on your inheritance. We planned to kill you on your birthday."

I can't believe I'm speaking to the same man from yesterday. "You won't get away with this."

"My dear, I already have. I'm sure that husband of yours is dead by now, and you will die, too."

"You fucking bastard." Tears pour from my eyes and my heart aches for Caspian. I pray with everything inside me that he's not dead. He can't be.

"On your death, I'll get back some compensation, and I won't have a wife to share it with anymore."

"Don't worry, I have the perfect death for you, my princess. I never got to bury your sister, but I will bury you."

He lifts the coffin lid, and whatever is propping me up moves me backwards until I'm lying flat.

Then the lid is descending over me. Peter's face comes into view before the lid closes, and I scream into the darkness that swallows me.

But this time, I'm awake in the nightmare of being buried alive.

CHAPTER 40
CASPIAN

There they are.

I sneak down to the jagged river rocks and hide behind a boulder. Guards line the entrance of the mouth of the cave.

This cave is roughly forty minutes away from where I left Elaine. It seems to be a mineshaft that's no longer in use for mining but definitely for other things—probably smuggling shit.

There are trucks down there, too. I'm trying to ascertain how many men I'm up against before I dive into battle.

I can see at least twenty guards surrounding the cave's entrance, and a few in the truck—too many for me.

I have one grenade left that I have to make count.

Suddenly, I spot Adrian and Peter walking out of the cave.

I focus on Adrian, really looking at him, seeing who

he is under the mask he's worn all these years. A storm rages within me, growing bigger with every second that passes.

He is my mother's killer. Him. He killed her.

My mother's beautiful face comes to my mind, the image stronger and more distinct than ever.

After my father found me in Russia and took me home, my mother barely left my side. It was months before she did, and only marginally. She's the reason I'm functional now because those nightmares I experienced at such a young age were enough to ruin me forever.

My mother loved me with all her heart, and I loved her the same. I sought solace in her love.

Accepting her death was the hardest thing I've ever had to do, but as the years went by I did it. I accepted that it was an accident, life happened, and so did death —things we have no control over.

However, knowing now that she was killed, and staring at the man who dealt death's blow, ruptures my mind, shattering me all over again.

He will pay.

Adrian will pay for every fucking thing he's done to Willow and me. And I will be the man to end him.

Adrian and Peter walk into the headlights cast by one of the trucks allowing me to see the big smiles on their faces, which means they've done it—they've killed my girl.

No... I refuse to believe she's dead. Although, what else could the victorious looks on their faces mean?

I shove the thought out of my mind. Willow is alive in my heart until I see for myself that she's not.

Now I just have to get to her.

Pulling the grenade from my pocket, I loosen the pin and throw it down near the cluster of guards. Once it blows up, I'll need to move.

I take cover and count down the seconds.

When the explosion rips through the air, I run out of my hiding space, shooting two of the guards in my way. The grenade took out a few of the guards but not enough. There are still a ton of them, and I'm still by myself.

Adrian appears ahead and spots me coming. He whips out his gun and starts shooting at me, but I don't slow down. I find cover behind the line of boulders leading down to the cave, continuing my pursuit by slipping between each one.

The motherfucker rushes toward me, too, just like I knew he would.

I can't see where Peter went, but he can't be too far away.

As Adrian bounds faster, growling like a wild hell beast, I decide to stay behind the last boulder with an idea in mind that will either kill him, or me.

Knowing he's breaths away, I wait for the last second then jump out and shoot when he reaches me.

It's perfect timing and I catch him by surprise with a bullet to his chest. I shoot him again in the same spot just to make sure I take him down.

He drops to the ground in a bloody heap, and I grab his throat, pressing my

gun against his jugular.

Adrian coughs blood and the motherfucker knows he has only minutes left in the world of the living yet he has the audacity to smile at me as if he's won, and I've lost.

"Where's Willow?"

"You're too late, too fucking late. I buried her."

A gamut of emotions assaults me and my hopes collapse. "You killed her." I hate the raw emotion in my voice. It speaks of my anguish and fear.

"I *fucking* killed her."

No. I don't want to believe that. Not until I've done everything I can to try and save her.

"You motherfucking bastard." Reaching for my knife, I bring it down into his neck. "That is for my wife."

I aim the gun at him again and shoot between his eyes, stealing the rest of the life from his body.

"That is for my mother."

I turn to run toward the cave to save Willow, but something hard hits the back of my head. It feels like a metal pipe.

It takes me down, and I almost black out.

I just manage to roll onto my back when Peter jumps me and places a gun to my head.

"You little shit. I've waited for this day for a long time," he growls. "You tried to kill my son. I will kill you tonight."

"Fuck you, I'd like to see you try." The odds aren't in

my favor, but I push against him, feeling my mind checking out on me from the blow to my head.

Click-clack. The sound of the hammer cocking on his gun ricochets off the walls of my heart and doom devours me as a menacing smile spreads across his devilish face.

"Goodbye motherfucker." As soon as the words fall from his lips, his head explodes at the same time that a powerful gunshot echoes all around us.

Blood sprays over me, and Peter's headless body drops on top of mine, revealing my father standing before me with a shotgun.

Behind him is a host of other Knights, including Thorne, who are fighting the guards.

I have back up. They're here. They came. *My father* came. I would never have expected him to come to my rescue—*again*.

Father shoves Peter's body off me and helps me to stand. My head spins and I'm unsteady but I try to right myself because I have to find Willow.

"Are you hurt?" His gruff voice identifies him as the devil I know, but as I stare at him, he looks like the father who rescued me from the well when I was a boy.

"I'm okay. I need to get Willow."

"Go!" he says and turns around to assist the team that has come to save me.

I make my way into the cave, staving off the effects of my injury and follow the path down to an amber glow. There I find a wide space with Oleg and Ilya's heads resting on a platform.

Across from them is a patch of freshly dug earth, and a shovel.

For the second time today, I grab the shovel and start digging into the earth. My heart doesn't stop racing, and I don't stop digging.

It's not until I've unearthed about three feet worth of dirt that I hear a mumbling sound, which gets louder the deeper I dig. Then I realize what it is.

It's her!

Willow.

She's not dead! But the motherfucker buried her alive.

I keep digging until I reach a coffin, then I move away the remaining dirt with my hands and yank the top off, freeing Willow.

She's screaming and crying with terror entrenched on her face.

"I got you, Willow. I got you, baby." I pull her to my heart, holding her close, grateful she's alive and I got to her in time.

I nearly lost her—*nearly*, but I didn't.

We have another chance.

She tries to talk but the words are swallowed within her tears.

I lift her out of the coffin and take the rope off her.

"Let's get out of here. It's over now."

Scooping her up, I carry her out of the cave, promising myself that no one will ever hurt her again.

~

THE NEXT DAY, we return to Boston and back to campus.

Things have been sorted out and the evidence gathered to close the mystery of the past.

Now I have one more thing left to do before I can truly relax.

Willow is sitting by the window bay in our bedroom, reading *Tom Sawyer*.

She looks better after the ordeal last night. I took her to the hospital to make sure she was okay before we left Bluff Island.

Although the doctors declared her fine by medical standards with nothing broken or damaged, I know she's not going to be okay for a long time to come.

Maybe never. She loved her godparents and thought of them as family. I know their betrayal has cut her at the deepest level.

An endless heartwarming smile brightens her pretty face when I walk in.

She doesn't know what I'm doing yet, and I want to keep it that way until it's done.

"I'm going to see my father now." I sit next to her.

"What has he said about St. Jude's?" Her brows lower.

I take her hands into mine and kiss her knuckles. "Don't worry about St. Jude's, Printsessa. You're not going back there."

She raises her shoulders into a shrug. "Despite what's happened, I feel like your father is going to insist on me going."

"Do you trust me?"

"Yes, I trust you."

"Then we don't have a problem, Mrs. Ivanov." I lean forward and kiss her forehead. "I love you."

"I love you, too."

I release her hands and wink at her, eliciting a curious stare which follows me as I walk out of the room.

I make my way to Raventhorn Hall, where I find my father in his office, sitting in the chair behind his grand mahogany desk, waiting for me.

I didn't see him again last night after he saved me, so I'm not sure what he'll be like today. He has all the evidence and knows what happened.

"It's over," he begins. "You got answers for your brother's murder, and you dealt with the three rogue judges."

"I did my duties. Now I want one more thing."

"What's that?"

"I want you to give Willow her freedom."

He stands and stares me down. "I can't let go of the past, son. I can't understand why you can do it so easily. I think it's a disgrace."

I knew he would say something like that. "Finding Lillian's bones negates the argument about Willow's insanity completely, but I had a feeling you would try some shit, so I came with backup."

"What do you have?" His lips curl into a sarcastic sneer making him look like a wild dog.

"Something that could get you killed, Father." I give him a merciless stare when the smile recedes from his face. "You had a very interesting call with Konstantin Putznez the other day."

That was the name of the man he was talking to on the call I overheard.

Just the mention of that name puts wrath on his face, as well as terror, because Konstantin Putznez is supposed to be dead. My father supposedly killed him three years ago after he murdered one of the brigadiers, who was also a Knight.

Konstantin is an enforcer for the Kosalov Brotherhood in Moscow. If you need him to kill someone —*anyone*—he'll do it.

I smile at my father's reaction as it worsens. I'm just getting started. What the fuck will he look like when I'm done?

"I heard you guys talking about the sixty million you're going to get for the deal with Tobias Rivera for the alliance with the Camorra."

"You spying on me, boy?"

"Play dirty and fight dirty. I had the call recorded."

Thorne recorded it. It was placed yesterday after St. Jude's contacted my father to let him know we hadn't arrived. He called Konstantin to reschedule their meeting but ended up saying just enough for me to use against him.

"You think you have me?" he taunts.

"I do. That kind of information would end you. You're not only dealing with a known enemy to the Knights, but you also lied about doling out a revenge punishment. As you are our leader, such crimes would be held against you at the highest level. The remaining judges would demand your head."

"So, you think you can fill my shoes as Pakhan?" Sardonic laughter rumbles within his chest.

"I think *you* can't fill *my* shoes. Do not think I won't kill you, even with my debt to you for last night."

"If you can say that then it looks like you finally learned to become as heartless as me."

"Maybe so, but the difference between you and me is I'm one motherfucker you don't mess with." I pull my knife from my pocket and hold it out toward him. He looks at the sharp tip of the blade and the sheen of defiance he exuded moments ago dissipates from his eyes. "I could be Pakhan. I could slice your throat for what you put Willow through and take the leadership from you right the fuck now."

I'm ready to lead the empire. Age doesn't matter when you're a Knight. What matters are skill, strength, and ability.

I have it all. I know it and my father does too.

That's why he's looking at me with that question in his eyes, asking himself if I'm going to kill him. He can see I'm no longer hesitant like I was weeks ago.

I'm not that guy anymore and now I know I would do it—I would kill my father.

I'm just not going to do it today.

Because of Willow.

She deserves normal. I promised her normal and she's not ready to be the wife of the Pakhan yet.

"What are you waiting for, boy?" He spreads his arms

wide, inviting me to take his life. "Don't disgrace me with empty threats or by second guessing yourself."

"I'm not. Here's what I want, Father. You hand over Willow's legal guardianship and set her free. Abolish any plans you have to ally with the Camorra and deal with Konstantin Putznez the way you should have. Do that, and you get to keep your empire, for the moment."

He looks me up and down, then begrudgingly nods.

"Agreed."

I thought so, but I have one more question for him.

"Why do you hate me so much, then you do things like last night?" He didn't have to come. Yet he did.

He gives me a crude smile. "I don't hate you. I hate that you remind me of who I used to be. The boy who switched places with his cousin so that he could live, the boy who defied his father to be with the girl forbidden to him, the man who fought for love."

We stare at each other, then I dip my head. He does the same.

"We're even here," I declare, although we're not.

We are far from anything close to even. This deal I'm offering him is far from satisfactory in relation to all he's done.

Admittedly, I know in my heart I have another reason for sparing him. It's because she wouldn't want me to kill him. My mother wouldn't want me to take his life and lose the last piece of my soul.

A life for a life—that's all I'm trading here. He gets to keep his so my girl can live hers.

"Yes, we are."

I leave him. When I get outside, I take in a deep breath of fresh air and feel like I can finally start my life with Willow.

The nightmare is finally over, and the darkness went with it.

EPILOGUE

WILLOW

Three weeks later

Today is my birthday.
It's the first one where I'm able to celebrate my freedom.

The only person I now belong to is myself.

Caspian got my freedom back from his father, and with it came a chance at the new beginning my soul was longing for.

Although the darkness of the past will forever be rooted inside me, I'm trying to move on, deal with my godparents' betrayal, and keep hope alive in my heart.

My family would have wanted that for me. They

would have wanted me to live, be happy, and accomplish all my dreams.

The last few weeks have seen me do just that.

My first act as owner of Dynamic Corp was to hire Lucian and Eilish's parents to run the company. Lucian's stepfather is now the new C.E.O.

As they'd all worked under Adrian and Elaine in the past and knew everything to know about the company, I figured they were the best people for the job.

Having them run things also means I can focus on my writing career.

My heart still lies with *Real Magazine and* my marriage to Caspian garnered me part ownership of the company. I look forward with the greatest anticipation and excitement to working there when I complete my studies at Raventhorn.

I also reinstated the partnership between Dynamic Corp and Ivanov Tech. That was for Caspian, not his father in the least.

I will never forget what that man put me through, but at the same time, I'm not a fool. I know what having such a partnership will bring for the future.

Of all the things I've done, the most sentimental was giving my sister the funeral she deserved.

That happened last week, and it felt like the closure I sought.

Now I'm here with my friends, starting the day with a quick coffee and cake breakfast.

This was Lucian's idea. He got released from the

hospital days ago, so he thought we could do this together to celebrate.

We've all had way too much coffee while we talked, and now it's time for cake.

Lucian opens the box of cupcakes he got from the bakery, and Eilish reaches inside for the cake with the pink frosting.

We're sitting by the river near the English building, and it's still so early there's no one around but us.

I have five more minutes with them until Caspian comes to get me to leave for our weekend getaway to Paris.

"We're going to have to do this again when you get back." Lucian looks from me to Eilish.

"Agreed. Let's do everything," Eilish bubbles. "I missed you guys so much. So many things happened to make me appreciate the friendship we have even more."

She rests her head on Lucian's shoulder, and I smile. They seem closer, and things are different between them, which is a good sign. I'll give them time.

"Me too," Lucian agrees.

"Me three," I say, taking a cake.

"Happy birthday, Red." Lucian smirks. "I hope this is the start of a new era."

I smile and raise my cake to that. They follow suit, and we each take a bite.

When I lower mine, I look up and see the man of my dreams walking toward us.

The brightest smile fills my face, and my friends look over at him, too.

"Looks like I have to go. Paris awaits."

"Have fun."

"I will."

As I rush toward Caspian, I think of all the birthdays I've had over the last few years. Some were terrible, others held that desolation of grief.

I'll remember this one the most because it will be my first with my husband.

Every time I'm with him, I remember how he saved me from destruction with his love.

❧

CASPIAN

A week later

WILLOW RUSHES AHEAD OF ME, running down to the cattail reeds in the meadow.

As I look at her beautiful smile and that vibrant red hair flowing in the wind, my mind revisits that day so long ago when we were kids.

Today, as I think back, I remember the significance of that day, and how many times I've dreamed of seeing her.

I'm not dreaming now. She's the real deal and better than any dream I could have—asleep or awake.

Although that darkness still clings to me, she is my light.

Willow stops and stares back at me. When I walk up to her, she cups my face and love fills her eyes.

"I love you," she tells me.

"I love you, too, Malyshka."

We fall into a kiss that speaks of forever.

The angel should never allow the devil to taint her, but this is what happens when the devil falls in love.

He loves fiercely and protects his angel with his life.

Thank so much for reading.

I'm so excited to take you deeper into this world.

Stay tuned for Lucian and Eilish's story next in Cruel Covenant.

Coming very soon xx

FAITH SUMMERS COLLECTION

Series

Dark Syndicate

Ruthless Prince

Dark Captor

Wicked Liar

Merciless Hunter

Heartless Lover

Ruthless King

Dark Odyssey

Tease Me

Taunt Me

Thrill Me

Tempt Me

Take Me

Original Sins

Dark Odyssey Fantasies

Entice

Tease

Play

Tempt

Duets

Blood and Thorns

Merciless Vows

Merciless Union

Cruel Secrets

Cruel Lies

Cruel Promises

Novellas

The Boss' Girl

The Player

Standalones

Deceptive Vows

ACKNOWLEDGMENTS

To my readers.

Always for you.

Thank you for reading my stories.

I hope you continue to enjoy my wild adventures xx

ABOUT THE AUTHOR

Faith Summers is the Dark Contemporary Romance pen name of USA Today Bestselling Author, Khardine Gray.

Warning !! Expect wild romance stories of the scorching hot variety and deliciously dark romance with the kind of alpha male bad boys best reserved for your fantasies.

Be sure to join my readers list *for some exciting, mouth-watering, seductive romance xx*

https://www. subscribepage.com/faithsummersreadergroup

Join my reader group -

https://www.facebook.com/ groups/462522887995800/